# Unfinished Business of the 97ᵗʰ Floor
Marisha Cautilli
Joseph Cautilli

http://jellingtonashton.com/

Events in this story take place one year, four months after events in Red Light Falling by Andrews, Cautilli, and Cautilli on JEA Press. In addition, they take place approximately two months post the events described in Attack of the Demonic Pillows by Cautilli and Cautilli on JEA Press and shortly after the events in All Juiced Up with Nowhere to Hide, by Andrews, Cautilli, and Cautilli on JEA Press.

Special thanks to Tobias Cabral and Roma Grey for their wonderful beta-reads of this work.

Special thanks to Jess Bickman for her wonderful editing of this work.

Dedicated to Yasmine Khelil Cherfi, who's discussions with me surrounding the Marked Ones inspired me to create this work! Thank you for being an awesome best friend <3! - Marisha

# Prologue

Hovercars led the streets to be blocked and turned into giant pedestrian walkways. Crowds from New Cyber Cities' twenty million people appeared as ants below, as Felicity chose the middle lane of three in a three-by-three stacked road.

Blue and red neon-filled the dashboard as the four engines, which propelled her hover quad, hobbled into Felicity's work garage. Her old machine rumbled and shook, but its insides smelled of cinnamon spice, which calmed her. Two yellow lights next to a dial flashed while the preset search program ran. It seemed stuck, so she tapped the glass to speed it up.

Deep inside, she figured a new quad was needed five years ago but not on a reporter's salary. There was always the option of asking her parents, but that led to feelings of guilt about not being more independent. If the woman were to give up her dreams as a journalist, her father would welcome her on the stock exchange with open arms and probably even bankroll her. The good life versus the fulfilled one, the choice always tempted her.

The newsperson tapped the flashing light harder, and her grey-blue eyes searched for the parking availability sign. It hung below some polyethylene pipes three feet above her and indicated a parking spot two levels up. One day she, like most, hoped for an assigned space, a simple sign of being off the bottom rung: Fat chance, maybe in five years.

From a distance, the spot appeared tight. She worried that her descent to the location would be a tough curve but skillfully angled gently in the quad. Her fingers lowered the music of Flock of Seagull's *I Ran* playing over the streaming jet. The fans buzzed loudly, and the engine ground as metal gears spun.

Turning it off, she stepped out, put some blue lipstick over her smooth olive skin, and puckered her lips in the compact mirror. The lipstick matched the blue nail polish she wore but contrasted with the gold tips of her nails and rhinestones placed in their center. Her make-up appeared fine, and the woman teased and put her blonde hair in a braid. Her grey-blue eyes matched her plain heat-dissipating textile turquoise blouse, denim skort,

4

and bedazzled blue eye shadow. She spun the small necklace around her neck. It was a nervous twitch, which the reporter developed over the years, and then slung her tote bag over her left shoulder. The young woman strutted across the garage to the elevator. Her biosignature unlocked the key-card gate, and the reporter stepped inside, rapidly pressed the button for the 97th floor, and then pressed it again.

Air conditioning caressed the woman's bare face as she sauntered to her office. Felicity's journalist workplace was of post-modern design with a tone of nature reform. The swirls of green and blue gave the feeling of a calm forest. The birchwood desk was oblong shaped and had a layer of turf to enable cooling. The sun (when it pierced through the clouds) reflected off the floor-to-ceiling windows with tempered glass. The reporter flopped into her egg-shell white egg chair. Immediately, the climate control system pumped a scent of blueberry, and the *Bioelectric's* cover of *As Time Goes By* blasted through the speakers of the plastic ovoid chair.

A copy of the New Cyber City Inquirer sat on the plexiglass office table. The headline read "Missing Robots Baffle Police." She wanted a front-page headline so bad she could taste it.

The chief of the journalism department, Michael Howe, entered her office. "My office five minutes," he grumbled. His pudgy belly fell over the belt on his pants, and the wrinkles of his shirt appeared like he'd slept at the office for the last week. Maybe it was the case. The man over saw both day and night shifts and never left.

"Sure, anything wrong," she replied. Mr. Howe was a fair man but often ill-tempered.

"We'll talk then," he offered while drumming his chubby fingers on her office door. At least she had an office. Many of the crew on the night shift still worked from cubicles.

"Ok," her insides quivered as he stormed out of the room.

Felicity drew out her fidget spinner and spun it. She knew her piece on the juice was late, and her leads were just about dry. Juice was the latest and most addictive of designer club drugs. She'd been chasing leads diligently for six weeks but felt like she'd been just spinning her wheels.

Felicity imagined the chewing out she would get or worse: he would be polite and nearly silent. At least the former meant she still had a career, while the latter meant they were planning to terminate her. *God,* she hated her life: too many deadlines.

"Computer," the reporter called. "Show me New Cyber Cities west end."

After a beep, a three-dimensional hologram formed in front of her, and her eyes studied the map. Lots of gang activity was reported in this sector. Many of the gangs were involved in running juice. Her story investigated the most infamous of them all. It was a dumb and cliched name, but they called themselves "The Marked Ones."

As a writer, she snickered at the childishness of the name but held it back, realizing the group's deadliness. Still, her work seemed fruitless. The gang appeared very decentralized, and she'd not even discovered its leader's name. Her contact with the police force either didn't know or was withholding the information from her. Maybe she'd try the old private detective again. What was his name? Johnson? He was dusty, but he had an ear to the street. The possibility danced in front of her, but it was probably another dead end. Okay, she would play the lead, but after this meeting.  She'd managed to make one contact in the gang, a Jorge Vasquez, but he was so low he never knew any of the important stuff. He'd told her about some minor event the police kept from her and the gang's plan to push out its rivals in the area, but he'd no details. He called it operation Tip of the Hat. *Silly name for a stupid group,* she thought.  Cringing, she saw the digital clock in her office: Meeting time. Whipping open her desk drawer, the newsperson dragged out her notepad, jaunted out of the chair, and the cat walked to the office.

Speed-walking, she passed through cubicles of new interns and veteran reporters on the night shift. The smell of fresh-brewed coffee danced around her. From three feet away, her boss hollered at a poor soul in the form of a newly promoted journalist, who sifted through the glass door.

The glass was thick, and she often heard others joke that the chief had gotten it to bomb and bulletproof in case someone retaliated for what the paper wrote. The death threats to the press were real and plenty.

Her body froze, refusing to take another step forward, and it took all her will to knock. The room inside fell silent, wholly drowned out by the chatter of reporters on cellphones running down leads.  A microsecond later, a call came to enter. The glass door slid wide, and two junior investigators quickly dashed past her. They appeared glad for her interruption.

"Miss Cruickshank," Howe called. "Please have a seat." The twelve by fifteen-foot room was the largest in the paper. The white plush carpet floor added a level of soundproofing, but far from enough, as her recent experience outside the door attested.

Behind a large glass desk, Howe sat next to her Human Resource Representative, Cohen Shay. The weird flower tattoo over the back of his hand still made her head spin when she thought about it, but it was nothing compared to the confusion she felt over his ugly tan suit.  Recently, Cohen entered a new chapter of life by marrying his childhood sweetheart, Gloria. The man enthusiastically spent hours at lunch, talking to anyone who listened about his hopes to have a baby girl. The day-by-day process of buying a home and nesting brought an exciting glow to his face. Felicity experienced the opposite effect at this point. The presence of HR sent her heart into her throat. *Oh no, were they going to can her?* Fear drove her to speak first. "On the juice story, I am still running down leads, but I think I am getting close."

"Good," started Howe. His baritone voice was amiable but formal, "right to business. The story is why we have asked you here. You have been on it for six weeks now."

"I'm sorry about that, sir," she interrupted. Her words were so fast that they blurred together. "It is taking longer than I thought it would." The HR representative nodded understandingly.

"Can you tell us where you are on the piece?"

"I've heard that an Officer John Jay," she babbled, "and a detective Johnny Johnson was involved with an incident not reported in the press. It seems like someone tried to kill the lead singer for the *Bioelectrics*."

"The *Bioelectrics* is a holographic band, Miss Cruickshank. They have no lead singer."

Felicity gulped, and an icy chill ran down her spine. "Yes, but the band is modeled off the movement of a He-Ran Jones. The programing work is done by her husband, Harold." She paused a minute, determining if her words were positively received, but the boss's deadpan face gave nothing away. She quickly added, "It was just the night after they played the Maenianum Maxus Primum Colosseum."

7

"They played a full week," her boss added, and the reporter felt sweat rolling down the swell of her back.

"Yes, but if you remember, the concert was cut short," Felicity quickly added. A sense of desperation gripped her, and the reporter hoped they saw the massive amount of work she had completed.

"What does this all have to do with juice?" The editor asked. His frustration was apparent in his tone.

"The word from my source was that they were trying to kill He-Ran and frame her husband."

"Why?"

"Not sure," Felicity admitted to a noticeable grunt from her boss. She sensed how this conversation was likely to end. She tried not to shed tears or become emotional. Her hand clenched and tightened, and she quickly added, "But I think there is a gang tie between the Marked Ones and Purt."

Her story caused the boss to lean his head in, his two eyebrows kneaded into one, and his face rumpled. "Purt? The religious network."

"Yes, sir," she replied. Her shoulder blades tightened, and the stiffness caused her neck to hurt.

"Any proof?" This time, the HR representative spoke up. She realized the man was probably concerned about libel issues. His controlled tone sent her reeling.

"Not at this point." A cloud of anxiety flew up inside her. She felt terrified her career was swiftly ending. When she was just a girl, the questions from either parent always felt controlled before the other foot fell, ceasing whatever fun she was engaged in.

"So, this is just speculation?" the editor huffed. "You need to have more than just speculation before you accuse one of the strongest religious groups in this city of crimes."

"I know, sir," she admitted. Her voice was tiny, and the veins in her arms strained. The tightness made her feel each swoosh of blood coursing through them. The reporter caught the look the editor exchanged with the HR representative.

"Purt does have a donation center and hostile on the docks. Pier elven," Her editor commented to her surprise, and he must have noticed her shock over this basic information, for he added, "Did you at least get it from your gang source?" The editor snapped.

Dread shot up, but she pushed it down, preferring to sound lifeless. "No, I did not get it from Jorge. He works at the docks and is much too low-level for that information."

"He's useless," the editor huffed exasperatedly.

"He gave me the Jones lead, sir," she wallowed.

The HR representative leaned in with soft eyes. "I'm sure you are working hard."

"I am," she said, "I've been trying to run down information on this gang. Just two weeks ago, before my birthday, I got a lead from Jorge about some plan to push the other gangs out of the area called Tip the hat or Tip of the Hat. I am trying to get a handle on what it entails. This won't be one piece but several, and the Purt story, could be the biggest piece of all."

The editor shifted his head. "Well, do you know that half the people who eventually get off that crap do so because of Purt's help?" Her HR representative sighed.

Her mind rolled in circles with no logical course to escape. She felt sure the termination comments were soon to come. "I know it," she added. Her breath shallowed, causing her to fear an impending panic attack. The reporter needed to stay focused and not get upset. She had to find the words to explain her research, but neither her HR director nor her boss appeared interested in a long explanation. They had questions and chipped away at her story and its glaring holes. *Maybe she would be better off selling stocks.*

"What the heck would be their motive?"

The walls appeared out of date and too dark—a scramble of emotions danced inside Felicity. A sense of those walls closing in on her caught Felicity's attention. "I'm not sure, but I think..." The buzzer went off on the boss's desk. He waved two fingers and the back of his hand for her to stop speaking. The HR representative shifted back into his seat and let out a relaxed sigh. Felicity felt her chest tighten. She wished she could sigh. She hoped the information she presented would put her in the clear.

He flipped the switch, "Yeah."

"Sorry to bother you, sir, but we got a delivery out here for Chinese for Ms. Cruickshank."

9

The boss appeared cross and shouted. "You ordered food during our meeting."

"No sir," her voice was a soft muffle. The minutes ticked by slowly, and some part of her wished that they would get to her dismissal, or hope shot up: maybe she was jumping too quickly to conclusions.

"She did not order any food," her boss bellowed into the communication port.

"The delivery guy is insisting. It's from Chin's."

"I've ordered from Chin's before but not recently."

"Go out and tell him to..." he insisted but seemed to change his mind. His nostrils flared, and he leaned back, placing his hand on his belly fat. "No, I'll tell him. See, a good reporter chases down a lead no matter where it goes- even if it is a misguided food guy delivering to the wrong place." She figured he offered the words in a teaching moment as if somehow, she should learn to chase down her leads more efficiently. She didn't care. A peaceful reprieve, if only for a moment, she welcomed it. The chief got up and left.

As he stormed into the cubicles, something wrong struck Felicity's mind, and she could not place it at first, and then a second later, it hit her: *Chin's closed about a year and six months prior due to the owner's death.* She leaped up and darted toward the door just as the bomb exploded. A wave of fire radiated out. She slapped the button as the upsurge of flame licked into the room. The glass slid close. The concussing sound rippled, and her ears rang as she hit the ground.

A wave of ball bearings slapped into the chief's glass-like rain drumming a window, and the woman hoped it was shockproof. The metal pellets could shred her to pieces. Small cracks formed, but they held.

Her body twisted to see blood staining the rug and a hand with a flower tattoo extended from behind the desk. Her HR representative wasn't moving. His arm remained sprawled beyond the desk, but his head lay behind it. *Maybe the reporter could reach him, and render him some aid?*

Resolved, she staggered to get up. Dark black spots formed at the periphery of her vision, and a tearing pain stretched in her side. Clutching it, the reporter stumbled backward, trying to find her footing, but a wave of dizziness forced her off balance.

She fell hard. Her skin felt the pressure of landing as it jerked her system, and her body undulated as if to bounce back. She wasn't sure when or how it happened, but blood trickled out from her forehead and rolled down her face. Her finger found its way up to the cut and probed it. Pain shot through her body and drops of blood coated her hand.

Her breath cycled in and out. The shallow sound echoed in her head: the only presence loud enough to rise over the ringing in her ears. Sobbing, she peered out the glass door.

The explosion destroyed the whole floor. Despite the sprinkler system flashing on, flames curled up the walls, licking the ceiling. Cubicles lay in chaos. Desks were flipped and broken. Felicity passed out.

# Chapter 1

Flashing lights danced in front of her eyes as they fluttered open. The robotic doctor peered into them with a penlight, observing and recording pupil size. She flinched back, confused and disoriented, but a second later, when the dull throb in her head reminded her of who and where she was, Felicity hoped no indications of nervous system damage were present.

"Take it easy, Ms. Cruickshank," the soft metallic voice of the robot insisted. "You are safe and in the hospital after a gang-related terrorist attack on your office. Nothing broken, and your temperature is fine."

Her arm had a sharp pain, and she looked to see an intravenous (I.V.) line running into her. Its needlepoint stabbed into the veins on her left arm. The robot reached over and dialed a white knob on the I.V.She felt an increase in the warm, clear white solution running into her arm.

"It's just saline mixed with a gene stimulant to increase your healing rate and some small amounts of growth hormone added," the robotic doctor reassured. Her finger reached up again toward the forehead cut and found it cured. She felt a sticky glue over them and figured it for liquid skin, which had replaced many stitching procedures over the last forty years. He tapped a screen, and on the glass table in front of her bed, she witnessed numbers and tables. The room sensors monitored her vitals and blood, so the robot could intervene if any abnormalities appeared.

"The others?" she mewed while her gaze shifted out the window. Red neon signs glowed with modern advertisements screaming for consumers to spend. She figured from the view that they were at least forty stories up. In the distance, the Haasting megacorporation's tower shone over three hundred stories disappearing into the body of clouds in the night sky. The clouds rolled into each other, cutting off the view of at least fifteen buildings. Even at night, she could tell a storm brewed.

"Most of the night shift. The explosion launched a wave of ball-bearings."

"How many?" the reporter interrupted, although part of her dare not know. Her eyes shifted back to the room and a clock on the wall. The digital display read four. Her fingers tapped the bedsheets. She wanted desperately to run.

The intervenous bothered her now. It had an odd pinch, followed by a burning sensation, and she worried the doctor had inserted it wrong into her vein.

"Twenty-six dead," the robot insisted. A flash of light drew her vision back to the window, cutting through the soft blue light of the hospital room. Even from her bed, she saw billowing clouds of darkness, and then lightning flashed in and out of existence, leaving only the dark and neon behind until the next flash repeated the cycle.

Felicity harkened back. "Did Howe?"

The robot drew back as if scanning a list. Yellow lights flashed on and off behind its ocular scanners. She stared at him with interest. "No, the chief editor Howe did not make it."

"Why?" Her stomach twisted. The rain blasted from the heavens and splattered on the hospital glass in gusts, then stopped to repeat with the next gust of wind.

"No one claimed responsibility," replied the robot.

"Then how are they sure it was gang-related?"

"They are not," the robot replied. Its gears whirred, spun, and its body rotated. "There is an Officer John Jay. He referred to it as gang-related, but no official announcement has been made." The robot paused and continued, "He asked to be alerted when you awaken." Inside, Felicity cringed. It was hit or miss if Jay's rugged face was there to comfort her or interrogate her. His strength made her draw up his face. It calmed her. The officer was handsome (high cheekbones and a square jaw like a pit bull) but not overly so (with the flabby cheek skin jowls of a pitbull) with solid Irish features.

"How soon until my release?" She glanced again out of her view—the neon lights scattered in the reflection of the droplets. The I.V. still felt as though it was stabbing her vein at the wrong angle, threatening to burst through on her arm. Concentrating on the lights helped her forget the pain.

"Chart says two days for observation," the robotic voice replied. "You need to fill out your food requests for review by the dietician." It droned on while pointing at the glass screen on a small table next to the bed, and it rolled over the table. Its movements reminded her of pacing, although she doubted the machine possessed the emotional programming for such an act. "We have you scheduled for a counselor to meet with you for some stress inoculation training and exposure therapy to deal with the ordeal you have just been through."

"I don't need therapy," Felicity grunted. Her fingers reached for her necklace. Its presence comforted her, but the movement released the stabbing pain from the I.V. The rain sounded like it was dying down some, taking away her distraction. She decided its time to ask the doctor about the I.V. "Doc. This line is very uncomfortable. Are you sure it is in me, right?"

He checked it, "It's fine, and as to the therapy -Maybe not now, but events like this interfere with one's emotional status later in life." Felicity knew the effects of grief. It had dogged her most of her existence, and she had always felt cheated when it came to love and loss. Now, she knew she would grieve the loss of her reporter community for the rest of her days.

"I'll seek it then," replied the woman. "Move up my release date to tomorrow, or I'll sign out against medical advice."

"That would not be wise," the robot replied.

The woman extended her tongue past her chapped lips, whetting them. "I have a job to do, and there is nothing evidence-based in therapy that is not playing on the state supporter mental health channel."

"The channel is doing it yourself, and many people find they need the relationship and therapeutic guidance. I know it might not seem like it, but your job can wait," replied the robot. "The corporation that owns your paper has granted you an emergency medical leave."

"How nice of them," she stated sarcastically. Here was the biggest story of her career, and she lived it only to be sidelined from investigating.

If the robot understood her tone, it did not let on, only replying, "Yes, it is." An awkward pause settled on the situation, not that machines could understand such things. The clunky robot continued its assessment and rolled from the room when completed.

Felicity drew the glass table to her bed and pressed its screen. Her fingers busily took to pressing internet links, anything to forget the hospital. Her screen's video display flashed in the background. Twenty messages and almost all were fans, wishing her well. So, she had people who read her columns, after all. The way her now-deceased editor spoke, the fact was sorely forgotten. She hastily zipped through the messages until she came to one. It was not a fan but a video message from her younger sister.

"Hey, goober. You had us so scared," the girl in the video, wearing a pair of goggles like an old 1940s aviator, gestured and made a shrug. "We went to the hospital and waited for a while. They would not let us in the room until you awaken. I am glad to hear the doctors say you are stable. I will be by  soon with mom and dad." The screen went dead. The message ended, now flashed.

A single tear overflowed in Felicity's eye. She wiped it back with her index finger and gulped.

Images danced in her brain of long ago. The scene played out with a sort of tempered quality.  She remembered, as a child, her father playfully carrying her and her sister into bed. Her sister hugged her father, and her mother came into the room to tuck the girls in and read both children a story. Her father dove into the entryway. His blue eyes stared at both his daughters. Then the scene shifted to a doctor identifying a strange gene sequence in her sister. Her parents were concerned and hid the knowledge from the start, fearing it was the sequence the Marked Ones sought. Inside, Felicity knew she had to keep her sister from the gang.

A sudden knock at the door broke her dream. "Excuse me, ma'am," said the old voice. She glanced up with watery eyes to see the bright smile of Officer John Jay.  Her body jerked, and the burning pain from the jolted  I.V. resting in her skin re-established itself. She winced from the pain but gazed up.

Her face brightened, and she slithered forward slightly in her bed, careful not to reaggravate the arm where the I.V. needle lay. "Jay," she huffed. The middle-aged officer entered.  A clean-cut, metro-sexual with an angsty surf punk soul who always knew just the right amount of cologne to wear, Jay was supposed to be one-eighth native American, but one could never tell from looking at him. He had solid Irish features and always appeared much younger than his age.  Besides his weird insistence on wearing soft-soled shoes, his one drawback as a love prospect was fourteen years her senior.

15

"It's good to see you again," Felicity smiled. Lean muscled, Jay had the look like one of those guys. If he put his mind to it could hurt a person severely in a scrap. Long thick, fingered hands appeared as he could easily punch through three sheetrock walls at once.

"Just wish I'd seen you before the attack," Jay said. That was Jay, in a nutshell, always business. Still, his husky voice had a soothing quality, which she could not deny.

"We cannot always be in the right place at the right time," she offered. Inside, she knew she could not cry yet. Nor could she tell him that if she was not so damn pleased the boss had stopped investigating the food order, Howe might be alive now. Hell, they all might still be alive.

"Do you think our friends set off the bomb?" Jay asked. He stepped closer and leaned in as if hanging on her words.

"Paper researched so many stories," she replied with a shrug. "It is hard to tell."

"What do you remember from the event?"

"Don't," the woman muttered, but Jay's soft accepting eyes flushed her with emotions.

"I know this is hard, but please try," Jay replied. The young journalist thought of her father and how he always seemed to know and ask questions that drove her to open up. She flushed and fought to catch her breath. The situation was developing too fast. The conversation with her boss, the final discussion, was too much to deal with at this point for her. The very thought of it exhausted her emotionally. The investigator needed to tell a partial truth. If she gave him something, he would stop the questioning.

"Not much," Felicity stated. "I was meeting with the Chief editor and discussing the story. He gave me the usual hassles about the deadline. Then there was a beep, and he answered his comm. They told him that I had a food delivery from Chin's at the desk."

Jay cocked an ear and then, with a kind, thoughtful voice, asked, "Chin?" He softly tapped his fingers on his cellphone, which recorded the conversation. "Aren't they closed?" His steely blue eyes studied her face.

Felicity felt her mind slipping away and her soul snapping from the stress of her joy in not having to answer questions that she failed to analyze the information at hand. "Yeah, for a year. I didn't figure it out at first, but it hit me after he left to retrieve my food." Her eyes swooped away toward the window as she tried to control herself. Her mind latched onto the blue light in the room. As she stated, the regret evident in her voice, "I should have been quicker, Jay." A single tear stung her eye and rolled down the side of her face.

As she suspected, Jay rushed in to save her from the pain. "It was out of context, my friend," he said, nostrils flaring with resolve. Something about their flare reminded her of Howe's moments before his death. It was both weirdly comforting and producing guilt. The net effect left her with a sensation that she owed it to Jay to hear him out. His eyes scrutinized her face, trying to determine if she was listening. "When things happen like that with only seconds to react, often we don't get it in time." Her face flushed. Her harsh glare softened, and she considered the situation.

"I guess," she replied squirrelly, but her belief in his words was low. Not the logical aspects of his phrase but her instincts and emotions held it off. *How would he know? He just wasn't there*, she thought. *If Jay were, he'd know her guilt.*

"Well, we know they were there to deliver the bomb to you. Are you working on any other stories at this point?"

"Nope, this is the only one," she confirmed.

"Let's start with that as a lead and then go. It could be something else, but I think the gang is at least as likely as not on this one."

"So, you plan to chase down that lead?"

"I'll stop by the gangs and do a brief interview. Review some files. I'll also keep an ear out for rumors and talk to a couple of my informants. You know the usual stuff."

"When can I meet with Detective Johnson?" Jay stared at her intensely. Maybe his gaze lingered a bit too long because Felicity worried. He searched her face to see if this event drove her bonkers.

"That loser?" chuckling a bit while he said it.

"Yes," she firmly insisted.

"Waste of time," Jay informed. "He's a private eye- not even a real police officer. Just street scum."

17

"I don't think so. I like to see him when I get out. See if he can put me on the right path." This was something she hated about Jay: his stubborn insistence. The officer was always so by the book and contending he was right. He even asserted at times like these when they both knew him wrong. Her life was too dangerous for his book. Indeed, right now, she could be living on borrowed time, and here Jay scoffed at a possible lead to help. *Far too rigid,* she thought.

"Johnson gives more wrong paths than right ones, but I understand." The thought of another line of dead ends for Felicity was profoundly disturbing and even somewhat depressing, but she owed it to the people at her job.

"Hey, I'll send an officer to be posted at your door."

"No, I don't think that would be necessary." The offer bothered her, although she was not immediately sure why.

"I'll feel better all the same. I figure you'll have a beat cop here in about two hours."

"Jay, it's a hospital. I don't need the police at my door. It will make everyone think I am some sort of criminal. Besides, I trained in Aikido."

"Black belt?" Jay asked skeptically.

"No, blue," she replied. "But I can always step on their foot or kick them in the groin or something." She chuckled.

"Not very high," he sighed, ignoring her laugh, and she glared hard at him with steely eyes. The officer eyed her skeptically, but he finally caved and said, "Alright, when she pressed finally. I'll not have the police here."

~

About an hour after Jay left, the nurse came in to remove the I.V. As she yanked it out, another round of burning pain (hopefully the last one) shot through Felicity. "Ouch," the girl shouted.

"Don't be a wimp," the old nurse demanded. She raised the newswoman's arm and motioned for her to press a cotton wad next to it.

"I wasn't," protested the reporter, but the nurse just interrupted her with a dismissive wave. After thirty seconds, the nurse yanked down Felicity's arm and lifted off the gauze. Once she was sure the bleeding had stopped, the older woman tossed it in the medical wastebasket and hurried out without another word to the patient.

Within minutes of the cranky old nurse leaving, a buzz came to the glass door of her room. "Come in," Felicity called to the door. It creaked open as a girl with long brown hair and blue eyes sauntered into the room. The windbreaker the girl wore around her body dripped with water.

"Wassup, sis?" The girl inquired while the girl's eyes filled with concern. Casually, she leaned in and kissed Felicity on the cheek. Water dripped from her hair onto the reporter's shirt.

"Hey Susan," Felicity greeted. "I see it's still raining outside."

"It's on and off for the rain. The whole hospital parking lot looks like a swamp!" The girls giggled. Susan, in most ways, was Felicity's best friend.

"Mom and dad?" The scent of her sister reached her nostrils. It was a mixture of musk and lavender.

"Yeah, they're coming later in the morning. Too much excitement, they crashed," the girl paused for a breath, "To their credit, they came first but could not get in because you were unconscious and undergoing tests. So, mom and dad sent me because you were still in a coma when they wanted to come," Susan stated. "Doing better?"

"A little. Still feel sorta out of whack...but better!" The newswoman stared at the curve of her sister's neck. The girl has such a beautiful shape to her. Perfectly symmetrical, and her yellowish-white skin was perfect in every way.

"I see you still are wearing that necklace I bought you for your birthday."

The newswoman reached up and twisted the locket on the chain around her neck. "Yeah, I keep it for luck. It reminds me that I have a family. Of course, they cannot stay awake when I am in the hospital" Both sisters laughed at their once pushy parents getting up in their years.

When the chuckle settled, Susan said, "Good to see you! How's the story coming?"

"Found a new lead regarding the gang. It's really suspicious."

"Ooh! What is the lead?"

"Can't say. Afraid to get sued for slander."

19

Abruptly, Susan rose and started pacing. "Ah, I see. What you just said just gave me an idea of what it is."

"Well, I think the nurse will give me some food soon. Up to you on whether you want to stay and vomit at hospital mush."

"Yeah, no. I've seen that stuff. It's quite gross."

"Can you fill my picture?" Felicity asked, pointing at the small brown plastic picture on the table.

"Sure, sis," she got up and strolled into the bathroom.

"Can you get some ice in it from the machine down the hall?"

"Not a problem," her sister added, strolling out of the room. Felicity heard her sister galloping over the hospital tiles. Calmed by her sister's presence, Felicity shifted in the hospital bed. Briefly, she closed her eyes, feeling like she finally had time to breathe and relax. Her fingers tapped on the hospital mattress. The rhythm was to an old Allen Walker song.

When the reporter opened them, a ragged man stood in the doorway less than fifteen feet away. His eyes were sunken into his skull, and he appeared like he was on drugs, probably juice. "Are you with the hospital?" she asked. He said nothing but rushed into the room. Her heart pounded so loudly it felt like it was bursting through her rib cage. In his hand, he held a knife. Felicity tried to block his arm and knock the blade aside. Her wrist struck solidly against the side of the man's hands, sending the weapon flying off into the corner.

The man rolled to retrieve it from the ground. Felicity yelled for help as he grabbed the dagger and lunged at her again. His lips spread wide, exposing his teeth. Timing her shot, Felicity struck him, and blood burst from his mouth and nose. Still, he pressed into her.

The knife lay inches from her throat. Its shadow covered her necklace. Sweat rolled down her assassin's face. His breath, warm and fetid, brushed her skin. Screaming, Felicity kicked up hard and managed to scissor lock the man's head. He fell back but rushed at her again. This time, the knife touched her skin. She held it back, but the addict pushed forward with his weight making him stronger. It pierced in but not deep. Blood trickled out, sending a massive wave of pain through her, but with the pain came strength, and she flung him back. He hobbled up, raised the dagger to his stomach level, and squared to try again, but her sister darted back into the room, having heard the scream. Susan came up behind the attacker and struck him repeatedly with the brown plastic picture, causing water and ice to fly with each swing. The assailant's shoulders flinched, and his head retracted from the blows. Felicity's body jerked as the ice water hit it.

The nurse rushed into the room and called for the doctors, hitting a code. Panting, the man curled over to the side of the bed and then plunged down the hall. The nurse picked up the phone and called the security desk on the first floor. When she reached them, she described the person who tried to assault Felicity. A cobalt blue LED code light flashed in the hallways of the hospital. The glass computer control panel squawked as a tracking light appeared on the wall.

"Oh, my," the nurse offered, staring at Felicity. "You'll catch your death. She marched out of the room and returned with a new white and blue floral print hospital gown. "Here, change into these." Felicity rose, and a wave of dizziness followed by a moment of nausea rolled over her. She nearly fell, and her sister grabbed her arm, helping the woman into the bathroom to change.

"Sorry about the water," her sister gently whispered.

Back in her room, the old nurse stripped the bed like a pro. She rolled out a fresh ugly grey linin sheet and placed it over the top, and tucked in the sheet. All the time, making sweet, supportive statements and praising the reporter for how well she and her sister acted. With her sister's help, Felicity returned to her bed to lie down while the nurse moved toward the tracking screen.

The nurse conveyed to Felicity that security figures were tracking the man using this system through the hospital. She pointed to two dots. They closed in on the figure running down the stairwell. Several other beads were on the screen. Felicity figured them out for additional guests in the hospital and wondered how security knew they were chasing the right person instead of some little kid. In the end, she figured there were cameras on every floor and down the stairwells. Security worked off the nurse's description.

Another dot appeared on the screen marked police. "Wow, they got here fast," Felicity remarked.

"Should have been quicker. He never left, been sitting in front of the building for almost an hour." So, Jay had sent the police to watch her. White-hot anger exploded inside her for a nanosecond, but she suppressed it. The correspondent chewed the inside of her cheek. Maybe on this one, Jay was right following the books. He'd been stubborn and inflexible but made the correct choice. It was hard to determine how she felt about this situation.

Susan took her place by her sister's side and rested a hand on her shoulder. It was firm, strong, and warm. The woman shivered at the girl's touch. Felicity felt reassured by the gesture and relaxed her head on the back of her sister's hand.

The woman's eyes' felt glued to the screen as she tracked the man who assaulted and tried to kill her. Behind him, security closed. He went into the tower, and they divided up. The three closed in on her assailant.

The nurse stepped next to the reporter. "It won't be long n..," she started saying but never finished. The glass shattered, and a bullet struck the nurse behind, exploding the woman's head. The blood doused both Felicity and Susan.

Susan stared frozen at the inert body. Her face greened like she would puke. "Down!" she screamed. With her palm over her sister's hand, she dragged the teen to the floor. Felicity rolled behind the bed. The newswoman racked her brain on what to do, then caught sight of an alabaster white three-and-a-half-foot drone hovering by the window.

Chapter 2

"Oh my god. Oh my god," Susan frantically panted. Then she heaved. The vomit spurted out, spraying her lunch on the floor. Her face was porcelain white, and her whole body trembled.

Knowing one shot from the drone could end her life, the reporter lay low and scanned the room: Moments ticked by as she assessed. It was a good ten feet from the bulletproof glass sliding door. The windows were not. They both crouched tight. Felicity heard the whir of a hover drone outside the building and worried it might have seeker rockets. If the missiles struck the room, they both would be ripped to pieces in the explosion.

A hollow feeling built inside her. The emptiness felt inescapable. *How had they found her?* Her eyes darted between her sister and the window.

Overhead, the hospital had switched to an active shooter code. The light flashed a brilliant orange. The bullets continued to fly into the room, striking the bed. Then she heard the machine click and understood. It was switching from bullets to rockets.

"Susan, look at me," the reporter said, grabbing her sister's face and lifting it. The girl's pupils were the size of pinpricks. "We got to jump toward the glass." Susan's head nodded. "On three. One…" Felicity never got to two. Panicked, the young teen tore from the ground, and the reporter followed her. They reached the glass door. It slid open, and they tumbled through just as the rockets hit. The room lit up like a ball of gold and orange as the door slid back with just wisps of flame, making it through the cracks into the corridor as it closed. Hot wind licked Felicity's cheeks.

The flame seared the back of Susan, who screamed in terror and fell to the far wall. She lay on her side, curled in a ball. At the far end, the robotic doctor clunkily rolled toward them. His metallic gears echoed under the sound of the flashing code and screaming alarm.

In the distance, roughly twenty feet away, the elevator doors slid wide. Jay appeared with the original assailant cuffed. So, he kept his promise and did not send someone to watch her. The officer just stayed. She hated his violation of the intent of her conversation and felt some guilt for doing so.

The robot reached her sibling and carried her away. A faint song played in the background: the *Bioelectrics*' cover of the old tune *Que Sera Sera*. The officer slammed the one perp to the ground. No time left to cuff the man. He flipped his blaster to stun and shot him. As the body spasmed on the floor, the policeman ordered him to stay, drew his laser, and rushed to Felicity's side. He flung her arm over his shoulder, the scent of his spicy cologne overpowering, and carried her back to the nursing station.

Plopping her onto the ground, Jay headed back toward the glass doors. He typed the screen, but the doors did not open. "Doc, is there an override code?" The robotic doctor mumbled something about safety, but when Jay threatened to toss him out of the other room's windows, the doctor relented, giving the officer the code.

As the doors slid back, Jay stepped into the room. Carefully, he paced toward the window, ensuring the ground was stable where his feet tread. He peered outside, but the hover was gone. His steely eyes cast down the long streets between the towering buildings of New Cyber City. With a loud huff, the tightness in his chest disappeared. The policeman raised his cellphone and radioed in the attack. He called for a unit to be dispatched to pick up the one assassin.

One sister was admitted an hour later, and the other left the hospital against medical advice. Felicity wished just for a moment to exhale and relax but settled on heading with Jay to the Scorched Wing Division for the recording of her statement.

~

From a three-block distance, Felicity saw the rebuilt precinct. Even this far, the perplexing design projected a sense of strength. The eight-story building rose proudly into the rainy night sky. A great curtain of mist hung around the structure, but massive columns of commanding white arc light shot up from the front of the construction, powerful enough to reach the clouds. Its extraordinary beauty replaced her numbness from the attack with a sense of pride.

The pink and red texture created by rows of small lamps in the fountain outside the area gave a sense of inclusion. It screamed that all were wanted. Recently, a statue of justice was placed square in the fountain's center. While Jay complained about it, the net effect on Felicity was a feeling of safety. Indeed, she felt safer here than anywhere else the newswoman could think of, even in her apartment, which was why she insisted on giving her statement about the assassination attempt now. Construction cranes, trucks, portable laser cutters, and three-dimensional printing robots hung in from of the building as it continued to get its renovations.

In its attempts to show dedication to law and order, the corporate council dumped massive amounts of money to rejuvenate the building. Even more, money flowed as Dr. Jennifer Lui, who held Robert Haastings' old seat on the council with the support of Rebecca Coke-Abe, pushed a bill through that allowed police to keep all money found and property seized in juice seizures. Auctions were frequent, and seizure money transformed the complex from decaying to state-of-the-art. Twelve white birch trees circled the building. Bringing a cleanness to the area, they made a pleasant, relaxing sight and added to the community's overall sense of freshness.

The central body was a multilevel superstructure. The face of the complex comprised a series of stacked eight rectangular blocks of prestressed concrete volumes, stacked by tubular

24

reinforced steel pylons organized around a central circular atrium. Everyone culminated in a bioluminescent green rooftop. Its face was onyx sandblasted concrete panels and areas of polished white concrete, which combined to create a checkerboard visual effect. The blocks were edged with blue neon running parallel to the ground and red running perpendicular. Perforated metal panels concealed equipment while still allowing airflow, and angled panels existed to border the windows. One block served as an area for arraignments and court cases that needed immediate decisions. Of course, the brass relegated Scorched Wing to the back.

The front of the edifice bustled with civilians and police officers entering and exiting the complex. Jay banked his quad toward the parking tower. The officer rambled on about precinct trivia. He certainly knew a lot, like the solar array atop the parking structure supplied over eighty percent of the lot's energy.

Her throat still sore from sobbing, the newswoman listened intently but said little. The occasional polite laugh did manage to escape her lips. Each time it did, Jay smiled enthusiastically.

The prisoner pounded from the back of his quad with the raw desperation that emerged from the lack of juice. The back was padded and soundproof to a large degree, yet Jay and Felicity heard the man throwing himself up and back against the sides and screaming so loudly It penetrated their seats. Jay licked his lips, cleared his throat in an embarrassing gesture, and dialed up the Blue Danube by the music.

Reaching the barbican, Jay glanced at the digital lights, which displayed the location and number of parking spots to drivers. Once his quad landed, the officer smiled and nodded at Felicity. The side of the quad rose, opening to the lot. She exited, and he moved to retrieve the prisoner from the back. Swiping his key over the lock, the officer pressed his finger to the quad. The machine immediately registered his identification.

Jay opened the evidence holder below the dashboard and extracted a sealed plastic bag containing the knife the assailant used. Then he cracked a joke with Felicity and moved to extract the prisoner from the holding tank at the vehicle's back.

~

Removing the junky, Officer Jay noted the man was groaning, sweaty, and shaking. His eyes were cloudy, and his clammy skin appeared ashen grey. He displayed all the signs of being in complete withdrawal. Many of the severe addicts died at this point, and Officer Jay felt terrible for the guy, but the creep's choices were his own. The thought left Jay with a nano-second of guilt. Maybe they should have run him to the hospital detox first, but the Precinct detox unit was no stranger to juice withdrawal. He gently pushed the guy to his side and walked back to his vehicle.

As he reached the back of his quad, Officer Jay glanced at the building. His experience at the new facility was different from that of Felicity's. Part of him missed the old design, but the sense of loss around his old friends made his heart sink. Sure, Reds seemed to be having a great retirement. A bittersweet feeling overcame him thinking of the man. He'd visited the man a couple of times to check in on him and was surprised his family had done so well. *When did he have time to have a family?* If Jay's sister did not work at the precinct- he'd never see her. But Red's retirement was just a tiny piece of the loss. The most significant element was his partner's death- Mikołaj. When the two were assigned together, Jay cringed because the guy was openly homosexual. It wasn't like Jay came from a family where that would bother him. His family was open and diverse, but on some level, it did. Over time though, the man proved to be one of the best friends Jay could ask. It helped that the guy was not flaming. Jay was even the best man when he married his partner. Now, Mikołaj was pushing up daisies – killed by a psychopathic serial killer. Then there were the crushing deaths just a few months prior of Agent Black and his robotic partner- 427. He always liked the robot. She had the wit and charm her partner often seemed to lack. His heart leaped at the thought of the two. He'd come to respect Black's crazy battle tactics and dedication to the force. Sadly both Black and 427 were killed when a strange alien mite landed on the planet from a comet. The whole situation reminded him more of something that a person would watch on the three-dimensional holographic televisions and not the reality he'd come to know. The one thing all three deaths shared- was a link to working with Detective Johnny Johnson. He hocked some phlegm and spat it out. He vowed not to let contact with that nut lead to his death.

~

Felicity noticed Jay seemed a bit flustered and strolled toward him. He told her to wait where she was while re-secured the prisoner's electronic shackles. If Jay pressed a small button on his key chain, the cuffs were designed to deliver an eight-volt thirty-amp electrical shock. The goal was to prevent the prisoner from running. Of course, the officer needed to have his body camera on during such events to ensure that the shock was proper.

Together, the three strolled up to the precinct. As they approached, Felicity drew back to admire the design. The government had taken a partition to the public. Separating the police department into sectors was already green-lit; however, the government wanted to keep it minimal for credit saving. Economically driven, they named sector houses, which for most got too confusing as the separation took in the whole state, not just the city. To lessen this confusion, names were given.

The Scorched Wing division's section of the building proudly displayed its new emblem. The neon red sign lit up in a holographic flame, its name, but the background was a blue neon patch that chilled the soul and spoke of calm in the sea of the chaos of life. The wings on the sign flashed with almost a spectral quality, making the place appear more like a nightclub rather than a police precinct of New Cyber City.

The pictures of the division's two captains hung on the wall. Captain Berger, a female in the mid-fifties, ran the day unit. Captain Mendez, male and early forties, ran the night division. Many thought the latter had the potential to make commissioner or at least deputy commissioner. Knowing his good chances made Mendez a "by-the-book kind of guy." He was Jay's report.

Passing under a security camera, Jay and Felicity with the prisoner entered through the street level ingress, passing a bomb-proof glass window and a metal detector. The officer on duty greeted Jay, tapped a few keys on his computer, and then buzzed him inside. The others followed. A large community room was the first place passed on entry. Jay passed the reporter off to one of the female staff officers, Elise Thompson, to get her statement, and then he continued with the prisoner toward the holding tank. Jay punched in a code, and the system completed a retinal scan.

A loud clunk occurred as the metallic door unbolted. Jay snapped on the light inside the room from an external switch and then placed the prisoner inside. He pushed the suspect forward, and every muscle in his body jerked. The man stumbled toward a cot. "I'll be back in ten minutes to bring your interrogation. Do you need medical attention for your withdrawal?"

The man nodded to Jay, and he tapped a small console. A red light indicated the need for a jail doctor to come and evaluate the prisoner. Jay worried from the prisoner's appearance that he would soon go into a form of seizure in which his brain's electrical patterns would become disrupted, and violent convulsions would occur. If that happened, the prisoner would not be able to be interrogated for at least forty-eight hours, and there was a chance he would not survive.

Frustrated, Jay hoped to have the opportunity to be interrogated but doubted he get the chance. It was not as if he even expected to get much out of interrogation. Over the last decade, he'd interrogated hundreds of juice users and dozens of gang members. Low-level gang members almost always knew nothing, and mysterious lawyers often showed up to get them off the hook. For Juice users, the prognosis was even less promising-most often, if they survived withdrawal, it was weeks before they were coherent enough to get information.

For now, it was a waiting game with the prisoner. Tired, Jay left to fill out the paperwork, pour himself some cappuccino, and brief the captain on the night's craziness. He was sure Mendez would be less than pleased.

~

From the room, Felicity waited to give her statement. The place, primarily done in deep stained brown wood, contained a long oak table where she sat. The walls were painted a soft blue color, which she felt was probably done by the community psychologists to give it a friendly feeling. The corner of the room contained a small dark black refrigerator with soda inside. Next to the fridge rested a white microwave oven, and on the far wall hung a vast holographic television. Two boxes sat on the floor filled with cheap toys for children. Some of the dolls lay on the floor instead of in the box.

She scanned the room and noticed the fresh green and blue streamers on the walls in the corner. A smile crept on her face. The station, at this point, had made an effort to ensure that visitors were comforted.

Her eyes gazed out into the hallway. The room's opposite was true: The fluorescent light glaring off the tile floor was disorienting. The division was huge, covering over sixty-five thousand square feet. Pandemonium traffic flowed, but the designers sectioned off by multicolored walls and gates gave it some wild sense of order.

The artsy array of colors, angles, and curves supported a calming effect. Computers, servers, routers, and old desk phones cluttered the corner of the room as if they were stacked and left. Each workstation contained a voice-activated computer, and most of the staff sported their iPods. Still, the work desk areas were a bit of a shamble (even crime didn't take a day off for the authorities to settle themselves in order).

Counting civilians, the building contained approximately two hundred personnel for any shift. Its night staff was the same size as its day. City planners made sure that each shift assigned at least one captain, ninety-three uniformed officers, eighteen detectives, five officers assigned to a community intervention team, and fourteen civilian crime-scene investigators. The basement was a crime scene investigation lab with the capacity to conduct DNA testing.

The defund the police moment led designers to set up a special division of community psychologists with access to two marketing personnel. The goal was to increase integration with community affairs to keep the pork. Their function was to design programs to ensure that the police were an integrated part of the community. A leftover from the old socialist government, the Corporate Council, continued the policy, firmly holding that policing was turned into occupation without the community's support. They often pointed to protests and riots in the early twenties and the feelings of some communities that they were overpoliced and under-protected.

Other staff included office support, three criminal profilers, and a specialized behavior modification division. The behavior analysts went into the community to offer crime prevention programs and consultation on cases to help ensure that all citizens would have a fair chance to be a part of the community's gains. Finally, they went into the schools for complex cases involving violent children and helped develop positive behavioral support programs.

An intensive behavioral health division also existed for cases needing specialized attention. It was not uncommon for prisoners to need medication services or for people with mental health problems to be given exceptional support if they forgot to take their medication.

Blending in elements of Asian and Ancient Egyptian into a traditional western station, the reporter admired how the place was kept so clean during so much action. As a reporter, Felicity had been at the precinct many times, even during its transformation. Her mind marveled at how much had improved in just the last few years.

While she waited, Felicity tried to call the hospital and speak with Susan. As it was outside of visiting hours, the hospital did not permit the call but took a message to deliver to the girl when she woke the following day. Felicity next called her parents to leave a message on their machine that she was no longer in the hospital, but her sister was. The day's craziness landed on her shoulders in the entire center as she hung her cellphone up. She brought her hands up, scratched the back of her head with fingers from both hands, rubbed her neck, and rubbed her face.

The female officer, who said her name was Arianna Gutiérrez, arrived to take Felicity's statement a few minutes later. Nervous, the reporter's hands fell on her chain and twisted it up and back on her neck. She briefly wondered if all crime survivors felt this way or something close to it. The two made small talk for several minutes.

"I like the room," she stated.

"The juice war has provided the department with some extra cash," the officer informed.

"I see," Felicity said. She crossed her arms and drummed her fingers against the triceps of her arms, "so you decided to decorate?" The reporter pointed to the lining of the room.

"Sometimes we decorate this room for department birthday parties, but those are actually for next week's dedication."

"Dedication?" the reporter asked, although she had the feeling that she should have known.

"Yes, the corporate council will be here to dedicate the new wing in two days. We are at the front of making the city safe from crime," the woman proudly added.

"Oh, it sounds wonderful," Felicity added. The forced delight in her voice indicated her sarcasm.

"I just have a few questions to ask, and then we can get to your statement," the police officer informed. The process lasted for approximately twenty minutes. Together they reviewed the information, and then Officer Jay arrived at the room. The reporter was happy to see him. Through this ordeal, his presence brought her a sense of safety.

"Love the decorations," the reporter stated when Jay entered.

"Yeah, it's the best thing since they added the bidet seats to the toilets," he said, and she laughed. "Well, I guess some of these guys could never get too clean."

"Oh, not Jay, too much information," she chuckled.

"I guess."

"How did the interrogation go?" Felicity asked, but Jay just shook his head grimly. "What happened?"

"Guy slipped into a juice withdrawal coma," Jay asserted. "I doubt we'll get anything out of him for the next two or three days." Felicity's face fell in her hands, and she sobbed bitterly.

Officer Jay waltzed over to her and placed a hand on her shoulder. She gripped his hand tightly. He was a bit of a dandy but seeing him in his element added depth and strength to his image. "I could be dead in a few hours, let alone a few days, if we don't find out what is going on."

"You're welcome to stay with her at the precinct. We have some holding rooms for people in protective custody to sleep, or we can put you into a witness protection program and place you in a safe house until things blow over."

"The safe houses are never a haven, Jay."

Jay cleared his throat, thinking back to when the safe house got overrun, and if not for Agent Black and 427, he might not have made it out alive. "I know," Jay softly replied.

"I know it is late, but can you reach that detective now?"

"He works the night shift, but I think he will be a dead end."

"Please, Jay? I got no other leads."

# Chapter 3

Two hours later, Detective Johnny Johnson sauntered down a narrow brown trash-strewn alley. Brick buildings rose on either side. Gand tags were readable on the graffiti-covered walls. The gumshoe's black faux leather shoes splashed in the mud, a line of quads danced in the slipstream above, and he staggered past a concrete cubist design coffee shop and to the bar and restaurant.

The stucco front appeared like a child-dripped sandcastle on the beach. The off-white color highlighted the motif.

He had rugged good looks with a stern square jawline for his age. Mid-fifties in appearance, his most remarkable feature other than his broad shoulders was his bionic left arm. The pale-yellow light highlighted his white hair and bulldog English features. He wore a black pinstriped Cardigan suit. Catching sight of Jay and the woman, he headed toward them.

Multicolored EFX LED lights lined the entrance. A soft piano played in the background with some sort of pre-recorded jazz. The place reeked of stale whisky and old vaped cigarettes, but a hint of cedarwood mixed with pine and flax oil lingered under it. It sported an aged fashion appearance with French sofas and love seats—the color scheme is a mix of reds and white ivory. The ceiling and walls were mirrored. The bar itself was upholstered with black plastic in the front. Behind the deep brown cherry wood bar, the top rested about three rows of neatly placed liquor bottles. Mid the second row slept an old-fashioned eight-track player, cassette player, and radio system combination. Top shelves bore a sign advertising rum brands with various cream-based drinks sitting on the shelf.

"Officer," the detective stated. "Good to see you." His bionic hand twitched—the gears in his micromotors ground. The two locked eyes, and Felicity found their expressions hard to read. Jay made no effort to extend his hand, but Johnson did. Reluctantly, the police officer took it.

"Johnny," Officer Jay said, "This is the woman I spoke to you about, Felicity Cruickshank."

Felicity nodded and twisted a small necklace from front to back, "Can I get you a drink?" She tapped her blue and gold nails on the glass and gave it a gentle swirl. The brownish-green liquid inside sloshed up the side of the glass and then settled.

"Just some soda, ma'am," the detective said.

Jay interrupted, "Johnny's back with his old woman, so he's back to being straight edge again."

The detective shot the officer a glance, but it never crossed his face if there was any malice. "Old Jay- Jay," the gumshoe started, "tells me that you've had a run-in with one of the local gangs." The reporter tapped the order screen, and the robotic bartender hobbled over, drew a bar jet, pressed the button streaming out a highball glass of coke, and pushed it toward the old detective.

She saw a small "x" tattooed under his wrist when he reached for the glass with his human hand. The letters P-H-H-C danced by each of the angles. She licked her lips and plunged into her tale. "I've been researching a story on juice, and it seems I've ruffled a few feathers."

"They tried to kill her, Johnny," Jay added. His nostrils flared with a strength that Felicity had not seen before. It made the man look ten years younger. "At least twice." The detective nodded. "We got a man in custody, and he is being interrogated now," Jay added, indicating to Johnny that the "real police," as he referred to them, were on it.

Scanning Felicity's face, Johnson appeared to be assessing her appearance more than the answer but made his statement anyway. "You must have gotten close to something," Johnny informed, and Jay gave him a look that screamed, "No kidding." They all chuckled. "Yeah, I guess it is obvious. Still, I think it creates a direction to start searching. Do you have a sense of what you discovered?"

"No, I hope it is related to my story on the juice," she replied. She licked her lips. "I feel I am getting close to how some of the networks are tied together."

Analyzing the woman's face, the detective thought to himself. *She is lying or leaving something out. This is too personal for her. She knows much more than she is saying, but she can keep her secret if it does not place me personally at risk. Hell, sometimes whole families have secrets.* He looked at Jay. Another

33

thought reached him: *Sometimes, entire families have secrets and don't even bother to tell their members.* It was none of his damn business, as Colleen, Jay's sister, once told him. The detective sighed and asked, "What were you coming to speak to me about?"

Felicity gazed at the man, and a long pause passed. "Gang in sector 13 at the west end of New Cyber City. You had a clash with them over a friend of yours?"

"A friend of mine?'

"The programmer for the *Bioelectrics*," she blurted out. "You served in the third Iraq war together."

The detective sighed, his tongue wet his lips, and another long pause ensued. "I think you have me confused with someone else." He twisted away, but Jay blocked him.

"The husband and his Chinese genetically augmented wife," her voice was vibrant, almost challenging.

"She is Korean and was raised by Irish people. Nice woman but not much of a cook," Johnson added, "and wants to be left out of this if you catch my meaning." His voice was firm and demanding. He glared at the reporter.

"I understand," the reporter replied. The old detective appeared to drift off as he clutched his gut, and Felicity remembered he'd suffered a belly wound less than a year before while working on a case. She glanced at Officer Jay and noticed him wince.

"Anyhow, Jay was there through most of it, so I am sure he filled you in on what happened after the incident." His voice contained a certain amount of bluster, then Johnson wiped the drool from the side of his mouth and took another sip of his soda. The Sisters of Mercy's *This Corrosion* replaced the piano jazz in the background as the bar transformed for the youthful night crowd. Four people totaled in the joint, and Johnny felt sure they could not hear them speaking over the emo-goth mix of sounds.

"Off the record?" Johnny asked, arching his eyebrows.

"Off the record." She replied.

"I mean it. I don't want to read any of this crap in your rag a month from now or ever, for that matter."

"Nothing about the Jones'." Felicity gave her a professional glare. The woman devoted her life to journalism, even went to college for it, and took the profession's ethics very seriously.

34

The journalist's words must have convinced the detective. He huffed and added," I'd spent some time tracking down the assets on the worker who sold Harold Jones and his wife out. He had many funds coming to him, and some of that money was gang cash. One gang kept coming up, the Marked Ones."

Jay knew the name but could not resist the opportunity to make a joke. "Sounds like pants at Border-Mart," Jay joked.

"No," Felicity added. "I ran into the name myself. They pick their members based on some genetic sequence."

"Well, that is just nuts then because, let me tell you, genes don't equate with talent," Johnny replied. His jaw slackened.

"Johnny boy," Jay shrugged and said, "I think they do." The three giggled.

"Anyhow, I found the leader of the gang's name is Renee," Johnny added.

"Renee, what?"

"What, what?"

"I think she's asking if Renee has a last name," Jay added.

Johnny stumbled, looking vaguely at them both. "On the streets, people, as you both know, often go by a persona and not a name. I don't even believe his name is Renee. Just some guy who was trying to capitalize on a French image. I suppose."

"I'm pretty sure he's a she," Felicity corrected.

"Whatever," Johnny scoffed, waving his bionic hand dismissively.

At the other end of the bar, two patrons screamed at each other in what could have been Mandarin, but no one in Felicity's group knew, for they didn't speak the language. One wore some camel hair coat, which left the man bathed in his sweat given New Cyber City's overall heat. The second, she turned away. He had a flower tattoo, just like her HR representative before his death. She twisted back to her company, and they waited until the noise settled down. "Where do we go from here?" Felicity finally broke the group's silence.

"I suggest that you go home and get some sleep. I'll put some guards at your door," stated Jay. He reached his hand out to touch her arm but stopped short, and when Felicity appeared angry added, "Look, this ain't my only case, and frankly, lady, you're absorbing a lot of my time. Now, I've done my part, and you're still recovering. The case can wait until tomorrow to continue. Go home, get some rest. Later, I'll head back to the precinct and interrogate the suspect, who we apprehended in the hospital."

"Well, maybe, I'll try," the newswoman replied, giving a soft shy smile.

"Yeah, Jay's got a donut shop waiting for him," Johnny smirked, and the police officer lit up with anger. Felicity chuckled. *Damn, this woman has more faith in Jay than he has in himself*, Johnny thought.

Joy Division's *Isolation* played from the jukebox. Felicity thought of the first time she'd heard the song. She'd heard it at her parent's home when she was a child. Unlike her, her father was a man of wealth and status. He had many parties and acquaintances. The song played at one of his many pool bashes with plenty of clients and friends. The song caused her to think of the emptiness of her parent's life. Still, he was never isolated nor had to turn to strangers for help. *Maybe stock investment would have been a better career choice?* She gave her glass another swirl, tossed it back, and slammed it on the bar.

Tired, Felicity refused to admit she'd reached an end but, given the twisting path of events, decided to go home and check her messages. She also had to call her office and find out where she'd be working now that the floor had been burned up. When the paper went on strike a few years prior, they'd had an office off the main floor, which they used for critical stories. The union even supported this because no one in the paper business, even the papers' online version, liked to get scooped. "Alright," the newswoman finally agreed. Still, the reporter could not escape the nagging feeling she was making a big mistake. Her fingers returned to her necklace and gave the locket a swirl. "Detective Johnson, I'd like to hire you for some work."

"Two hundred credits a day plus expenses, ma'am," the detective replied, and Jay appeared horrified.

"You're steep, Mr. Johnson," she stated. Her mouth felt like cotton, and her lips stumbled. "I'm not sure my paper will reimburse."

"I'm worth it. Besides, I already worked the discount in ma'am," he stated. "Sort of a professional courtesy."

"I guess you got me over a barrel, Mr. Johnson," she elongated his name. "You're hired. I just got one last question for you before I go."

"Well, ma'am, ask as many as you like if you're paying."

"Do you know of any connections between the Purt Network and this gang, the Marked Ones?" An expression of shock crossed Officer Jay's face.

"Well, Miss," the detective stated. "The Purt Network openly hates the juice, but things aren't as they always seem. I know that Harold had some questions, but nothing we could prove. Before a robotic officer, I knew, died, 427- she told me about an alleged link to a Rev. Kathleen Cosbin with Purt" He shot a glance at Jay as if begging the old officer to say something, anything but Jay was silent. The officer's face darkened, and the sorrow grew boldly visible.

Noticing the glance, Felicity stated, "Jay?" but as the words escaped her lips, Johnny screamed to get down now. He drew his Smith and Wesson ion blaster and fired over the bar toward the two men who previously were arguing. They returned the fire. Jay shoved Felicity down behind the bar.

Green and orange laser fire flew over her head while the air filled with hissing and sizzling sounds. "Jay, what's happening?" Laser weapon attacks were rare post a Supreme Court ruling in 2043 in which lasers were not found to be covered under the second amendment. This ruling led to the rapid creation of intelligent lasers that needed the human genetic code to be fired. This did little to increase the number of killings as plenty of semi-automatic weapons permeated the street. It just left the ion and laser batch mainly limited to the police, and after retirement, the guns were energy drained and recycled not to work. The exception, of course, was the detective class, which had registered ion weapons heavily regulated, especially in New Cyber City.

"The guy with the tattoo drew a weapon and targeted you," Officer Jay replied.

"The tattoo was just like the one my HR representative had on the night of the bombing," Felicity informed. She glanced up, and Johnson continued to return fire.

"Interesting," Jay called. "It could just be a coincidence, though."

"What about this Kathleen Cosbin?"

"I worked that case with 427 and her friend Black. We had a case, but when we got to the grand jury to get an indictment, everything went to pieces and blew up. She's dead now, though. Listen, you stay here; I'm going to try to maneuver around toward the side to get a shot off."

"Jay?"

Dark onyx-colored smoke and heat flooded the bar from laser strikes. The few remaining patrons fled for the doors. "Listen, Johnny's taking this all on his own, and he's badly outgunned without my help." The reporter glanced over and caught sight of the detective, who was pinned down. He had no clear shot at the other side as they ducked behind a plush pink couch. His opponents were trying to coordinate their attacks to draw him out. Still, he boldly exchanged fire.

"Oh," she nodded. Jay 's lips quivered. He took a huff and rolled four paces. Blasts circled him as he drew the fire from Johnny. One explosion from laser fire would fry him like a turnip. He landed on his back, and a green bolt sailed over his chest while staring at the ceiling. His mind whirred like a machine, and he rapidly calculated the angle and fired.

His laser blast hit clean off the glass and bounced and struck one of the assailants between his neck and shoulder. The man screamed and burned. The second man rose just an inch to see what happened. It was enough to place his head over the couch. Johnny didn't need to be told what to do. He fired and blew the man's head off. The walls crackled from the laser strikes and some fires caught.

Their success was short-lived. Two more men wearing coats decided quickly from the stairwell. At the front of the bar, the sounds of multiple people entering curled Jay's skin. "Johnny, we need to book it out. Fast!" Johnny nodded, while Jay rushed over and grabbed Felicity. The three-shot toward the restaurant end of the bar. The sounds of heavily armed gang members darting through the bar and knocking over furniture kept the group moving.

Johnny flung the swinging door to the kitchen open. A waitress dropped a plate of food, and Johnny felt terrible they would probably take it out of her pay. She screamed as they made their way out of the bar. They pushed inside, and Jay tossed the woman his card- saying, "I'll cover it. Call me."

The chef huddled in the corner as they rushed toward the backdoor. As they ran, Felicity screamed and threw the necklace off her neck. "It burned me." She yelped.

"It what?" Jay stared, confused.

"The necklace. That thing burned me," Felicity replied, panting.

Catching an ancient microwave running, Johnny yelled, "I got it, Jay – you keep going."

"Leave it," Jay screamed as he picked up his small walkie-talkie looking electronic. Jay ordered for police backup as he dove behind a stove.

Trying to pick the necklace up, Johnny felt his hand burning, and he quickly flipped it to his bionic. Behind him, the swing door from the restaurant flipped back and forth—a vast burly man hobbled toward them. "Move," Johnny screamed to Jay, who pushed Felicity out the back door and motioned through himself.

Simultaneously, Johnny and the intruder fired at each other. The man had to fire down toward Johnny, who was still on the floor. His angle was wrong and hit the detective in the foot. Set, Johnny had an easier shot. The ion blast from his Smith and Wesson sent the man flying back through the swinging doors. He leaped for the alleyway. His foot stung, and his toes would not bend in his boot.

Outside, Jay and Felicity grabbed the detective, one on each side, and together they helped the hobbling man forward down the darkened alley. Jay swiveled on his hips in a three quarter's turn, laying down cover fire to prevent gang members from exiting the bar. They reached Jay's black and white hover a block away and stumbled into Jay's quad. Within seconds they were airborne.

"We'll circle until backup arrives and then try to re-enter and arrest the suspects," Jay stated, exuding reassuring confidence that the reporter felt.

Full throttled, the ship raced through the azure sky. As soon as he placed the airship on autopilot, Jay screamed, "Johnson! What was that stupid maneuver about?! You could've blown it for us!"

"Had to get the necklace, Jay-Jay."

"You nearly got us all killed for cheap junk jewelry! This is why I hate working with you!" Jay shouted. The anger grew inside him. His face was flustered, and the veins bulged out of his neck. "Your bad decisions killed Mikołaj."

Suddenly, a wave of guilt drowned the detective. *Was Jay still mad at Mikołaj's death?* Johnny frowned. It hit him in the gut like a solid punch. But he and Jay had interacted on many occasions since the event. Most of the interactions were positive. *Had he kept it from Johnny all this time? Had he been trying to deal with it, and only now were his coping patterns failing?* An unstable Officer Jay was the last thing he wanted at this point. The detective knew one thing, this was not the time nor the place to clear the air on this matter.

Taking his finger on his human hand, Johnny felt the necklace. He held his breath as it seared his finger. *Best to keep it in the bionic hand,* he thought. His metallic fingers clenched around it. The faux flesh felt like it could melt while Jay continued to rant in the background. Johnny was unsure which was hotter: the necklace or Jay's temper, but he did know one thing- unlike Jay, the chain was cooling off. Finally, Johnny said, "Calm down, dude, before you blow a gasket. You don't understand."

"No, Officer Jay's right on this, Detective Johnson. It is just cheap-junk jewelry."

"That got hot near a microwave," Johnny replied. "Don't you see- it is a tracking device." They scoffed. "Okay, a cheap one but a tracker nonetheless."

"Detective Johnson, my sister gave me that for my birthday. I doubt she is trying to track me." Felicity felt her heart flutter. The inner quake shook her to the core, and part of the reporter worried it split her in two. *Could the gang already have gotten to my sister?* She thought, her heart rate rising. No, that made no sense. Her sister helped her at the hospital. She hit her assailant multiple times with the pitcher. She'd just have to figure this all out later. Susan would not knowingly betray her. Yet, the facts rested before her eyes. *The facts,* she thought *but not the context in which they occurred.* She hated the detective for carelessly bringing the situation up without clear evidence.

"Maybe you should ask her how she got it." Johnson insisted.

Felicity realized Jay was right. This Johnson guy was a loser who would lead her down the wrong path, costing her time and energy. Maybe even her life. She got ready to fire him, to tell him off, but bit her lip as Jay interrupted.

"Even if it is a tracker, and that is how the gangs found which hospital she was in," Jay scoffed.

The detective's face relaxed. "And bar," Johnson added.

"And bar," Jay steadied himself in admission. "Isn't the best move to destroy it or leave it behind."

"No," Johnny stated. "I might be able to hack it and follow the signal back to the source. We can leave it behind after I get where it is sending mapped out."

"How do you know it is not just sending to some satellite?" Jay insisted. "And you have spent months telling me you could not hack into things with that bionic arm of yours."

"Yeah, about that," Johnny's face slackened. "I sort of lied."

"I knew it," Jay announced. A bright glow emerged on his face as if he had just cracked a case, and Johnny worried his revelation might have helped Jay break a few.

"As to the signal going to a satellite- that would be good. I want a directed signal, but these things tend to be short-wave transmitters. If so, it will blast out a signal, and a receiver will find it."

Johnson spent the next ten minutes trying to figure out the tracking device in the necklace. Bending a metal fold, he managed to peel off the back, exposing a small chip. Fidgeting with the surface, the detective undid a thin copper wire next to his bionic arm's main fiber optic cable. He licked his lips and called over to Jay, "I think I found an entrance. I need to concentrate on my work."

The officer cleared his throat. "Well, go for it," Jay staunchly replied. The detective nodded in affirmation, huffed, and linked the ends of the wire to the chip. Electric blue energy arched out and circled his arm. "And Johnson, we're being followed."

"Can you give him the slip?" Felicity butted into the conversation.

"What difference would it make?" Jay replied. "They'll just pick up on following us later. Just don't want to sail close enough to us for a shot. Maybe, I put the siren on and force him to land- give him a piece of my mind."

# Chapter 4

"Better to let it go. Call back up and see if they can take care of that," Johnny replied. "Take a side road- somewhat darker and narrower. It'll stop them from pulling alongside us." Jay nodded in agreement.

"Don't let them get below us or above either," Felicity added. Her heart pounded from an adrenaline surge. Jay reached the comm, clicked it on, and contacted the station. Colleen's voice sounded on the other side. Jay guessed his sister was working dispatch.

"I got a cruiser within three blocks," she stated. "You just keep flying. I'll have them force them down."

"If they find anything on them," Jay replied, licking his lips.

"I know. Bring them into the station for questioning."

"Good idea," Johnny said, "but I doubt the foot soldiers will know anything."

"Hell, if I had my way, we'd be bringing the whole gang in," Jay said. "Just get back on that tracker, Johnson."

"Right," Johnny nodded, let out a chuckle, and returned to the microchip in the necklace.

"Ms. Cruickshank," Jay called politely, "Why don't you get some rest. It's been a long day." But as he said the words, his eyes caught sight of something rising in the distance. It was still about one hundred fifty feet below, but its ascent was swift.

The reporter's eyes went wide as Jay pondered aloud, "Drones aren't allowed in the slipstream. What the hell are they doing?"

"Jay, the drone nearly killed me in the hospital," Felicity screeched. Jay's face twisted in a mix of horror and disgust.

"Damn it! Jay, dive on it," the detective whipped his eyes up and screamed. As much as Jay said he questioned Johnny's judgment, Jay gave the former soldier turned detective deference at life and death decisions. He floored the hover jets as weapons rose on the drone and rammed it. The police hover quad smashed the drone into pieces. The reporter gasped, and Jay shouted, "Johnson shut that damn thing off, or I'll toss it out the window!"

"On it," Johnson called back. Hover lights in the slipstream fell through the window and danced on the chain while it dangled and twisted. *How many people had died because of it?* Now, was he wasting precious time and leaving himself to be counted amongst its victims. The thoughts tolled in his brain.

Heart pounding, the reporter felt wide awake, but Jay told her she needed to calm down and get some sleep. "We can handle it," he announced. His self-assured voice relaxed Felicity, looking for a reason to believe anyone. Her life was entirely out of its normal rhythm. This had been such an exhausting trip; she could collapse at any second.

Felicity curled in the back seat corner, and Jay caught sight of the cruiser speeding under them, heading back toward the tale. The reporter cried, which relieved some of her built-up anxiety and tension.

Soaring through the neon lights, Jay lost track of time as he watched below from the slipstream. He stretched his neck, careening it to peer out the side window, and rubbed out the stiffness—the elegant stacked buildings powered into the sky. In many ways, it appeared as if staring at the surface of computer chips. The dials on the console spun, and lights flickered on and off. With a deep huff, he clicked on the satellite navigation. Then came the bad news. "Officer Jay," the communication link called, and both Jay and Johnny immediately recognized the voice of Jay's sister Colleen. Jay grabbed the commlink and pressed the button.

"Yeah, Coll," the officer replied.

"Just thought you'd like to know," she stated. "we sent a squad of five quads to search the bar. The place burned down, took the firing squad almost an hour to put the thing out. They came up empty, Jay."

"Understood," Jay replied, and then the information got worse. Johnny finished fiddling with the device. He peered at Jay.

"It's a short wave," Johnny informed. "The good news is I think I can jam it."

Jay grunted at arriving at another dead end. "Maybe we could use the thing as a trap," Jay finally offered. "I mean, we have it, and they are tracking it. What do you think, Ms. Cruickshank?"

"Jay," Johnny replied. "She's dosing off, but you know the next play here: We need to be talking with her sister." He let out a yawn.

High above New Cyber City, the black and white pierced through the neon blue, red, and green lights like a fish darting through water in a stream. Holographic advertisements danced on the streets of the business districts. Inside, Jay's hover, black and white, possessed a lemony scent. Jay placed on some old opera music. The aria Mozart's *Der Hölle Rache Die Zauberflöte*.

Felicity resisted the urge to vomit in her half-sleep state, but Mozart was just one more frustration of the day. A tear formed in her eye. The reporter wished she could become invisible or shrink so small that she'd disappear—anything the reporter could do to escape the previous night's horrors. The woman lost so much and now time ticked away. She wondered how much time before the gang identified her sister possessed the gene sequence.

The reporter fell in and out of sleep in Jay's quad. Halfway asleep and half awake, she thought about a memory of when she was little. Felicity's kid-self sat on a bench in a lovely park. She was playing with her braided blonde hair when a black and white cat caught her eye. The girl snuck closer to the cat, watching it stalk its prey: a grey pigeon. It moved slowly toward the bird, step by step. The bird pecked and strutted, seemingly unaware of the cat's presence. The hungry cat made its move. It leaped, grabbing the pigeon by the back of the neck and shaking it. The bird's wing fluttered out to the side. It was about half the cat's size. The cat clenched the pigeon in a suffocating and flesh-tearing grip. The pigeon struggled to get out of the cat's grasp as it hit the cat right in the nose with its wing, causing the feline to let go. The cat backed up just an inch or two. The bird repositioned itself to face eye-to-eye with the cat. With eyes locked, they stared for about a minute reading each other. Then the predatory feline leaped again at the bird, and the pigeon flew away. The cat wouldn't let that be the outcome and chased it. No luck as the pigeon flew off into the clear blue sky, something the young Felicity was not accustomed to then.

The cat turned to face Felicity. They locked eyes as it walked toward her. Instead of begging for attention from the girl, it turned and walked beside Felicity, wanting nothing to do with her.

45

Felicity woke up. The journalist felt like both the cat and the pigeon as they represented her situation: both hunter and hunted. She was hunting for answers and on the run from the gang.

"Hey Jay," Felicity said as she stretched out her body and twisted her neck.

"What?" He replied, panting.

"I know you seem tired, but I just had a dream!"

"So- what," he replied. His voice was rushed and a bit ill-tempered. He stretched out his leg from the console. His hands were on the steering wheel, clenched tight enough to turn his knuckles to whiten. "People dream all the time. They usually don't mean a thing. It is just the body's way of getting rid of amyloid proteins, so your brain does not suffer damage."

For a minute, Felicity admired how bright Jay was, especially for a beat cop. "Yeah, I get it. But sometimes, when the brain dumps its toxins, the relief brings up images. I think I got one of those images. It was very inspiring."

"Oh great, a motivational dream. I hate when people bring up something like that to stimulate the crowd."

"Yeah, but we gotta keep going. Time to see my sister."

"Are you sure?" Jay asked.

"Yeah, from now on, we chase down every lead and hope it brings us another. We push them as far as we can until either we run out of leads or get the answers we seek."

"Or get killed," the old detective added.

"Or get killed," the reporter acknowledged. "Thanks for the positive words there."

"Well, I have no plans for dying," Jay said, "As Patton once said to his troops, your job is not to die for your country. It's to get the enemy to die for his."

"I think you missed some vulgarity in that quote, but point noted," Felicity stated. They nodded, and she added, "Tell me about Reverend Kathleen Cosbin."

"What do you want to know?" Jay replied.

"Papers wrote a psychopath killed her."

"Well, the story printed Is not the way it happened. Press often doesn't have the complete picture."

"Give it to me," she stated.

"I'll tell you what I can, but the file has some stuff I am not allowed to disclose as it is an ongoing police investigation." As Jay said it, Detective Johnson moved his finger to his throat as if making himself gag.

"So, how did she die?"

"Her driver killed her," Jay stated. "Shame, he was a nice guy. He's dead now."

"Why did he do it?"

"She got his nephew addicted to juice," he informed.

Shock spread across the reporter's face, and the words fell numbly from her lips, "What?"

"It's true," Johnny added, "427 told me."

"You were closer to her than I thought," Jay added, wondering why the robot would betray such classified police information.

"You know I linked with her, Jay." Confusion lifted, and it all made sense to the officer, and it quickly became replaced with anger and shock.

"You got it from the link," Jay replied. His mind immediately turned to Detective Black, 427's partner, and an urge rose to protect the man. "Damn, that is a violation of her privacy."

The old detective's face grayed and appeared hopelessly sad. "Robot is dead, Jay." His face tightened and as if knowing Jay's fear added, "And so is Black." Word was Johnny hated Black because of the scars the abusive police detective left.

"You know what, you're an ass," he huffed with disgust, "and not just for what you said, but you've been holding out on me, Johnson. The way I see it, that is obstruction of justice and prison time." Detective Johnson knew it was pointless to argue with Jay when he reached this state. The guy was tired and cranky, but worse. He knew Jay had stored up a lot of information, choosing to look the other way on the detective's many occasions of slip shot processes. The book was not something Johnny Johnson prided himself on following. The situation could turn brutal quickly, and what was worse, Johnson had nothing to gain from it. Still, his friendship with Jay was vital to him, and they were in a hover close to four hundred feet in the air. There was no place for Johnson to go. On the plus side, he would be his own man again and earn his living by his work, not the occasional tosses from the police force. Overall, the relationship with Jay rested supreme, at least for now.

"What do you want to hear, Jay?" Johnny barked. "She loved him?" Jay appeared stunned, like this was too overwhelming for him. "Well, she did, and dang it, she had a right to keep that private."

An overwhelming sense of scorn rose in the police officer. "She was a robot Johnson," Jay spat. "Just a confused bunch of wires." The man's cheeks flared and reddened in defiance.

*Johnny thought the petty point, but the guy seemed invested in it.* "Think what you like, but it was what it was. You were there. He died in my arms."

"No, Detective Black died in the robot's arms." Jay took a deep breath and added, "Johnson, you've told so many goddamn lies you can't keep them straight. Don't you dare destroy a good man's reputation with your lies" Angry, Johnny bit back the truth? He'd walked through so many machines that he was unsure which lives were his and which were theirs. Deeply hurt, Jay always took Black's side over his, and the detective huffed. The force covered up for each other. It became so predictable that he anticipated it. Still, the truth was Jay always expected him to hurt Black's reputation, but after being in the robot's mind, Johnny could not even find it in himself to do that. Well, to hell with covering up for the abuser. The argument was going nowhere. He let it go.

Johnson gazed off and then said barely in a whisper, "We fought like hell to get out from those critters."

"And what did you do with them, Johnson?"

"What do you mean what did I do?" Johnny asked. "We destroyed them." Johnny lied. It came quickly and simply because preventing genocide was a more significant cause in his mind.

Jay huffed, "Did we now?" His voice was flat and distraught. "Johnson," Jay barked. "I am so sick of your crap. You have your secrets, and people get killed because of them. It happens repeatedly. If Mikołaj was alive, I swear he would...."

"What, Jay?" Johnny interrupted. *The detective thought, is he trying to pin Mikołaj on me?* For a moment, Johnson flustered, inarticulate. He huffed to gather his thoughts. So many raced in his mind, and it felt overwhelming. He forced himself to cut to the basics and drop his emotions. "He was the most decent man I knew, and I'm sorry how he died. If I had the chance to trade

48

places with him, I would have. This is the way life is: People die. It makes no sense. There is no honor, glory, rhyme, or reason."

Frustrated, Jay cursed under his breath. "He had plenty of honor and glory. It was all cut short, and his poor husband has not been the same since! If you had told us what Haastings Corporation was doing, the situation would never have happened. Now, he's dead!" Jay sucked in a massive gulp of air, and Johnny thought he saw saliva dripping from the man's incisors. "The hospital is just up ahead. When we land, I'll take Ms. Cruickshank inside. I suggest you take a walk and get some air." Bordering on swinging back to rage, Johnson nodded but inside, his chest tightened.

~

From the sky, white light circled the hospital. An odd array of ambulances hovered in front, dropped off patients, and quickly dispatched. "I called ahead," Jay announced. "They were not too keen on us stopping by outside of visiting hours, but I managed to talk them into allowing us to speak with your sister. I told them it was official police business, a matter of life and death."

"You broke the rules, Jay?"

"What makes you think this is not a matter of life and death for you," Jay coldly replied. "I need to tell you something. It is not such great news."

"I'm listening," Felicity stated, worried the night would worsen.

"Yeah," the officer breathed. "Okay, well, your sister does not remember anything about today's attack." Felicity appeared shocked. "Her long-term memory appears for the most part intact to the doctors, but she has a gap." The woman huffed and cried. "Now, this is a common thing. It often clears up in a few days after the trauma. Don't worry." The reporter fell into his arms, and he hugged her.

"What if she doesn't gain her memory back?" Felicity sobbed. "How do we find out who's trying to track us with the necklace?"

"It's alright. We'll find out," Jay said. "She remembers most things. It is just the immediate attack."

~

The two entered the hospital, and Johnson strolled around the building, waiting. His heart briefly fluttered as he dealt with the

49

understanding that maybe Jay was worried about winding up dead if he worked with Johnson. *Could he really blame the officer?* It happened more than a few times, *but if he only knew me,* Johnny thought*, or maybe he did.* Mikołaj always had Jay's back, and now he was dead, and worse, on some level, the guy believed Johnny responsible for his death.

His mind flipped it over as he crossed outside the white light glow of the hospital. It was more likely that Jay, ten years Johnny's junior, was trying to impress the lady. Superficial was more Jay's style. Not like the guy would ever break the rules and ask the woman out, but maybe he just wanted to appear like the head bull, the big cheese, the knight in shining armor. *Sure, the officer would eventually realize life had passed him.* Johnny chuckled loudly. He'd learned long ago that his life did not play some vital, critical role in society. The knowledge freed him to explore what he felt made sense, and so he drifted over to a park bench to call his wife.

A convenience store rested across the street, and after the call, the detective went to get himself a chocolate bar and some cocoa for some quick energy. The crunch of fried jellyfish appealed to him. He debated picking up some fried jellyfish chips but decided against it. The night was drawing on him. He drew out the necklace and continued to study the workings. Maybe the design held a clue, but the way his luck was running this evening, he seriously doubted it.

~

The cool, climate-controlled air engulfed them in its icy embrace as they walked through the doorway. Chilled, Felicity gave a tiny shiver. At the security desk, Officer Jay found a team of nurses waiting for her. The sound of their shoes clunking on the tile floor echoed forth.

"Good evening, ladies," Officer Jay said, raising a hand in greeting. "We are here to speak to one of your patients."

"I want you to know this is highly improper," the first nurse inline stated. She tugged at her white uniform, making it even stiff.

"We know," Jay replied respectfully. "If it were not an emergency, we would not be asking for the interview. As you know, the suspects, in this case, are wanted for multiple terrorist actions, and we have no reason to believe they are done with their attempts to kill yet."

"I see," the second nurse said. "So, which patient do you need to see?"

"I need to interview a Susan Cruickshank?"

"She is still undergoing treatment, but it will be done in about half an hour."

"We'll wait," Felicity interjected. She and the cop took a seat. Half an hour quickly passed as Felicity binged online videos on her Megasmart phone and read magazines to kill time.

"Ms. Cruickshank is ready," the nurse said after thirty minutes quickly passed. "You can see her now." Chattering, they strolled past the desk. A door beeped, unlocked, and slid wide.

The nurse led the duo to the room where Susan lay. Chilled air piped through the vents. The low whir of the climate control machine played continuously in the back. The room smelled like mango. In the background, electronic music played on the speakers. The hospitals created rooms to be the most relaxing and healing possible. The temperature was always kept at a comfortable but chilly sixty-eight degrees.

Felicity gave a subtle half-wave to her sister. Susan gazed up, and a smile crossed her lips. Felicity rushed over and hugged her sister, who yelped. "Watch. The back is like a bad sunburn."

The reporter's gut dropped and twisted. It felt for a nano-second like her soul was wrenched from her body. "I'm so sorry," Felicity cooed. "I'll make it up to you." Life was far from perfect, rarely pretty, and never ideal. Even with that reality, she needed to make this better for her sister and those on the ninety-seventh floor where she worked. The reporter felt overwhelmed with unfished business, her life filled with so much red and debt.

"It's fine."

"But your birthday is coming up soon," Felicity's voice cracked, and the last bit barely made it over her lips.

"I'll be out long before then. I'll be healed in a week. The doctors have me on growth hormone to regrow the skin, some stem cells to enhance the healing and steroidal skin creams. I don't remember the attack. Doctors said it might never come back." The reporter was impressed with how positive and spirited her sister was. Even when they were kids, Susan was always full of life and fun. She was the cool kid at school. The kid, all the children, wanted to hang with, unlike Felicity, who was a bit of a nerd and neglected mainly by her peers.

Jay waltzed into the room, "Ma'am, Susan, I need to ask you some questions."

"Sure, anything."

The group chatted, and Susan explained that she'd gotten the necklace from a store called Sequins. A friend, Dennis, took her to the shop. Initially, she wanted to get her sister a ring, but he stated the necklace looked better. The chain did not cost much, only seven credits, but it was all Susan could afford. Indeed, she'd gotten a discount on it. Neither Felicity nor Jay told her why they were asking questions and the reporter just repeated over and over how beautiful the necklace was, and it was the perfect gift. She did not want to upset her sister. They talked for about an hour before Jay indicated that they had to go. Felicity promised she would return the next day to see her sister.

When they left the room, Felicity told Jay that she barely knew Dennis, a heavy-set kid with sapphire blue eyes, except that he went to school with her sister, and they were friends.

After the interview, the group returned to the police station for a debrief. They picked up Johnson. He swirled his coco in his hand, and they headed back to the Scorched wing Division.

~

"I'll run down the jeweler in the morning," Johnson stated. "I'll see if anything turns up."

"I can track this friend of her- Dennis down," Jay added. "My shift is ending now, and frankly, I'm exhausted. I think this is a great point for us all to go and get some rest. Ms. Cruickshank- I can have a police officer take you home and station two police quads outside your place. It should be enough to keep you safe."

"Please, Officer Jay," she stated. "The Marked Ones will expect me to go home."

"We could arrange for a safe house," Jay replied.

"I'll take her," the voice came from the archway entrance to the room. It was Jay's sister, Colleen. She was Jay's older sister and mostly worked at dispatch in recent years after nearly dying in a gun battle on the street. The desk job was not a choice but a recommendation from internal affairs, who felt her temper contributed to the shoot-out. All who knew her understood the last as a complete fabrication. Sure, Colleen had a bad temper, but she'd always conducted herself with the utmost dignity and

52

completely respected the people of New Cyber City. Her story was the subject lunged for her, and she drew. An excellent shot; she'd taken out four before realizing two were unarmed. Her brother held it was for the best, as she had family, and her death would destroy them. She told Jay to grow up.

Jay gritted his teeth. "That would place your family at risk," he replied.

"My husband has taken our son out of town for the week. They are at a free-roam virtual reality event," Colleen replied. "What can I say? The kid loves HADO like his dad." Felicity felt the arrangement might work, and she'd be glad to escape all the testosterone flowing headfirst between Jay and Johnson.

"Just the two of you, alone. What if the gang comes?"

"Jay, maybe you could ask Captain Mendez to put Natalie Ryder on the case," Johnson interrupted.

"Oh great," Jay replied. "One of your clan on the case is supposed to make things better. Besides, Ryder and her partner Jan are working on a huge case in addition to their overwhelming caseload."

"Jay-Jay, not everyone in my group is like me."

"Mr. Johnson, that's not exactly denying that there's no one else in your circle like you. You realize that, right?" Felicity matter-of-factly added. "But I understand. Ms. Ryder can join the case too."

"She's involved with an internal affairs investigation. Two of the newly ordered robots went missing at the factory."

"Wow, when was that?" Johnson added.

"A few weeks ago," Colleen replied.

"Yeah, our future replacements," Jay scoffed. "The type they eventually hope to replace us with, so the department thinks it was an inside job."

"I heard about those," Johnny added. "They are cool with the solar skin."

"Solar skin?" Felicity asked.

"Yeah, they charge from the sun. It is pretty intense."

"Whatever," Jay replied. "You should read the papers more, Mr. Private Dick."

Johnny's face twisted as if he were biting his tongue, but he added, "Natalie would be perfect for your group. You should ask her."

"One condition," Colleen added.

"Okay, what is it," the reporter asked.

"I hold your phone," Colleen replied. It seemed like an odd request, but Felicity turned her MegaSmart phone to the woman officer.

Leaning into Jay, Johnny whispered so no one could hear, "She'll only like you if you find a way to like yourself." Jay's face flushed with anger.

The officer stepped slowly back. Irritation and some embarrassment flushed his face. How could his professionalism be questioned? But he managed to whisper firmly. "Detective, you are barking up the wrong tree. You don't belong in this lane, so piss off."

The detective strolled off, mumbling, "Guy just doesn't know himself."

~

A half-hour later, Colleen hauled the car up in front of her house. Her neighborhood boasted a diverse array of architectural styles.  At least three on the block had been designed more familiar to the southwestern portion of the country with adobe brick in front. Most homes stood from the last century, but Colleen's older two-story Colonial contrasted with most of the block. Its two stories high rectangular facade design with a yellow wooden front immediately caught a viewer's eye and drew them to the structure's steep, pointed roof. The central entry door was marked by the distinct paired windows on either side.

Fifteen years prior, with the birth of her son Maska, she'd moved from an apartment here with her husband, Steve Yazzie. Her mind thought of how young they were and how quickly the time had passed while she set her to hover down and waved to Jay, whose hover fluttered overhead. He landed as well to give a quick check to the house. The necklace was left safely with Detective Johnson, who stated he would chase down a few leads he had on it. A typical solar floor pathway, which met a concrete pavement, led to the steps.

After a quick check of the place, Jay yawned loudly and bid the woman goodbye. He told Colleen to call him on his cell if they needed anything and then left.

"Yay!" Colleen stated. "You gotta rest up first. You're on the run, but you'll be safe for now. How about a girl's night when Natalie shows up?"

Felicity flashed a grin. A girl's night together sounded fun. "Got any movies?" Felicity asked.

"I have some Nicholas Sparks flicks we could make fun of," Colleen cheerfully replied. "But let's wait for Natalie before we do all that fun stuff!" The officer strolled over to an old fashion fireplace. Holo-screens replaced the area where flames used to burn. The senior officer pressed the button, and a heatless fire burned. The crackle of the flame was soothing, and the colors mesmerizing.

The news reporter felt herself drifting into the flames. She sucked in a colossal breath, and her whole body relaxed, but a feeling of homesickness came with it. She felt terrible.

Colleen's place was very nice, but part of Felicity wanted to be home now. Safe in her tiny apartment and the warm jets of her jacuzzi shower. Its water pounded heavily, relaxing her flesh. But the sane, rational part knew she couldn't be. Her apartment would be the first place that the Marked Ones would search. So instead, the reporter resigned herself to being at the house of Jay's sister in a quasi-witness protection setup.

The two sat on the couch and chatted. "Tell me about your brother, Officer Jay."

"He's a good guy. If anyone were going to crack the case, it would be him."

"You think there is something here to crack?"

"Our mother always said there were special things inside Jay. He was just unaware of them. She always said there was super good in both of us. He's very bright. He'll figure it out."

A half-hour later, a knock occurred at the front door. Colleen rose to answer, and she saw a flash of headlights as a quad launched away. A young police officer around Felicity's age, Natalie Ryder, came into the house. "Hey, Colleen," the woman stated. "Jan drove me over," Natalie chatted with Colleen. Officer Jan Heisman was a fixture on the streets, having been with the Force for ten years, and Colleen remarked it would be nice if she stayed, but Natalie said with her third kid, the officer tended to avoid overtime as much as possible. "So, I guess we will settle for the rookie," Colleen laughed. "It's not like anything is going to happen anyway."

"Colleen, we always have you," Natalie offered, but Colleen downplayed the idea. She waved her hand, stating she was only a desk officer.

"Little old me, you're supposed to be the quick shot in the department. What is it two seconds?"

"Something like that." Colleen stared at the woman, who hated to brag, and then she caved, "Actually, 0.145 seconds."

"That is drawn, aimed, and fired?" Colleen asked.

"Yep, and re-holstered at the hip," she replied.

"Fantastic," she joked. "I feel much safer. We should call you high noon." The woman glanced at Felicity. The reporter, through the exchange, felt an increased level of safety.

"Believe it or not," the rookie added, "Detective Johnson taught me."

"But he only has one arm," Colleen said in mock disbelief. Natalie nodded with a sense of pride.

Some of the mannerisms and ways Colleen talked reminded Felicity of her brother Jay. The two women entered the living room, and the young officer approached the reporter.

"Officer Natalie Ryder," she introduced. "And you must be Ms. Cruickshank. Younger than I expected."

"So, what did you expect? Some middle-aged woman with wrinkles and a potbelly?" Felicity chuckled as Colleen brought out a large bowl of popcorn.

"How is the case going?"

"Which one," Natalie asked. "I carry a big caseload."

"The missing robot one."

"More press hype? You know your ilk wastes a ton of my time."

"Not my story, sorry."

"It's ok. We got a few leads but nothing specific. Probably a guy wanted to take one home as a housekeeper or something. We'll find out." The three chuckled. Natalie sounded so confident; it was hard not to take her seriously. "Hey, let's see those flicks you were talking about."

The three spent the night watching bad films and eating popcorn until it was time to sleep.

"There is a guest room down the hall on the third floor," Colleen said. "I already set up the bed, so all you need to do is crash and sleep. Would you like a beer?" Felicity shook her head. "It'll help you to sleep."

"Nah," Felicity replied. "I feel like I can sleep for a month." Colleen tossed her a stuffed tiger and a pair of black pajamas.

"This will help you feel safe. It always did for my son." She smiled.

"Sure, offer the victim a comfort object. Trauma one, oh one," Felicity glanced at it. "Okay, give it to me." After all, the reported felt there might be something to that psychological first aid and self-care stuff that New Cyber City budgeted for training the police.

The tiger felt soft like cotton. It looked old and rugged, Tattered like it had gone through a lot with its owner. Time and many uses had scratched the plastic eyes, and an opening showed the fluff inside the animal. Felicity cuddled it like she was a little kid again. It reminded her of her old stuffed caracal from when she was little. She offered out a soft giggle.

The woman tried to watch the film, but it was too slow. On more than one occasion, the ticking of Colleen's old fashion clock woke her up only for the swishing drone of the ceiling fan to guide her back to sleep.

The plot seemed unrealistic to Felicity, who kept fighting hard not to dose off. She'd typically feel bad about her behavior, but she noticed that Colleen and Natalie had the same problem. Maybe they all had tough days, or unrealistic blonde girls falling in love with super caring and infinitely patient guys tested their reality limits. Of course, plot twists involving ghosts and acts of god in a movie, which was supposed to be realistic, broke the limit to the point where the reporter rose and excused herself.

"Shower's just up the steps and down the hall," Colleen informed and pointed toward the back of the house.

The bathroom smelled of old mint soaps, formaldehyde, and soft scented body oil. An old computer hook-up played Kentucky Blue Grass in the corner. Knowing Jay's Native American heritage, Colleen's music choice surprised the reporter. Maybe the simplicity of the music gave her a calming sense of humanity. The hectic life of officers was recently kicked into overdrive when New Cyber City threatened to triple its mechanical force and cut human officers. Once Jay mentioned that most of the police force feared machines would push them off the Force. Probably a worse fear for the desk and dispatch crews.

The woman lit a mirror by the sink and stared deeply into it. She ran her finger over the mostly healed helices-shaped cut on her forehead, which she acquired in the bomb blast at her work on the ninety-seventh floor. Then she guided her hand down and exposed the cut, just under her neck, which the assailant in the hospital made, trying to stab her. She'd placed an adhesive strip over the amount, hoping to hide it from hospital staff out of fear they would not let her sign out, and the robotic doctor would instead inject her with some crazy tranquilizing cocktail to keep her. The thought of fighting the robot caused her a brief chuckle. Her finger touched the cut. It prodded the area, wondering how the scar tissue would appear. Finally, her gaze drew sad again, as her body felt naked without the necklace from her sister. A slight pang of guilt and sorrow blended as she worried about Susan's memory loss and her scarred back. The words, "they might do a small skin graph," echoed in her head, and she sighed.

A knock on the bathroom door brought her out of her doldrums. It was Colleen just checking to make sure everything was okay. "I'm fine," she lied, and the middle-aged woman on the other side strolled away.

As Johnny Cash's *Solitary Man* kicked out over the speakers, Felicity stripped down and dove into the shower. A warm trickle of shower water glided over the reporter's body, melting away the day's tension. She cried and scrubbed her skin and hair, hoping to remove the sense of repeated victimization and attempts at victimization with the dead skin. She felt a sense of shame. As a reporter, it was her job to hunt down the truth; now, she found herself hunted. *What would her peers on the ninety-seventh floor think?* They'd think it couldn't just be about her. She was too small a fish to deserve all this effort.

So many emotions overwhelmed her that she rapidly put on the pajamas that Colleen had given her. Half in a dream, she staggered off to her assigned room. The guest room was oak wood around a sheetrock frame. The sparsely furnished inside contained a queen-sized bed and an end table on either side. Behind her was a closet, but she did not glance in it. Instead, she dove into the warm bed provided. The minute her head struck the pillow, Felicity fell into a deep sleep.

# Chapter 5

Sun piercing through the blinds woke Felicity the following day. Her mind replayed the explosion as she lay in bed, and her guilt flared up again. A real reporter would have analyzed the situation instead of feeling pleased for a break from the boss's interrogation. She realized Howe had visited her dreams while she slept and told her she had failed him and not to yield again. The goal was to catch his murderer. Her hand crinkled the sheets tightly in a ball.

The reporter tried to rise from the bed, but her back strain caused massive pain. She lay there in pain, and the doubt set into her. Everything happened so quickly after the bombing that she had no time for self-doubt. Now it crushed her. *Had she missed something more significant about the case? More than just the Chin reference. If she caught it, would her friends and boss be alive? Was that what Howe was telling her.* Unsure of the time, she twisted on her side, fell out of bed, and hobbled down the steps of Colleen's home.

The soreness of her back caused her to wonder if it was from all the running she did the previous day or if she'd slept wrong. The tendons of the backs of her calves ached, and she knew that was from running. The reporter stopped in the bathroom, turned on the faucet, and threw cold water on her face. The splash of water somehow made her feel alive and real. Her hand found the towel and patted it over her cheeks and chin. Then she relieved herself and headed down the stairs.

When she reached the bottom, an overwhelming smell of eggs, bacon, and steaming coffee coming from the kitchen greeted her. Laughter filled the air as Colleen and Natalie joked. She staggered toward the kitchen.

"You missed half the day already," Natalie, who wore the dark blue police pants with a light blue police work shirt, informed her. The New Cyber City patch was displayed over the triceps on the shirt. The whir of the kitchen fan over the stove caught the reporter's attention. She glanced at the delicious food. Her stomach grumbled.

"Yep," Colleen added, dressed in a white shirt with dark black pants. "It's one-thirty." The reporter noticed the two solid brass bars pinned on Colleen's collar lapel as she escorted Felicity to the table and drew back her chair. When Felicity sat, Natalie waltzed over with the frying pan and shoveled two eggs onto the plate while Colleen went and retrieved orange juice.

"Sorry, I guess my body betrayed me and kept me asleep. It wasn't so good, honestly." The reporter tossed some pepper on the eggs and then stabbed her fork into them as Natalie brought over some bacon and Colleen delivered some fresh toast.

"Nope," Colleen replied. "You betrayed your body by getting up. Healing is important. Sometimes, it is just good to lay there and let it happen."

"I really can't believe this gang's efforts to try and kill me," Felicity said, soaking up the running eggs with the toast and taking a bite. The eggs tasted marvelous like her body craved them but lacked awareness of its needs from the shock of the previous day's events.

"Honey," Natalie replied, "They know if you figure out who they are, well, they are going to jail, and no one ever wants to do that."

"Yeah, it's like that old song *Seven Spanish Angels*- better dead free than in the joint," Colleen joked.

"I wonder if Detective Johnson found out anything after leaving last night," the reporter asked.

"Johnny's a bright guy," Colleen added, and something in her voice hinted at more than just admiration.

"I am surprised you say that given how much your brother seems to hate him."

"Jay can be very stubborn, but he and Johnson have made some great busts working together."

"Yeah, and Johnny likes working with him. I know because he tells me all the time," Natalie added.

"Tells you?" Felicity questioned.

"Sure, his daughter and I are best friends and have been all our lives," Natalie informed. The reporter just nodded, stunned by how small the world around the police force seemed to be.

"Jay goes on shift at four," Colleen added. "We could head down to the office then."

"Okay, but would it be possible to take me home so that I can get a change of clothing?"

"Not safe," Colleen added. "Much better if you gave us the keys and we shot by and picked your stuff up."

"Okay," the reporter stated, "But I think I will call Johnson."

"Not from your MegaSmart phone," Colleen interrupted. "I powered it down yesterday."

"Why?"

"Satellites can track it," she stated, "and I did not want those nuts coming to my home if your phone went off. I left it in holding. Consider yourself unchained." The older female officer grinned toothily.

"Makes sense, but I need to work on my story," she stated. "I have an informant in the gang, and I was hoping to contact him."

"Well, he couldn't be much of an informant," Natalie retorted with a huff. Felicity locked eyes with her, saying, "well, he failed to tell you they planned to blow up your entire floor."

"Good point," the reporter replied, scooping more eggs into her mouth.

"So, what's his name?" Colleen asked.

"I can't tell you," Felicity added, biting her lip, "reporter never gives up a source." She reached over, picked up the orange juice, and took a big swig.

"Yeah, I figured," Natalie stated. "Anyhow, maybe Colleen can take you into the office, and I'll stop by your apartment and get your stuff. Give me your keys or combination."

"It's a handprint scan," Felicity replied. While she knew it was part of the police's trauma training to make people feel safe, the reporter was impressed with how secure, nurtured, and connected to the officers she felt after only one night.

"Seriously," Colleen rebuked.

"It's an apartment. I can't afford much. So, I guess you're going to have to take me."

"Or buy you some new clothing at the store and bill it to the department," Natalie replied, picking up her MegaSmart phone and reviewing the morning news sights. "Looks like it is starting as a busy day. She pointed to a story, the papers are covering the bombing of your place, and they pulled out a body from the Delaware river- a local dock worker."

A sense of worry flushed over Felicity. Her body ran hot and sweaty from head to foot. "Dock worker?" she asked.

"No one important, just a Jorge Vasquez."

The reporter's heart sank. They'd found out her informant, but how? "Oh shit," she called out. "That was my informant."

Colleen stared at her in disbelief. "He was your...."

"Informant," she stated.

"I guess they are cleaning up loose ends," Natalie sighed, putting on her police hat.

"Does your ethical sense of confidentiality follow a person past the grave?" Colleen asked. "I mean, I like to figure out how he got caught and, frankly, if he told you anything that can help us track down his killers."

"I'll call Jay," Colleen affirmed. "Finish eating, and we'll stop and pick you up some clothing."

~

The trip to the boutique clothing shop lasted about ten minutes. Felicity refused to let the department pay for her clothing. She was a grown woman with a decent but far from great salaried job and could take care of herself. Colleen balked at the use of credit cards, they were too easy to track, so Felicity paid in credits. Unfortunately, this form of payment greatly limited her options.

Knowing just what she could afford to purchase, the woman decided to allow the computer program to dress her from head to toe in matching gear. Her women escorts all remarked about how sharp she appeared and how her choices of denim matched her blue bedazzled eye shadow.

"Get a windbreaker," Colleen said before they left. "It's supposed to be foggy tonight and chilly."

"Welcome relief from the heat," Natalie added, and Felicity agreed.

Even though the reporter knew she was safe with the officers, the previous day's events left her feeling uncertain. Her mind played tricks on her, and she was paranoid about being followed. Thus, Felicity was happy when they finally left the shop and hovered at the department.

On arrival, her first stop was holding to retrieve her phone. The place smelled of fresh brewed hot coffee. Officers shuffled through the room.

Felicity pushed through the desks of officers at the Scorched Wing Division. While most of the precincts sported ultra-modernist, high-tech designs, this division seemed proud to not.

She remembered Jay once describing it: "The police need to be different from the military, else it goes from community service to occupation."

Most of the patrol people in the precinct functioned out in an open-spaced area. Each metal desk bore a computer. Walls were covered with old-fashioned paper and posters, except for the far northern end. This end displayed a holographic map of the city, showing current images in real-time based on a satellite feed. White erase boards were in various corners with blue and red ink scribbled on them. Some offices were sectioned off by glass and wood-colored metal. The mall set up a new holo-screen to project images into the center of the room. The place had a homely appearance to it.

Officer Jay's desk had a plant on it. Nothing fancy, little more than two vines straggling out of the pot and over the side, but it was enough to distinguish his desk from the others. In addition, he was the only desk that she could tell with a comfortable black reclining chair. She noticed the chair sported both heating and massage functions.

The MegaSmart displayed three calls from Detective Johnny Johnson. She wondered what he discovered at the jeweler, running down necklace leads. She flipped open her phone and dialed. A voice on the other end of the line said, "Johnny Johnson, Private Investigator."

"Mr. Johnson," Felicity began. "It's Felicity Cruickshank. I hope you are well today."

"I am doing just wonderful, ma'am, and yourself?"

"I am a little stiff, but hoping news from you will loosen me up."

"I hope so as well. Listen, can we meet in say a half hour. I promise not to take long, but I believe I've picked up some valuable information.

"Well, Mr. Johnson, I am under protective surveillance. I was hoping you could swing by, and we can chat. I got a ton of irons in the fire."

"Yes, ma'am, I can swing by the precinct in an hour and a half?"

"Sounds good to me."

64

"Okay, and ma'am, can you ask Officer Jay to be present. It would save me having to give the information to both of you at separate times."

"Will do," she replied.

~

An hour and fifteen minutes later, Felicity raced to the community room at the precinct and waited for the detective's arrival. She hoped his lead bore fruit but more importantly, she hoped he'd reached the same conclusion that she had, which was that her sister had nothing to do with the attack at the hospital.

The light in the room was considerably stronger than last night. The reporter figured it had a setting for times of day and night. Now, it blazed in full daylight mode.

Thirty minutes passed, and the detective had not arrived. Jay straddled into the room. "We got a call from Johnson," he stated, and worry rose for Felicity. The list of potential catastrophes mounted in her head, and the woman fought them off as just by-products of her recent ordeal. She feared he wasn't coming. She feared he dropped off the face of the earth. Everything felt wrong. "He asked us to set up a video conference because he got detained on a work matter."

"Oh."

Two officers brought a computer into the room and hooked it up. Felicity slumped into a chair and waited. Jay used the program to dial a number when they completed the setup. It rang four times, and then the answer chirp occurred.

The computer screen kicked on. The sweat-coated face of Detective Johnson appeared. His drenched shirt matted to his skin as if he'd been running. A white arc light seemed to bore down on him from an above-lighting track. Behind him, a double paneled white French door rested. Two large porcelain vases with green scrawled birds in flight embroidered sat on either side with a table. On the table sat a statue of a large black panther. The sculpture appeared to be gazing out a window with white painted wooden blinds. The floor was faux wood with a large white Persian rug. "Sorry I could not make It in person. I got some trouble brewing at the shop. I'll get to you all as soon as I can."

"We understand, Mr. Johnson," Felicity stated, trying hard to suppress feelings of betrayal for the detective she hired.

"I ran down some leads," Johnson stated. "First, let me reassure you. I don't think your sister was directly involved in your attack."

Felicity heaved a big sigh of relief," Thank you, Mr. Johnson, "she stated with a nod.

"Your sister's friends got some gang ties. They wanted you tracked. He went to a jeweler, who had done mob work before, but the electronics were far beyond what he could achieve. There was a man- Timlin, who provided the electronics. Timlin worked freelance and owed a favor to a friend of mine. I planned to visit him."

"Great," she replied, but then Jay's huge frown entered her peripheral vision, leaving her voice sounding somewhat unenthused.

"Anyhow, there was an assassin hired to take out your floor," Detective Johnson said, "My contact heard them speaking to the guy on the phone. This guy spied on you for about a week before he tried that bombing attempt." Felicity thought she saw the French doors shake on the video screen as if someone was yanking them. For a nano-second, the detective went quiet and stared at the door. It rumbled for a few more seconds, and then it went silent. In the instant which followed, Felicity worried Johnson might be killed, and her leads would be gone with him. A wave of guilt immediately replaced her fear: a man had placed his life in danger for her, and she was more concerned about the information than his life. Patience was difficult.

Seconds ticked, and Johnson shifted back to the computer camera. The anxiety of the situation compelled Felicity to speak out first finally. "Who was the assassin?"

"Don't know. The only thing my contact heard was they planned to make a final payment to the guy, and he called back at the last minute to cancel. The real payoff got reworked. The assassin is going to pick up his payoff around midnight."

"Who?"

"I didn't get a name, but I got the location of the drop," he offered. "I'm texting it to you now." He tapped his communication link, and the reporter heard a ping on her MegaSmart. Almost immediately after the registry of the arrival of the information, a crackle of laser fire echoed through the computer from behind

Detective Johnson, "Work calls. Sorry, ma'am, I got to go. I'll be in touch soon."

"Mr. Johnson," she started while the detective drew his Smith and Wesson, but the video link clicked off.

Jay strolled to the refrigerator, yanked open the door, drew out a cold can of soda, and tossed it to her. "Thanks," she said, cracking it open and chugging down a huge gulp.

Officer Jay waited for her to finish and said, "I need to see your MegaSmart, Ms. Cruickshank."

"I'm going," Felicity announced.

"It's not safe," Jay charged. His body shook with anger.

"It's my damn job, Jay, and I hired Johnson,"

"What does that mean?"

"It means Johnson's information, and I am providing it- so I am part of it."

"Pictures would be good for your career."

"Good for my career and family," Felicity replied, hoping that Jay missed the last. His eyes furrowed as if reading her face and then shook it off.

"I need to speak with the captain," he huffed and left the room. Mendez, a divorced man recruited from Brazil to add to the force, quickly climbed to heading up Scorched Wing. He'd had an incredible career so far, and many expected him to be commissioner someday. His job was fast-tracked; his relationship died. The early arguing quickly gave way to profound indifference. When his wife asked to return to Brazil, he knew it was over and offered to buy her the ticket. The only thing left in his life was the force.

Fifteen minutes later, Jay returned grumbling. "Three teams," he stated. "Six people for a job that takes two."

"Hey Jay," Arianna Gutiérrez drawled, "It seems like we will be working together again."

The officer grinned, "Yeah, we also have Ryder and her partner."

"This ought to be fun," Arianna continued.

"Just a boring stakeout," Jay replied, grabbing his black police pee-coat and throwing it over his shoulders. Felicity had to admit for an older guy, he looked great. "Come on," he called to her. "Let's go."

67

Felicity's face brightened. They headed out to the police quad tower.

~

The foggy air did not lend itself easily to surveillance. New Cyber City could be a dangerous place under the best of circumstances, but it created a more significant challenge with the added limitations to visibility. Three hovers glided through the air. The fog refracted the neon lights in multiple directions. Blue and green scatter over the ship, painting it with a glow. Water condensed on the glass windshield, further limiting visibility.

When they reached the street, the quads dropped from the slipstream and initiated landing protocols. Their lights cut to the ground piercing through the platinum fog, exposing dozens of fallen leaves on the solar road below. Jay and Felicity landed in front of an old convenience store long since abandoned. Felicity was sure that it was more of the mom-and-pop type variety than a big chain when it lived. The darkened front window to the shop boars a crack line through the glass. The graffiti covers the walls and some of the glass.

Most of the rest of the block consisted of single-family homes, each with a lawn and semi-unique flowerbeds containing some odd array of red and yellow flowers. Almost all the houses had a cherry tree in front, although a few chose oak instead. *A pleasant neighborhood*, Felicity thought.

The reporter smelled the dampness in the air. The moisture was so intense that it seeped through the quad's glass. She hesitated and turned to Jay. His stern and chiseled face refracted the glow of the yellow streetlight. Worry lines creased his brow.

"How long do you think until the shooter shows?"

"Johnson said around midnight, right? Outside of his information, I have no idea," Jay replied. The first two hours passed wordless, and Jay sat rocklike with few gestures or moves. Felicity cast an eye over the other quads. Glistening water dripped from the unmarked vehicles on the street lined with single-family homes. She rotated her neck back to face Jay.

Officer Jay peered through his MegaSmart camera function into a house midblock. "Mikołaj used to hate watches," Jay spontaneously offered, "but he always said he loved the company."

"Why did he hate them?"

"Never told me to believe it or not. I think it was all the eating we did. We used to get cases of cashew nuts and pick at them for hours."

"Sounds pretty intense,"

"Yeah, and of course, there was the coffee to keep us awake and the cartons of Buddha's delight for him and General Tso's Chicken for me."

"Sounds like a real pig fest Jay," Felicity added.

"Yeah, I miss those days."

"You guys were close."

"We were. You never realize how great a guy is until they are gone. There were times I hated him. Nothing big. You know, when the little things get on your nerves."

"What kind of things?" The reporter glanced over at him. His face, etched by the refracted pale-yellow streetlight, appeared harsher and stronger by comparison to their ordinary looks.

"His trust in that street walking buffoon of a private detective Johnson for one thing."

"The guy always had a way of getting under my skin, but Mikołaj would preach- give him a chance. He knows his business. Hell." Jay made a gesture of disgust.

"He liked Johnny Johnson."

"Or maybe he just liked to preach. I never quite figured it out after twenty-five years. He used to have such a preachy side to him. It really would tick me off. Now, I'd give anything to hear him preaching about what I needed to be doing in life," he breathed and drew out a bag. "Cashew nuts," he offered.

"No thanks," she replied. "I don't really like them."

"Yep, life is always changing," Jay chuckled, sticking his finger into the bag, dragging out a nut, and tossing it into his mouth. "Salty," he said, as his teeth cracked the shell. Jay chewed for a minute and then spat the shell out the quad's window. Enjoying the crunch, he repeated the process several times, and then his eyes narrowed. He lowered the bag of nuts into his lap and raised his MegaSmart phone. "I think we got movement. "

"How many?"

"I count two," Jay replied. "When he hands the second the money, we'll move in."

The radio in Jay's car snapped and crackled. "Jay," Arianna Gutiérrez spouted through the microphone, "I think something is happening."

Jay picked up the mic," I do as well. As soon as the money goes into the can, I think we move in."

"Affirmative," Officer Gutiérrez replied, and her Latino accent was very pronounced.

"I see him as well," Natalie Ryder announced. "Just give the signal, Jay-Jay."

The man with a black faux leather briefcase strolled past the trash can. His hat hid his face, and his collar extended up. Initially, he did not seem concerned about the can, barely glancing at it. Then on return, he placed the briefcase into the can and started to talk.

"He's placed the bait," Officer Gutiérrez replied.

"Wait on it," Officer Jay announced.

"Jay-Jay," Natalie called, "check out at four O'clock behind us. We got company."

"What now," Jay called, swiveling in his seat to see a hover drone floating in the air.

Felicity whirled around and drew out her camera to catch a few shots. Jay's eyes searched the drone, assessing its purpose.

"I think it is just a standard spotter," Jay remarked. "I believe it is scanning the area, ensuring we are not here."

"So, what's our move?"

"Nat, can you jam it?"

"As easy as saying it."

"Wait until we get the suspect in visual."

Ten minutes passed, and Felicity felt she could use a bathroom break. She was ready to ask Jay about it when a grey hooded person wearing a tan trench coat entered the block. "Might be our perp," she stated to Jay, who nodded.

Jay drew his gun and flashlight. "Almost game time," he called to Felicity. "Ready to get off your butt and to work."

The woman grinned back and raised the camera. "I'm ready to get some shots."

Officer Jay picked up the radio, "Ok, Nat, jam it."

"She's on it," replied her partner Officer Jan Heisman.

The quad side door rose in the instance the drone fell from the dark sky, and the lights of solar-charged streetlamps reflected off its blades, flashing briefly through the fog. It hit the ground behind them, disabled as Natalie planned. The others emerged from their quads. They approached the figure from three different sides- two in front, one behind, and one on the side.

The team's flashlights all converged on the figure moving in the darkness. "Excuse me, sir," Jay called as he darted toward the assassin from behind. After downing the drone, Natalie emerged from the quad, ten paces behind her partner.

In the foggy night, the trench coat flung round, and the assassin whirred, drew a blaster from the left side, and fired. Three blasts headed Jay's way. He dropped his flashlight and barely managed to dodge.

One of the blasts struck Jay's hover. Cursing, he yanked his weapon and fired. The team drew from the front and side of the figure. All fired at will. The scene seemed chaotic to Felicity, who was confused about what was going on.

A whirlwind of events followed. Immediately, from the form, it was clear the assassin was not a man but a woman. Two shots struck the killer, and she snapped back over the top of a flowerbed and onto the pavement. The assassin got off another round mid-spin, which hit Officer Jan Heisman. Her face went wide with pain, and the woman screamed, falling back to the ground.

"No," Natalie yelled and rushed toward the body. The screams from the body indicated she was still alive.

When Jay reached the assassin, the woman flipped over and kicked up to his head. Her legs wrapped around his neck. She jerked him down with a flush, and he realized she was wearing a black laser block vest.

Jay pinned the assassin down and slapped on the electronic cuffs. Felicity caught sight of the flower tattoo on the hand on the fat puffy part between the thumb and index finger. She quickly snapped pictures of it as Jay yanked off the hat. The woman's long blonde hair fell over the sides.

The face with its thick lips, etched little nose, and high cheekbones was familiar. Maybe a thousand times, Felicity greeted it before, but it did not relieve the shock. The assassin was Gloria Shay.

"Jay, I know her," Felicity said, and the words fueled the officer's speculation. Her hands shook as she continued to flash pictures.

71

His words became flustered, but he managed to get out, "How? Who?"

Sweat glistened off her skin. Officer Heisman hit the ground. Blood spurting out into the air. "Officer down!" Natalie screeched into her hand communication system. The blood caught Natalie's face and beaded in drops.

Coughing, blood spurted from Jan's mouth. The officer rolled on the floor, screaming out in pain. "Stay with me, Jan!" Natalie called out. Jay trudged over and glanced down at the officer. Waves of sadness filled the officer. He knelt and grabbed the officer's hand. She squeezed tightly, and her nails dug into the officer's hand.

"How long to the hover?" Jay shouted. Natalie looked at him. "We might do better running the woman in our quads."

"Ambulances would have medicine and robotic paramedics."

"Massive trauma," she stated, "Tissue necrotic around the wound."

"Applied pressure to the bleed," Officer Arianna Gutiérrez yelled as Jay thrust the prisoner into her arms. She nodded, staring at the weakened and barely alive body.

Grudgingly, Jay started to give the order to override, but fate stepped in, and out of the corner of his eye, he caught sight of the hover ambulance dropping out of the slipstream. Ensuring no seconds were lost, the robotic doctor jumped off the side and landed on its blow-up balloons next to him. He touched the screen of his diagnostic scan.

The flat line of the screen frightened Natalie. Jan was in cardiac arrest. In a moment, all hope rested with the machine doctor. Natalie clenched her fist.

The robotic surgeon stabbed an adrenaline needle into the woman's chest and instituted emergency medical procedures. Laser scalpel in one hand and cauterization laser in the other, its hands flew in a desperate attempt to save the woman in a situation where every second counted. It laid electrode sensors all over the woman's body and ripped open her shirt to reach her chest. Felicity flinched but never stopped taking pictures.

"Give the woman some dignity," Jay spouted and reached over to cover Felicity's camera. At first, she thought he would

72

grab it and, as she had seen him do before, slam it into the ground and step on it, but he didn't.

"I'll delete those," she stated.

"You better," Jay screeched.

The robotic hover landed, and an electronic emergency wheeled the cart out of the vehicle. It was less than an inch thick and amazingly slid under Jan. The cart raised her about four inches off the ground and transported her back to the hover. "I'll ride with her," Nat said. "Can you take my hover back?"

"Sure," Gutiérrez stated, nodding to her partner to take their airship back.

Flustered, Jay strolled back to his hover. Felicity dashed to join him. When the side door opened, she flopped inside. Jay tried to start the vehicle, and it didn't start. "It was hit," Felicity wanted to inform him, but his gaze stunned her into silence. A hard-cold reboot of the engine sent the quad spiraling into the neon sky.

# Chapter 6

The reporter sat with her head resting in her hands at the table in the community room. Tears flowed freely down her face. Colleen entered the area and placed an arm on her shoulder. Felicity rolled into it and started crying. "How is Officer Heisman?" the reporter asked with desperation.

"She's in critical condition," Colleen informed. Her voice reflected a cold detachment. "We notified her family, and they rushed to meet her there. Natalie is at the hospital as well."

"Oh," Felicity tried to say, but the words died on her lips.

"Gloria Shay," she added, "was taken to the infirmary here. She is in bad shape but should make it. If she doesn't, well, no big loss. It would just be good to interrogate her, though."

"I guess she was how they knew about my story?" Felicity said. Visibly shaking, she raised a hand. The adrenaline of the firefight wore off, and the realization of the scene settled into her.

"Her husband probably told her about you working on the gang piece."

"Why?"

"Seems like Gloria Shay had a dark side, or maybe a light one. A sort of religious drive that caused her to tell them."

"So, she had connections to Purt?" Felicity scoffed. Before her work as a reporter, she had no feelings about Purt. Still, after researching them as a reporter, only disdain surfaced for their fake religious hype and their driving people to evil deeds for their financial gain.

"Yes," Colleen added. "I was running through her files and purchases at the captain's request. She was pretty high up in Purt and a true believer."

"But her husband died in the blast," Felicity felt the urge to remind them of how her HR director passed, and then she remembered something odd. The day she went to HR and her boss, they intended to terminate her story and probably her employment. If they had not attacked, Purt might have gotten everything it wanted. Now, it stood on the verge of scandal and ruin. The universe did have a sick sense of irony, or maybe someone up there just laid his hands on the scale. "Guess their life wasn't a Nicholas Sparks flick," she chuckled.

Colleen shot her a harsh stare, and she figured the joke was too soon. Especially with Jan fighting tooth and nail to cling on to life. "How is she tied to the Marked Ones?"

"That is less clear."

"Oh, well, at least your department can start to take down Purt."

"Not as simple as it sounds. No group is responsible for the behavior of one member," Colleen added.

"But you know," Felicity interrupted.

Colleen spoke over her, "I know nothing about Purt's role in any of this. I do know about Gloria Shay's role."

"Where is Jay?" she asked.

"He's interrogating the guy who tried to kill you in the hospital," Colleen stated.

"Without me?"

"Last I checked, you are not on the police department payroll," Colleen firmly stated, "so, of course, without you."

Felicity realized her comment had probably crossed a line. This was her first time dealing with so much death. She found she lacked the skill to communicate how intensely bad she felt and her desire to help.

As if sensing the reporter's desire to help, Colleen added, "Anyway, I came to see you about the tattoo?"

"Sure, what about it?"

"Jay said you saw it before?"

Felicity's voice dropped one full octave, her tone became a whisper, and her eyes rolled back as if she had fallen deep in memories. "Yes, I first saw it on my HR representative- Shay's husband and then I saw it at the bar where we had a shootout with some men."

"Do you have a photo of it?"

"Sure do," Felicity said proudly, drawing out her phone. "Let me tap my phone to yours and transfer it."

Colleen drew out her phone, and Felicity did the transfer. "I'll be back," Colleen said and left.

~

The overly cool climate-controlled air blew directly on her neck and back. Felicity wanted to get up and move but did not

75

have the strength to pull it off. Six long hours had passed since Colleen left to track down the tattoo, and the officer had not returned. Worse still, she knew that Jay and Colleen were scheduled to get off work four hours ago. Not only did they come to claim her and take her somewhere safe to sleep, but neither seemed to come by and say goodbye. She felt alone, abandoned, and trapped by the cold wind blowing on her.

The air droned on, almost hypnotic in its churning, swirling sound. The reporter let out a tear and a small cry like one caught in purgatory. As if on cue, Officer Jay waltzed into the community room. "Jay, you're still here?' Her mood brightened slightly, knowing he had not forgotten her.

"Colleen and I decided to pull a double," Jay calmly stated. "She's still trying to run down the meaning of the flower tattoo." His staunch clean-shaven face peered at her.

*Obviously, a five o'clock shadow would never dare mark his looks.* Felicity thought. "How did the interrogation go?" she softly asked.

"Couldn't do much. He slipped in and out of consciousnesses, mostly babbling nonsense."

"Hmmm."

"I hate being played," Jay replied. "Especially when people I am attached to lives are on the line."

"I'm sure the junky will crack."

"Not him," the police officer folded his arms over his chest. "Things aren't adding up. Do you got something you want to tell me?"

"What are you saying," the reporter replied. Her back and neck hurt from the time she'd spent with the air blowing across them.

"It's simple. You're lying- not by what you say but what you're not saying. You owe it to those you worked with to be more truthful."

"What- no, what are you saying." The sting of tears in the back of her eyes made her wish more than anything to be far away from the police station. Hell, she would run if it were possible to find a safe place to hide from the gang.

The officer's face hardened into an icy steal, and he pointed his finger at the reporter. "How many bodies have to stack up before you start leveling with us?" Jay shot.

"What do you mean?" Felicity replied.

"You're as bad as Johnson," Jay shouted, "I mean, I want everything, and I want it now."

She nodded. "Really don't know anything, Jay."

"Why did you start researching the Marked Ones? There are about a hundred gangs in this city, most of them running juice."

"I was assigned the western sector," she said defensively, "they are a big gang there."

Jay locked eyes with her. There was no trace of sorrow or remorse etched on his skin or eyes. She knew he was reading her pupil size, searching for a lie. "Western sector has at least twenty gangs," Jay said. "I want the whole truth."

"My sister," she acknowledged.

"What about her?"

"She has an odd genetic sequence," Felicity cried. "My parents thought it might be the one the gangs used to target for membership."Jay took a step back. All knew that genetic manipulation was outlawed after the failed Mercury Project in the mid-2020s. Still, natural variations existed, and it became illegal in many places to remove those sequences.

"Might?"

"The doctor at the hospital hinted at it when they profiled her," the reporter continued. "About six weeks ago, when I started this story- I used my job to look into it. I met Jorge then, and he gave me some leads."

"Alright. What sort of leads? He put me onto the He-ran story. But it has not gone anywhere, and he told me there was a plan to push other gangs out of the area. He called it- I can't remember under this kind of pressure."

"Give it a minute," Colleen offered, and Jay waited.

"Tip the hat or Tip of the Hat," She chuckled at the memory.

Jay paused like lights were going on in his eyes and then dimmed out only to go back on. "I heard something like it before. It sounds very familiar."

"It could be a billion things,"

The word a billion caused Jay to suck his teeth. "Rival gang-related? Are you sure it is?"

"What do you mean?"

77

"You saw the green toilet paper hanging up on the walls in the conference room." He pointed at the streamers.

"It's not actually toilet paper, Jay," Colleen informed him. "You know that, right."

"Yeah, whatever, but that isn't what I am talking about right now. You saw the decorations."

"The Hat," he glanced at Colleen. "It's what the department keeps calling the meeting planned for the Corporate Council in our conference room."

"Yeah, I remember the captain says we are tipping the hat to them to get more cash." And then he drew back, "It could be a hundred things. I don't know…."

"An attack of some sort on the meeting?" Colleen asked. "Bold might be close to a thousand people there, and the security will be airtight. They are heading for a quick arrest."

"I got a bad feeling on this one," the reporter interrupted. "I have been in airtight places before, and they found a way to get to me. Taking out the council would be a huge move."

"Ah, it's suicide,"

"But we are the legitimate rivals for their turf. We hit them all the time. Kill their members and jail others. Hell, we even help others get off the crap."

"How long until the ceremony?"

"Two hours or so," Jay replied. "It is scheduled for eight a.m."

"One hour and fifteen minutes until the start," Colleen added. Her eyes looked glassy, weary from the long hours of the third shift. "Berger is coming on soon. Mendez is probably gone. I'll contact her with our suspicions."

"He'll laugh at us without any proof, "Jay added, and he paused, "but we have a credible threat."

"They could call off the event," the reporter stated.

"Not a chance," Jay informed. "Too much of the top brass is riding on the impact this will have with the community."

"He could heighten security and round up some of the gang members and push on them," Colleen replied, "This is a process, and I fear we haven't given them much time," and they all agreed the Captain needed to know.

"One last thing," Jay twisted back to Felicity, "How did you know about Purt's connections to the gang."

Felicity's eyes froze in shock. "I'd rather not give up my source on the information."

"Lives are endangered here," Colleen sincerely added.

"Yeah, but the guy has helped me a ton, and he did it by accident. He slipped up in a conversation and probably did not realize he did it. I just don't want to get him in trouble."

The officer's eyes hardened, and he appeared ready to shout. Colleen slapped Jay hard. "She has a right to her sources Jay."

"Yeah," he gulped.

The catering staff arrived in the room, rolling in two warmers. "We will have to give this room up," Colleen stated. "We have a place upstairs for cat naps- I'll take you there," she said to Felicity. "Don't worry. I'll wake you after the talk with the captain."

"Shouldn't I come to the captain with you?"

"No, he's a busy guy and somewhat cranky. Most of all, he doesn't like reporters."

~

Exiting the elevator, Colleen escorted the reporter past a pine wood banister to a barracks-style room. It sported several old fashion bookshelves lined with law books. The far corner bore a desk with an old-fashioned computer on it. Next to the desk lay a couch with aqua-marine silky sheets and about a dozen randomly colored and shaped throw pillows. In its center, eight bunk beds going three high rested. A couple of the bunks were full, but plenty were empty.

The officer escorted Felicity to one of the bunks and asked, "Top, middle, or bottom?"

"Bottom," Felicity decided and flung herself underneath, hoping resting on a soft mattress would take the kink out of her neck and pain from her lower back. The bed was lumpy, and the springs were in her back, but she didn't care and was asleep instantly. Colleen withdrew and headed back to meet Jay.

The two officers went to the captain with their information while the reporter waited in the community room. They knocked on Mendez's door. The middle-aged half Latino and half African American waved the two off, saying, "Real busy now!"

"Would not come if this was not important," replied Colleen.

The captain's office was state-of-the-art. It sprouted the best in computer video displays and gave him a city view. "Alright, come in."

It took about fifteen minutes to explain the entire situation to the Captain. He huffed, yelled at them for not discovering the information earlier, questioned and probed the data, and then tapped his MegaSmart phone and ordered a doubling of security. He also placed five teams to go and round up all known gang members related to the Marked Ones. He insisted on people with even minor casual contact with the gang. "This is beat the clock," he told his officers. "The officials are starting to arrive now. The press is setting up cameras. Catering staff has been working since six a.m. on getting the warmers for food and appetizers ready."

~

Felicity filed in with the rest into the community room. She felt a sense of desperation, knowing the teams would barely be rounding up gang members at this point, and here things were with the community brag event at hand.

In the background, Kool & the Gang's *Celebration* played, and waiters offered people appetizers.

The reporter rolled around the room, her mind playing tricks on her as she imagined everything that could go wrong. Her eyes scanned and assessed the area. She gazed at each of the reporters and then all the catering staff. They were easy to spot, for they wore traditional and spotless white uniforms with white gloves. They even wore the funky tall white chef hats. Her paranoia worsened, and something now bothered her more and more. Within ten minutes, the speeches would start, and the police were no closer to solving the situation.

A spark went off in her head: *The tattoo.* She'd seen it on a gang member one at the bar and on Gloria, who had Purt ties. *Maybe it was the Marked One's mark?* Or perhaps she was being silly. It was on the hand in those situations where people wanted to kill her. Of course, her HR representative had the same tattoo, and he was not a gang member as far as she knew. Catching the sight of Colleen in the corner, she called over to her. "Can we interview the catering staff?" she asked.

"Why?" the officer responded.

"A couple of the gang members wore a flower tattoo on their hands. It might not mean anything."

"But it could be a lead," Colleen passed for the officers to take the catering staff out of the room, just as the police commissioner rose to the podium to start the speeches.

Felicity saw the camera lights go on and Collen, a few other officers, and Jay leading various catering staff members out of the conference center. One of the caterers lunged toward his cart in the exit's opposite direction.

A millisecond of indecision occurred as Jay weighed the option of drawing his gun. Killing a man over a simple mistake caused by maybe forgetting to lower the warmer on the soup would have substantial negative implications and impact on the police force. It probably would lead to protests and people screaming about police occupation, so Jay shouted to the man, "Hey, this way."

The man rose from the table, spun, and drew a plastic pistol. Jay gasped and pulled his weapon, but he lost the jump. The man fired his gun. It was clunky and poorly three-dimensional printing.

Grumblings rippled through the crowd. The gun exploded on firing, and the bullet struck Officer Arianna Gutiérrez in the shoulder. The woman flew back in agony.

Instantly, Colleen drew her weapon and fired. The officer's bolt struck the man. He flew back to the table and screams rippled through the audience. Some started to exit the room quickly, but the camera crews rushed toward the explosion to get the scoop. The caterer wobbled to stand and drew himself up with the table cover on his catering station. The metal warmer lid dropped, exposing a blob of clay, several glass electrodes, and several copper wires running into it.

"Jay, it's a bomb," Colleen yelled while she fired again, finishing the perp. Unlike shooting a perp, bomb disposal was not her area. Cut the wrong wire, and they could all be dead. Jay thrust his weapon back into its holster and darted forward.

The reporters frantically panicked and screamed to cut different wires. Some shouted to cut the red wire while others chanted for the blue one. Jay hated the pressure, and worse, knots in his stomach grew from the mixed input. Out of the corner of his eye, the officer caught sight of Officer Asia Thorpe waving and escorting people from the room. *No time for them to get away,* he thought and glanced at the explosive device.

In less than a nano-second, he scanned the bomb and, with lightning reflexes, drew his blaster, flipped it on a thin beam, and fired. The orange blast struck his target dead in the center between both glass cathodes, blowing a hole clear through to the other side. After he fired, the gun felt heavy in his hand, as a moment of dread over his decision washed over him, but it had paid off.

~

A bomb disposal team rushed into the room. The team studied the munitions and transported it into a large containment metal bin. An hour later, a report was issued. The glass electrodes were filled with small amounts of radioactive material. An explosion would release the material and contaminate the whole precinct entrance. Not enough to do much harm but to invoke the fear a dirty bomb had been used and show the police as worthless and weak. A typical gang turf war maneuver makes their competition or opponents appear weak.

The reporter sat in the noisy precinct in the reclining chair at Jay's desk. The hustle of patrolmen's movement and detectives completing paperwork droned in the background. The heat function applied to her back, combined with the gentle massage, kept her in a state somewhere between sleep and awake. A soft hand fell on her shoulder, startling her awake. "Jesus, Colleen," she muttered. "You scared the crap out of me."

"Sorry, I didn't mean to." The woman's gentle soft voice contrasted in the reporter's mind with the image of the cold and calculating shooter who cold blood killed the caterer barely two hours earlier.

"Where's Jay?" Felicity asked.

"With the captain,"

"So, the captain must be pleased Jay stopped the bomb."

"Maybe, but it's likely he might be taking Jay's badge."

"Why, he saved us all and this building."

"He took a huge risk shooting the bomb."

"Jay knows munitions."

"Maybe, but his actions were impulsive. Especially for him. He never takes risks."

"He probably saw something and went on instinct."

"I know my brother; it was like he was someone else. Almost daring." Colleen stated. She let out a soft chuckle. "He's been different lately. Probably related to the deaths."

"Death of his partners."

"Big part of it," Colleen huffed, "but also Black and even the robot, 427. He's never quite gotten over it."

"Psychologists sometimes call it unfinished business. He wanted to save them, but he couldn't, and now he's finding it hard to accept."

"Who knows, might be that psychological mumbo jumbo," Colleen replied. "Maybe in the instant of seeing the bomb, he decided he would either save us all or blast us all to hell. Probably let fate decide." The sister shrugged and said, "Although it was a good shot. "

"Yeah, it really was. Sometimes, people have an inner mechanism that kicks in in times of serious trouble, and they know the right move."

"Angels, ghost, and hands of god sort of thing?" Colleen suggested.

"Or like an outside writer is authoring their destiny."

"Or two conflicted authors," Colleen replied. The reporter glanced up, and a pause occurred.

Colleen switched the subject. "We were able to run the tattoo back to a shop on the east side."

"How?"

"Most tattoo designers use a signature. It's an ego thing. "

"Do you know what it means?"

"Not yet. I guess it is just a cold design some people use to scare the victim before finishing them. Or it could have some grand meaning- Natalie plans to find out by going to the shop."

"So, she's back from the hospital."

"Yeah, she needed to get back to work. Besides, it'll help her get her mind off her partner."

"How is Jan?"

"Still in critical care," Colleen informed and then, jumping to a new subject, added, "Any word from Johnson?"

"Nope," Felicity replied. "It's like he dropped off the earth."

"Well, it's been a long night. Lieutenant approved, you're heading home with me."

"Okay," she started but did not finish. The captain's door flung open, and Jay came out. He was all smiles, and several of the patrolman and officers shook his hand because of his decisive action.

The reporter rushed up to him. Colleen staggered behind her. "How did it go," their voices almost came in unison.

"A commendation and two days' mandatory vacation to be taken immediately."

"He suspended you," Colleen said. "That bastard."

"I'm okay with it. I understand the point. He wants me to have time to see the company shrink before I return."

*I'd love to be a fly on the wall for it,* Felicity thought

"But what happens to Felicity's case while you are gone?"

"He transferred it over to Officer Ryder."

"The rookie?" Colleen stated, and her eyebrows rose into an arch.

"Well, he seems to think she is more 'stable' than I am," Jay made air quotes when he said stable, but Colleen did not reply. So, he finally added, "You don't think."

"You're going through a lot, Jay,"

"It was standard plastic explosive, Col. It needed a detonator. I saw that and fired between what I thought was the detonator."

"The cathode tubes were full of radioactive material."

"Misjudged that but was aiming to get between then. I never planned on hitting them, and believe it or not, I'm an excellent shot."

"We know," they both said in unison this time. "My bro, the psycho, "Colleen added with a hint of pride. They chuckled.

"By the way," Jay said to Colleen. He dragged his hand through his hair. Even from this distance, the reporter smelled the hint of almond in his locks. It was probably from a gel or his shampoo. "Captain wants to see you. Something about discharging a weapon in the station."

"Great, I'm sure he'll pin a medal on me and force me into early retirement," she huffed.

"Don't joke," Jay told his sister.

"I'm not," she replied and headed to the captain's office.

Seven minutes later, Colleen exited the meeting noticeably upset. Tears streamed down her face, and her shoulders sagged.

Murmurs started to fill the police chamber, and Jay thought, *Oh my god, the chief canned her.*

Briefly, Felicity realized she still needed somewhere to sleep. Her mind drifted to thoughts of her boss telling her to "Just go home and sleep" during a case she'd had a few months back. Sleep was essential, and the reporter needed to be somewhere she felt safe to do it. "Am I still at your place?" Felicity asked.

Clearing her throat, Colleen coughed, trying to get the curse out of it. "Of course," she replied and broke into a heavy sob but quickly muffled it back into a constrained refrain.

"What happened?" Jay asked his sister. He knew his sister was less agile than he was when it came to arguments with the boss. He figured it for the tears, but then she spoke, and his heart wrenched.

The words passed through her lips, barely a whisper. "Jan passed."

Jay stretched out his hands to hug Colleen, but she drew back. The gesture stung Jay, but this was no place for an emotional scene. He understood her anguish, for it was his own.

# Chapter 7

Spirits still somber, Colleen and Felicity left the building. Dense skyscrapers hid the early morning sun, but the effects of its light were present. On most days, the rich powder blue sky transformed people's spirits, but not today. Jan's death left a cloud hanging over Felicity and Colleen's head, which felt impossible to shake.

A soft hot breeze whiffed through the reporter's hair and caressed her cheeks. The wind was dusty, containing the debris of all the city construction. Sand in the mouth experience annoyed her. Felicity occasionally made attempts at conversation, but halfhearted replies greeted her effort. On most days, they were often platitudes or non-sequiturs. She decided it best to let Colleen have some space and focus on the warming day.

As they hobbled toward the train, the sky brightened, and the newswoman suspected that the powdered blue would be gone and replaced by a hazy white by midday. Colleen stopped, drew a white monogrammed handkerchief, patted her forehead, and then offered it to the reporter. Felicity shook her head. The officer folded it and placed it back in her pocket.

Somehow, the length of the trip served to mock the news reporter. Her chest clenched, and she needed to force herself to breathe. It felt like the final shreds of her dignity were being cast aside. The endless trip home in a silent world of grief forced her to think of her lost colleagues. Soon, she'd have to live with the guilt of surviving a meaningless attack when all else were dead. Even compartmentalizing, a part of her knew it would be an adamant thing to live with, and the thought frightened her. She pushed it away. The reporter forced her mind from the "why me" scenario, which she knew would grind her soul. It was too difficult for her to accept the truth: she wasn't unique or gifted, but a random lucky dice roll placed her behind the bomb-proof glass. Indeed, if her story had been timely, she'd not been called in to be fired but be dead as a rat feasting on Decon. *Not now*, she demanded of herself; *analysis can wait*. It was only proper to find justice for the slow first and how many dead kept coming for this story.

The reporter longed for a cool shower with soft Piña Colada soap. Her aunt took her to a unique bath shop when she was young. Felicity fell in love with scented soaps and has used them ever since. Her mind danced with the image of a cool rainfall shower dumping buckets of water on her head. She would create a good lather and rinse away all the pain and grime of the last week, not just from her skin but her very soul. *No doubt the day is beautiful, though*, crossed her mind.

The city's vast solar arrays were set for a good energy production day, which meant less fracking and probably no earthquakes. Indeed, since Haastings announced it would reduce its overall level of hydraulic fracturing, the frequency of earthquakes had substantially subsided. But how long would it last? Even peaceful days reached an end.

For now, the two stared at the distant solar collection panels, wishing its power could infuse them and lift their depression and grief. Felicity wanted to be in her mother's arms again. To go back to an innocent childhood, where all fear and sadness were miles away.

The large tower measured over four hundred fifty feet high and stood equipped with over twenty-three thousand mirrors. Many arrays sat next to urban agricultural greenhouse farms, carbon-capture giant air purifiers, and pumps to move water from the river into irrigation systems.

They turned a bend, which gave a purer view of the sky. Felicity squinted in the outdoor sunlight. She raised her arm to block its sting from her eyes. The city smelled of dust and grime, but there was no brown photochemical smog today. The groan of the distant air purifiers squeaked.

Air-born dirt floated, creating difficulty breathing. The air quality had improved over recent years, and people stopped wearing filters some ten years prior.

They strolled in silence for ten minutes, reaching the vast maglev tube. The landing for the train had a ruckus of conversation as crowds pushed through, mostly going to work.

Colleen opened her thermal water bottle and sloshed the extraordinary substance down her throat. She still hadn't spoken. The reporter noticed the deep grooves on the officer's face.

The maglev's doors slid open, exposing a gust of cold air, which enwrapped Felicity. The cabin reeked of pine cleaner and other scented chemicals, hiding the smells of the sweaty passengers. They flopped exhausted into the soft bronze faux leather polyurethane seats. The reporter kicked her feet up on a crisp dark grey mat.

Colleen dozed off on the train, and when she woke startled a few minutes later, the reporter could tell it was not something the woman often did. All signs pointed to emotional exhaustion. Why not? The recent death of Jan must have wiped the woman out. The thoughts lingered in Felicity's mind. The events of the last couple of days continued to shock her. She lost all her colleagues and could be killed at any minute, yet she seemed to be holding it together. Maybe she was just in shock. With her life on the line, she had no time to lament. At least for now, completing her business, no, it was more the business for her entire crew: the whole ninety-seventh floor drove her. She'd morn but only when it was over. Maybe she would take a month and just visit the shore, collapse on the beach, and sleep.

Arriving at the stop, the two hobbled off the train and headed to Colleen's place. Colleen closed the white flat panel shaker made of composite wood shutters from the inside. The house smelled of a soft lilac today, with a hint of lemon wax.

Colleen pointed to the rocker. At first, Felicity appeared puzzled, but after a reassuring glance from the officer sat. She felt the sweat roll down her back. Struggling with the lever to her easy chair, the reporter finally got it to recline. Quickly, she punched the button, the massage function rumbled, and she hit a second button causing the chair to rise to eighty-five degrees of heat.

~

Two long hours passed in mostly silence before the rookie arrived. The air was that of awake. A tremor of isolation rumbled through Colleen as she pressed a hot mug of coffee in her hand. With her palms, she turned the cup in circles. The aroma of hazelnut provided small comfort. Her pattern was playing out: she would withdraw and feel intense loneliness. Still, the time felt helpful to Colleen. Even the mood suited her. While taking small sips and breathing in the smell, she talked with Jan in her mind and searched to find peace with the situation. Probably, the precinct psychiatrist would think her nuts for it, but it worked as her process. Colleen believed death never really left a person. She'd remembered an old tribal elder saying, "When someone died, they could capture your soul and not return it until you made peace with them." The stolen soul matched the deadness she'd felt inside. The officer wondered what Jan would demand of her to return it.

Natalie spoke, and it whipped Colleen from her thoughts. "I touched her face," Natalie stated, closing her eyes. "It was so cold and hard. I felt so helpless."

"I am so sorry," Both Colleen and Felicity offered. Colleen's outstretched hand touched the officer's shoulder. Natalie melted into her firm grip but then twisted and drew back. Her fierce eyes met the reporter. A carnival of decay danced within their empty shells like worms eating through their spirits.

"And you -vulture," she spat. The venom spewed from her reddened eyes. "You're here to get the story for your paper? Are you planning to slip off and phone it in?"

Felicity took a step back and stared at the rookie in disbelief. Anger burned up in her blood. The betrayal meshed into the fiber of her being. She hadn't even thought of it and now hated herself for not thinking of it. It was her damn job. She backed out of the room to let them both speak.

"You shouldn't be so tough on her. If you remember, she was there- not to mention the death of all her co-workers started this case off," Colleen's voice was firm and soft.

"Yeah, we need to know who our friends are," Officer Ryder professed.

"Our friends are who they have always been, Natalie."

"It's clear we are in a race to stop this gang, or they plan to kill us. They are cop killers. Haven't you learned anything from the attempted bombing of a police building?"

"You think I need to be told," she replied. "Hell, I am ready to take the Marked Ones off the damn street once and for all." The look in Colleen's eye told the story. This was not the Colleen Natalie had come to know. This was a more primal Colleen. The one she'd heard about from those working on the force, and frankly, the thought of this woman scared her.

"Nah," she offered. "You don't need to do that. It is my responsibility."

"Rookie," Colleen said with a scowl. "You don't know what is happening. Leave it to those of us who will get it done proper."

"No, I'm in, but when it comes time to bring that Renee down, I plan to pull the trigger," Natalie said. Her body barely hid the fear turning to rage building inside.

Tough guy talk and lawlessness offended Colleen, who jerked back. It was almost like the old Colleen disappeared, or maybe she just pretended to disappear. Law and order Colleen emerged. "Rookie," Colleen glowered and harshly insisted, "I don't want to hear that talk. We serve the public, and we will bring these criminals to justice, but we are not the jury and executioner squad. Got it."

"I don't care," Natalie's words emerged barely above a whisper, but we're like vile filth added to the air. Acrid, they burned away all sense of friendship and compassion. *What vile sat inside this rookie? What lingered behind the beautiful eyes and perfectly puffy lips?*

Colleen watched the woman tremble with hate. People wear the mask of decency completely shredded into pure hatred from the grief. A silence ensued for an awkward minute before the older officer spoke, "They can take your badge and gun for even suggesting it. They'll investigate your past and bring in the hordes of psychiatrists to study your childhood. Hell, they'll even check into your relationship with the detective."

"She was your friend too," Natalie punched out the words like a fighter on the ropes after a right cross. The message was clear the woman expected, no demanded,  to know the older officer to be at her side to kill to make the situation right.

The rookie hated hard, and Colleen could tell. It was a revulsion the older officer knew intimately. She did not say anything for a long minute and then carefully chose her words. "We worked on dozens of cases together. She was a fine officer." Colleen used her hand to fan herself as she waited for the climate control to bring the room temperature to a more bearable eighty degrees.

"She thought the world of you and the law is an unfair process. The killers will just get an attorney and push free, especially if it is Purt with all their political connections."

The older officer's expression didn't change, but she crossed her arms. "It's all we got."

The rookie's eyes bugged out. "Who speaks for the victims? Who speaks for the dead? Who speaks for Jan's family? Damn it. She was my partner- my family. Her life meant something!"

Colleen reached over and grabbed Natalie. She wrapped the rookie in a hug, and Natalie sobbed loudly.

"Don't worry. We'll find the louse who called the shots. No matter who it is. We'll make sure that they fry like the Cohen chick," Colleen reassured with all the faith and trust that her voice could muscle, but even saying the officer knew the system offered no guarantees. The corporations owned everything, even the government, and treated their own with special care. Still, the words comforted Natalie.

~

Officer John Jay changed into his civilian clothes. He planned to take his two days of vacation immediately after stopping by the tattoo parlor. His breath shallowed, and his heart rate slowed. He wasn't about to go into the place half-cocked.

No, he figured the best play was to enter and ask to see the tattoo book and then ask about it.

Inside, the place was chilly. Climate-controlled air was fan blown through a ventilation system, which had to be nearly three decades old. It hissed and buffeted against his skin. The disparity between this shop and the newer ones on the east side of town was striking. The "Marked Ones," if they used this place, clearly did not have contact with the billions of credits Purt possessed.

A metallic voice sang in the background, sounding like an old DJ mix typical in the early part of the twenty-first century. Possibly an Alan Walker remake by a synthetic band.

"Do you need some help," the gruff voice came from the doorway. A goon, six foot five with tattoos covering his body, stood at the darkened brown trim and paneled entrance. Behind him, yellow light shone, obscuring his face. Above, ruby-colored disco lights danced on the ceiling.

"Thinking of getting a print," Jay said.

The artist stared at him. "You don't seem the type," the figure stated and waved him over to the black plastic polyurethane mix-covered upholstered chair.

"Maybe not," Jay replied. "Got a book of your work?" The man heaved out a book over one hundred laminated pages. Jay flipped through. It took ten minutes to discover the design, which he sought, was not there. "I am looking for a specific design. A friend told me to get."

For the first time, Jay got a good look at the huge man. The goon was older, and deep lines etched his face. Tattoos lined his biceps and crawled up the side of his neck, over his cheeks, and twisted at the top of his scalp. He cracked open a can of beer, took a swig, and then shuffled toward Jay. "What kind of design is that?"

"Flower tattoo that looks kinda like a daisy. Here." Jay pointed to the area between his thumb and forefinger. "Something yellow with a black center." The goon's eyes widened.

"Odd tattoo," the man mutters. "Not very masculine."

"I'm brave enough for it," Jay coldly insisted.

The artist winced. "I don't...." The man started, but Jay quickly interrupted.

"Renee told me you do?"

"This ain't the procedure, and Renee knows it!" anger exploded in the man's voice. The words came from the pit of his stomach.

"I'm sorry. I am new at this. As you said, I'm not the type to get such a tattoo."

"Yeah," the man boomed, "you're about twenty years too old for that one." The tattoo artist shrugged, huffed a deep breath, and continued, "So when did you decide?"

In his mind, Jay searched for an answer. He knew he needed to play on, but the play was not apparent. "I have been thinking for some time. You know I'm marked."

"Yeah, but even of the marked, very few of you cross over. What's your name? I'm Hector Nguyen."

"Sam Douglas, and it's a tough decision to make," Jay said. He extended his hand. They shook, and the off-duty officer sat in the chair. The man drew out his heavy tattooing laser, and Jay worried the thing was not sterile. *What the hell was he thinking?* He was suspended, and it was not like he could just arrest the guy and bring him in now for questioning. If the captain found out, he could get fired. The artist reached into his pocket and drew out a piece of gum. He opened the wrapper and stuffed it into his mouth. "Frankly, they needed me at this point, and I thought I could be of some use." *Maybe Johnson could give him a job playing second fiddle in his detective company.* The thought made him cringe.

92

"Look, the less I know, the better. I'm not your priest. Six thousand credits," the man insisted and held out his hand.

"I was led to believe this was gratis or not such a steep price."

"You're joining the cross-over group between Purt and the Marked Ones. What the hell you call it: The Flower of Justice." Jay just nodded, and the man's voice stumbled in disgust. "I'm just performing a risky service. I need to get paid. This ain't a charity boss. So, do you want my artistry or not? It takes a lot for the circuits to work from ink, dude." The man raised his leg and placed his foot on the small stool near Jay.

"Hey, give me a couple of days, and I'll get back to you," Jay replied, trying to sound indecisive as if he needed to check the price out and reconsider from there. In his head, Johnson laughed at him.

"I will have to report this to Renee, and she'll be furious," the artist barked.

Jay got off the cushioned metal chair and walked toward the man. He tried to regain some of his blusters, but he had a phobia around needles. "I know, but I am not one for needles." The officer made himself shiver to make the fear appear natural and hoped it was convincing. The information he had gotten was worth something. At least it was a starting point.

"Last guy who told me what you said- well, they found him at the bottom of a river. You need to make sure you treat Renee with the respect she demands."

"I'll go grovel now," Jay chuckled. He let his eyes dart side to side. Better to let the guy think he was chickening out than to get a gang tattoo. He marched out the door, allowing it to swing closed behind him with a swat causing the bell to jingle.

~

Nerves frayed; Felicity sat grumbling in the other room of Colleen's house. Her feet extended on a soft red Ottoman. The conversation with Natalie had left her both nervous and exhausted. The reporter shifted uncomfortably. After a few minutes, she got up, wiped the tear from her eye, waltzed to the bedroom, stripped off her clothes, and flopped on the bed.

Her mind wandered over the events of her life. Shimmering images fought to control her consciousness, but nothing breached her awareness. Maybe wishful thinking, but the woman felt she'd missed something. She scolded herself for her poor self-reflection. Analysis and reflection are two critical skills of a good reporter. Where had her talents gone?

Her job was a reporter, and she was damn good at it. Maybe not too good since her boss was seconds away from firing her before he became toast. The thoughts flooded her with embarrassment. She failed at her job as a reporter. The one job she wanted her whole life. No hope or dream could change the situation that almost unfolded in the office that day. Her whole body tensed at the thought, but it was the truth and stayed with the feelings of embarrassment, failure, and loss. Her face flushed warm.

Maybe she wasn't going to be let go. What if her boss just wanted to demote her? Being a columnist wouldn't be so bad. She would get to write about how she felt about this week's hologram pageant.

*Pfft, my ego wants to act up. Freud would love all the defense mechanisms there,* Felicity chuckled. *I guess I must face the truth.*

One of the things she built her life around was having some internal honesty, and this might have been the place for her to start to get it back. Why not? It was the moment she had lost honesty with herself. But the reporter quickly corrected herself. Her internal honesty existed in the minutes before the explosion. During her conversation with Jay, when her lie of omission occurred that she lost reality with herself. She needed to come clean and tell him the embarrassing truth. Damn all this rumination. Too much time was spent on self-distraction. She needed to confront it, accept it, and move on. At least, that was how she felt at this minute.

Her attention drifted back into the room. A videophone rang. Colleen's high-pitched voice rang out when she answered.

~

After leaving the shop, Jay was on the phone with his sister relaying the information. They discussed his visit to the tattoo parlor, and she didn't like it. "This case has got me worried about you, Jay. You're acting more and more like Johnson every day."

"Well, no need to get insulting," Jay chided back.

"Please, Jay, watch what you're doing. Far too much personal risk. You need the badge to put food on your table. You know the corporations love to break you, specifically, and put you in the damn indentured servants' program for not meeting your bills." Her words wrung true, as Jay had been a thorn in the corporate council's side for some time now.

"I know, but I feel I owe it to Jan's family and all those who died in the two bombings to bring this to a quick end. We got to get the Marked Ones off the street," Jay replied, and a bit of the fear over what he'd done escaped from the part of his mind. He compartmentalized it, but he'd felt himself go white.

"You got a soft heart, bro," Colleen chirped. A sense of inner balance in her delivery. For a moment, Jay felt his sister was fronting strength for his sake. After this morning's events, maybe it was her best attempt to convey that all would someday be well, but both knew it wouldn't. They could obtain no peace on the matter. When senseless violence struck, one just learned to live with the pain of dead friends.

"Anyhow, I know what the tattoo is about and wanted to share it with Felicity, Natalie, and you."

"The girls are asleep little bro, but if you tell me," she sighed, stroking back her hair over her ear, "I'll let them know when they get up in a few hours."

"The tattoo is some cross-over group between Purt and the gang. He called it- The Flower of Justice." The name almost forced a scoff from Jay. They'd done no justice to his police family. They had committed a heinous crime with their cowardness, but he contained himself the best he could. His mind drifted briefly back to his partner, Mikołaj, and his tragic death by Turtle Dove. The pain seared into his soul for the rest of his days. Even the end of the man's killer did not lessen the pain. Indeed, it only removed some anger, which allowed the hurt to flare even higher.

His sister's words snapped him back. It was for the best. Over time, He came to prefer his heartache to live in silence. "This is great. It looks like you finally have hard evidence they are tied together."

The officer grasped a sense of pride as the case was advancing. "Yeah, I'll have the captain have a detail pick the guy up after getting off the phone with you."

"Captain isn't going to like that you went. Especially given your suspension," the sister replied.

"It could be a problem," Jay acknowledged. "I'll tell him I stopped at the shop on my way home. I was in the area. I was so upset with the mandatory vacation I needed to express myself with a tattoo."

"You didn't get one. Did you?" Colleen nervously asked.

"No," Jay replied. "They wanted 6,000 credits- over a month's salary. It's way too much for an honest cop like me."

"Why so steep?"

"Besides all the illegality, he suggested it had something to do with the tattoo acting like a circuit."

"Interesting," Colleen stated. "Maybe when they bust him, Scorched Wing will chase down that lead."

The officer recognized the logic of her words. "Well, if Mendez don't fire me first. I mean, I plan to honor the suspension and all. I just needed to get that one thing out of my system."

"And now that it is out?" The sister side of her came through on these. She was trying to give him direction or point out something she felt was obvious.

Jay paused and chewed his lip. The message was clear: Nothing was out of his system. Finally, he snarled, "I guess everyone is expendable. Maybe if I get fired, I can offer to do investigative work with Johnson."

Colleen laughed and stated the obvious, "Bro, you hate the guy." She planned the words as a defense to get the officer thinking. Thus, she was unprepared for his comments.

"I know," Jay replied. It was soft but said it all. Ever since they were kids, Jay always played straight with her, but for all his anger at the detective, Colleen never thought of him as having hated the man.

Her voice grew reserved. "Hard to convince him. It's close to your home but at least six blocks off any direct route."

"I'll just have to try my best. Maybe tell him I always wanted a tattoo and figured now was the best time to get one."

~

"Was Jay on the phone?" Natalie asked when Colleen got back to the living room.

"Hey, didn't see you," she replied. "I thought you were getting the first round of sleep."

"Yeah," I was too 'wired' to get some shut-eye." The women stared at each other as if exchanging silent thoughts.

"It was Jay," Colleen offered. "He played a lead and seemed to have picked up some information on the gang."

"What sort of information?"

"He found their tattoo artist."

Natalie's face crested into a slight grin. "I am not a hundred percent sure. I need to get to my notes at the office, but The Flower of Justice. It was the group's name we were trying to get a beat on for the missing robots."

"It all seems so scrambled," Felicity could get perfectionistic, and she had to keep herself on guard of it blocking her completion of important stuff, which might not need such a level of detail.

~

Before he crossed the street to his apartment building, Jay stared up at the concrete, steel, and glass complex structure. The stacked, highly pentagonal geometric form with pitched roof and individualized copper-clad decks with a brown and blue glass color palate screamed postmodern. It was a mixture of old and new, much like he felt his life had become. Had his life come to this? A twelfth-floor room with a terrace and garden staring out on the park as its most prominent feature. Hell of a selling point, but what did it mean in the score of things. Maybe he wondered beyond this what was his mark on the world. In many ways, he was a markless one. Jay bit his lip, strolled inside, waved to the front desk, and hobbled toward the elevator.

The first five floors of his building were galleries and offices. His express elevator quickly bypassed them and swung open at his floor. Aquamarine lights lined the hallway but could not disguise the gaping hole in the ceiling, exposing an extensive array of pipes. Construction drills hummed from the apartment three doors away. He believed the place was a condo, unlike his rental.

The doors on either side of the hall were reinforced with mental plating. And as he passed through the hall, he heard one of his neighbors, a man he barely knew, cursing through his door. His fingerprint unlocked his door, and the magnetic gears drew it open. The middle-aged officer stepped inside.

He drew out his gun. It felt heavy in his hand but no more severe than the responsibility of carrying it. He stripped off his shirt and drew his badge from his pocket, tossing it on the table next to the gun.

His impeccably clean floral-scented room was small, twenty by fifteen feet, but designed so that it tangled spaces where the relationship between the indoors and outdoors was ambiguous and even surreal. As he walked to the outdoor garden, he picked up three darts sitting room the side and hurled them rapidly to the board, barely shifting his eyes to aim. All three struck the bull's eye.

He passed in front of his three bookshelves. The dirty, molded books were mainly centered on genetic engineering and astrophysics, his two biggest hobbies. Indeed, his interests often alienated him from most people on the force. He found it hard to indulge in the activities they found relaxing. His mind often wandered to philosophical life issues.

Reaching the table, he lifted a bottle of cognac and poured out a glass, gulping down the contents. His job felt like trying to drain the ocean with a teaspoon most days. Today felt like less than even that. "Computer play Don Cherry- *Old Gold Band*." Instantly, it complied. He swirled the almost empty bottle, poured a second glass, and gazed at the faded brown wallpaper covering his living room. A single tear escaped his eye as he called out, "May you rest peacefully, Jan." He whipped back the glass, wiped the tear from his eye with his left hand, strolled to his bed, and collapsed. Briefly, his mind whirled at how the woman had died. He felt a surge of guilt and could not even find a way to blame Johnson for this one. Soon, blackness took him. The odors of the bar invaded his dreams, but thankfully no images.

Six hours later, he woke, legs hunched up, fell out of bed, showered, shaved, and dressed. Glancing in the mirror, he splashed on some soft-scented spicy aftershave and headed toward the door. His eyes fell on his badge and gun. His heart twisted. Should he take them? He was suspended, and while going to his sister's was fine, the man doubted she'd let his head out to do any policing. Still, she served as a safe house, so an extra gun and badge could not hurt. Jay grabbed both and hit the hall. Not sure of how the night would proceed, he decided to take his old quad.

The private black quad with a lightly tinted glass of Jay's piston rods spun and clattered. The solar machine was battery-operated and a dozen years old but worked reliably. Indeed, Jay had often referred to his "girl" as Old Betsy. The quad was well past its prime, still flying with a joystick instead of the latest cyclic control, which transmitted instructions to the rotary blades. For this reason, his quad found it much harder than the newest one to pitch and roll. The officer had saved the better part of the last three years for an upgraded model when Betsy finally died, but he had a few to go on an honest police officer's salary.

Now, the blades beat, and his vehicle lifted into the sky. He'd make one stop at the market to pick some groceries up for his sister.

~

Colleen wandered the house and into the bedroom, stripping the sheets off the bed. She vacuumed the floor. When things changed, even for a brief period, she felt her life in chaos. One more day, and her house would go back to normal. One more day, her husband and child would be home. She hung plastic beads in the room's entryway. Scattered sunlight reflected off a mirror, and the officer stared at herself. She thought to herself, *a decade to retirement, and I still look gorgeous*. She had to. It was in her genes- the modified ones anyway.

"This was your last night staying here," Colleen informed. "My husband and kid return tomorrow night. They plan to place you in a safe house. Jay and Natalie will guard you. Any word from Johnson?"

"No," the reporter replied. "He's still missing."

~

Jay arrived seven hours after the call. Colleen was happy to see him, but her face was so hollow and pained that it hurt Jay to see her. She appeared exhausted and empty. "Hey Jay," her voice offered a false cheeriness.

In his left arm, Jay carried a brown grocery bag. "I thought I'd bring these so you guys have enough to eat."

"Jay, my refrigerator orders food when we run low," Colleen insisted. "And I hate Cheese Its," she huffed, pointing to the box sticking out of the bag and knowing Jay loved them.

99

"You can never trust technology with things like this, and the department paid for it," Jay replied. "Besides Cheese, They are awesome. Even the name sounds- well, cheesy."

Felicity was in the doorway and thought to herself, *He is a sweet guy, but who would have thought he was such a Luddite.* For her, it brought up a wave of how much anyone knew anyone else. She stopped her brain from walking down that path, knowing it was just a smokescreen to avoid talking about her failure, to be honest with him. Her heart sank, and she needed to woman up.

Taking the groceries, Colleen strolled into the kitchen to unpack them. Jay started to follow, but Felicity seized the opportunity and stepped in front of him. "Jay," Felicity stated. "Do you have a moment?"

Jay's sister shot him a glance. "It's okay, bro." She insisted. "I'll pour you a brandy." He nodded at his sister and turned to the news reporter. "Yeah," Jay stated, sitting in front of the fake fireplace. "What is it?"

*I should tell him*, she thought, *I have to, but what would he think of me.* "I have something to tell you, but I am unsure how."

"It's okay. I got time," Jay replied.

"The day of the explosion," Felicity stated.

"I see. Great!" Jay replied. "Have you got something?"

"No," she huffed. "Well, nothing new at least, but I've been holding something back, and it's really been bothering me."

"What is it?"

"Why it took me so long to remember Chin's was closed. I was just caught up in the moment enough that I didn't realize it until it was too late. He was interrogating me hard, and I knew I would get terminated."

"It sounds horrible," Jay empathized. "But as I said, the information about Chin's restaurant was out of context. Now, it makes even more sense why you did not put two and two together immediately." This was something. She always liked Jay, his empathy for others, and his ability to understand them in the context they were in at the time. "More importantly, you should have told me sooner!"

"It was not related to the case, and frankly, I just did not want you to see me as oblivious."

"You're not oblivious if you were able at least to get a gateway into the gang's actions!" Jay seemed to know what to say

100

and when. His words could not shake off Felicity's guilt even a little. He felt awkward. This "emotional thing," as he termed it, while the department trained him to do it, he still did not feel great at it.

"See, that's the issue. I didn't find that gateway in time, and on the day of the bombing... well, I was going to get fired." Her voice turned rushed and pissed.

"Why would they fire you?"

"The business is just that. I was way behind in getting a publishable piece. "

"But you knew so much," Jay offered almost consolingly.

"I thought I did, but when I went into the meeting, even Mr. Howe seemed to know that Purt had a building on the docks."

"Wait, what? Say that again?"

"Howe knew Purt has a building on Pier Eleven," She repeated.

"I pass by Pier Eleven all the time," Jay stated. "If they have a building, I would've seen it. Where on Pier Eleven did he say it was?"

"He said it was a donation center."

"Just a bunch of abandoned warehouses on eleven. Are you sure he said eleven?"

"I may suck as a reporter, but I'm not deaf," she countered.

Jay drew out his Megasmart phone and spoke to the artificial intelligence program. It linked directly into the computer system at the Scorched Wing Division. The system told him the address, and the two swiftly drove to the coordinates. When Felicity saw the buildings, she froze. It was the place with the French doors from where Detective Johnson had phoned her.

"I'll get Natalie to assemble a team," Jay replied. "And see, when there are no secrets, things always work out better." He nodded, and while he was a sweet guy, the "I told you so" moment frustrated her.

"Jay," a voice came from the back, "You're going nowhere. Have you forgotten that you are still suspended?" Colleen approached him. "Besides, Natalie already left." Strolling into the room, she handed him the drink.

"Left?" Jay replied. "But she is supposed to guard the house." He swirled the brown fluid in the highball glass and took a swig.

"She'll be back," Colleen said. "She's picking up a pizza at the mall."

"Nearest mall is five miles from here." Jay's words hung in the air for a minute. "Ok, what is she really doing?"

"Went to the mall to check up a lead she had on the Flowers of Justice. Something about a hit on robotics. And yes, she is bringing back a pizza."

"I can still call her and catch up," Jay insisted.

"Standard radio silence protocol for this one. Her contact might panic if she's on the phone, thinking she's calling him in for a pickup and night in jail."

"Why would he think...."

"Because lil'bro," Colleen locked eyes with him. "She had him arrested before."

~

As Natalie left the house, the late-day sky was cloudless grey. In the distance, factory smoke billowed up to the heavens. She headed toward the glass skyscrapers—the spired roofs like needle points: a single bed of nails for the gods. Leaping on the train, it soared through the glass vacuum tube belowground Within ten minutes, and she reached her stop some file miles away.

The corridor on the side of the train opened to a dozen others, all of which appeared the same, but from experience, she knew the mall's direction. The area had thousands of people filling the station. The crowd was thick enough. She'd have to twist and wind her way through. People argued and negotiated prices with street merchants in stalls of the underground market part of the larger mall. Ad drones flew up to her, scanned, and then played an individually tailored holographic advertisement for her based on her age, shopping history, and demographics. When one finished and flew off, another from a different story flew up and did the same. She scoffed, thinking *they used to be able to do this on every street before the don't disturb laws went into place.*

The packed mall forced her to squeeze her way through the crowd of shopping consumers. People were milling everywhere, entering boutique shops to purchase high-end fashion at cut-rate prices. Others milled about sloshing down a soda or chewing hotdogs.

Amazingly, everyone appeared frustrated, tense, and tired as they milled around. It caused Natalie to wonder how anyone sought this as a preferred activity. Behind the crowd's rumble, the swash of a vast water fountain placed in the ceiling roared as seventy thousand tons of water cascaded into an artificial lake at the mall's center. The rushing water's best thing was how it cooled the entire shopping area.

Her destination was in the small electronics shop next to the arcade in the basement. There she hoped to find Johnathan Carver, a crooked-nosed man. He had severely broken it in a fight some years earlier.

The escalator lets off on the lower level, down with the fast-food restaurants, fashion clothing shops, taser tag, the arcades, and many kids. The place smelled of mold, french fries, and beer. She headed for the coffee shop. Bright cobalt and red lights reflected off old red rugs worn and stained. At points, they mixed to form a ghastly passion purple. A scheme of wires crisscrossed overhead.

From a distance, she caught sight of the crumbling electronic shop. Its window was painted an opaque grey, and its dirty white pained brick side could have used a heavy power wash. Posters on the outside announced sales of the latest virtual reality video games, which could be easily downloaded online, but the shop offered steep discounts if purchased there.

A couple, one with spiked greasy black-haired with orange-tipped goons and the other blonde with a crew cut jelled into tight short spikes, stood on either side of the shop. Both men were very tall and fit—typical low life with studded polyurethane faux leather biker -jackets. One had three tiny metal skulls dangling from his collar. *Punk rockers*, she scoffed in her mind, *with nasty oily complexions*. Their faces with empty eye sockets reminded her of a trip she'd taken to Mexico City some years back for a day of the dead festival. Primarily, their sunken eyes created an empty stir within her. *Maybe they were juicers?* As the officer neared, they approached her, probably ready to beg for cash. She whipped out her badge with absolute conviction, and they parted to either side.

She scampered into the electronic shop. As expected, Carver's scrawny butt stood behind the counter, reading a standard business printout of the day. In his late twenties, he had short-cropped buzz-cut black hair. Next to him was a cute blond, possibly twenty-five. Wearing blue work coveralls, a spiked black imitation leather choker, and white latex gloves, she stood close and peered over his shoulder, obviously flirting. Her giggles were intense, and her hands took every opportunity to touch his arm.

A bright blue light shone behind them. The wall flashed a screen, which offered the biometric data of everyone in the room. The surveillance system creeped the rookie out. Carver's eyes fell on her, glancing back down at the sheet. "Busy officer," he shouted as she approached.

"I need to speak with you now," Natalie demanded. He nodded to his co-worker. With a twinkle in her eye, she chuckled and walked off to the other side of the room, sorting through items on the shelves near the entrance.

"So whatcha need, officer," the man asked, closing the metal lid on the data chart. Natalie drew out her MegaSmart and tapped the glass. A picture of the flower tattoo came up.

"This tattoo has electronic properties to it," she said. Her hand reached and grabbed the back of his head and pushed it closer to the picture.

His eyes rolled, and the man appeared mildly annoyed. "It could," he replied. Stepping closer to the screen, so her hand fell away.

"Not in the mood today. If your scrawny ass lies to me, we are heading right downtown for some serious hours of discussion." She had no time for one of his bullshit spiels.

"I'd lose my job," the man replied. "I got bills to cover. Kids to feed- but you know that. You want me to wind up an indentured servant."

Their eyes locked. "You better tell the truth then," her icy voice caused him to shudder visibly. Silence ensued.

He broke it, "I think it could."

"Why didn't you mention it before?"

"Ah, I don't."

Having no time for his lies or excuses, the officer asked, "Could the design trigger something on the robots?"

Nervous, Carver hummed and hawed. She pressed the button. "Yes, it could be wired up to serve as a starter or a dozen other things the damn engineers could have designed it. It is a chip design."

"Can you read it?" she pushed as her eyes drifted up to the creepy scanner on the wall. A dot on the monitor turned red, indicating the subject's pressure and pulse rose. It was behind Natalie by the door.

The flirty blonde drew a throwing knife, hurled it, and killed Carver, spiking him directly in the center of the forehead. Blood poured from the wound as the body collapsed. In one motion, the flirt darted out the door.

When the knife hit, Natalie flinched, her face paled, and she spun toward the woman, the gun was already drawn, but it was too late. It took all her self-control to stop from firing, as she had the flirt's back, and departmental policy was not to fire at fleeing suspects. She cursed herself for flinching and gave chase.

The rookie bolted out of the shop in hot pursuit but quickly bumped into the two oily-skinned punks, whom she scattered before. In her head, she cursed their timing. As the officer twisted passed them, she dashed up the escalator two steps, bumping into multiple people along the way. One in a tan suit, mid-forties, with thinning hair, pushed her back and said," Excuse you." She drew her badge. Wisely, he stepped aside, but the crowd had folded in her path in front of him. The murderer was no longer visible.

She grabbed the guy who blocked her and twisted him around. "What the hell," he screamed. Her mind grasped that the two punkers were probably running interference, but she was unsure if this man was doing so.

"Interfering with a police investigation and allowing a murderer to escape, you're under arrest," she bellowed and glanced back at the crowd forming around the shop. The two punks were gone, or she'd arrested them as well.

The man continued his protest, but she quickly shushed him. The murderer was getting away, but the rookie was not out yet. Her hand grabbed her MegaSmart, and she tapped the police app. "Commandeer, the ad drones," she spoke.

"Thumbprint required," the phone called back. She placed it on the screen. "Confirmed. Please provide a sixteen-digit authorization code." *Redundancy*, she thought. *I hate this shit.* It was the price of using the Earth Corps computer system by local police. As a child, she'd often felt a thrill at how the older man Robert Haastings spoke of the importance of redundant systems to protect rights. Now, she hated such maneuvers because, for all practical applications, the twelves seconds it took for her to state her code into the machine for it to read her voiceprint and numbers let the killer get twelve more seconds away.

The advertising drones stopped mid-hover. As the law required a small red blinking light to emerge, civilians knew it was a police scan. They soared through the area, analyzing the crowd. She watched on her MegaSmart. *Where the hell was the perp?*

Disgust welled up in her. How had the woman beaten the system? From behind, the guy whom she arrested grumbled more. Half listening to him and half with eyes on her screen, the officer occasionally nodded and said, "uh ha..." or "hmmm."

Four minutes passed. Maybe the perp went into the lady's room. She would check when her backup arrived. "I had no way of knowing. You never identified yourself," the man protested, and she laughed. His face bristled with anger, "Do you know who I am? My lawyer will have me out in an hour, and I'll sue for you to lose your job,"

"Good luck," she snarked. "You have the right to remain silent."

"I'll break you so bad," the man called out while she picked out her MegaSmart and called for backup, "You'll be downtown begging passers for a credit." The rookie continued to Mirandize the man.

A crowd formed around the electronic shop. There was crying and more than a few gasps. In front of the store, she raised her badge and dispersed the crowd. The rookie returned inside with her collar, clutching adhesive yellow police tape from her utility kit across the entrance, reviewing the video feds for the mall, and waiting for her backup.

Her eyes darkened at the feed. She closed her eyes and scanned her memory. She'd heard of this maneuver before but could not remember when. Disgust rose. Two minutes later, the mall flooded with local law enforcement from the Scorched Wing Division. One of them carted off the perp while Natalie spoke with Captain Berger.

"Watch the feed, captain," she told the older woman. "I gave chase to the sadistic killer. She is here plain as day but now watch what happens once the gloves are stripped off." The rookie pointed to the screen as the blond woman vanished from it. The shocking image visibly frustrated the young officer.

"How?" The captain's perplexity was evident in her voice.

"Some sort of disruption," she insisted while lifting a water bottle from one of the mall's vending machines and taking a quick swig. "But look at the seventy frames just before the glove is completely off."

The image was clear. "Some sort of tattoo. Yellow."

The rookie nodded. "Flower. I suspect it is disrupted the image. I'm checking her old employment files for her address, phone number, etc."

"Victim?"

"One of my informants. A good one. Divorced three years back, two kids. His child support payments, family's sole means of support."

"Jesus," the captain replied. "Unfortunate. What led to the divorce?"

"Married very young and grew apart."

"Oh," the captain said like she understood the story or at least heard it a thousand times.

"Yeah, they started to drift apart after he came out as bi-sexual. His wife said she never had a guy who was more a woman than she was. Things went downhill from there."

~

At the kitchen table, Jay chucked a few Cheeses Its into his mouth, savoring the rainbow of cheddar flavors. The news reporter chuckled, staring at him. "Have a few," the officer stated, holding the bag toward her. His cheap Swiss cologne mixed with the full-flavored cheesy smell of the crackers.

"Nah," Felicity replied, waving the salty, cheddar crackers away. He drew back the bag and picked up the cards, shuffling three times and bridging the deck. *The man certainly knows who he is,* she thought, as she sipped her bitter Grande Expresso from a ceramic cup. The reporter enjoyed the smell much more than the taste.

"Don't tell me you're watching your girlish figure," he said and then offered the cards for her to cut.

"Nothing wrong with that if I was," she stated back while cutting the deck, "but in this case, I'm just not hungry. I feel like my whole system is out of whack."

"I know the feeling," he said, dealing her five cards down for a round of draw poker.

107

Just then, Colleen entered the room. She wore her full police uniform. "I thought we were just staying here tonight," Jay stated, raising his cards to see two jacks and some junk.

The newswoman stared at her and tossed two poker chips into the pot. "Call," Jay said, adding two in, while the news reporter asked for two.

"Nope," Colleen replied. "There was an incident at the mall."

"Not the mall where Natalie was," Jay gasped, bringing the cards to his chest, unsure whether to finish the hand.

"Sadly yes," Colleen replied, "I called a judge friend of mine and got a search warrant for the warehouse." Jay dealt himself three cards, keeping the pair and tossing everything else. He picked up nothing.

"Really," Jay's jaw dropped, "Surprised Purt usually blocks anything related to their issues. And for Johnson? Who would step to the plate for him?" Every lie or half-truth the Purt network disseminated was purposeful and focused on control. The problem with the web as they had so many judges, police, and politicians working for them that nothing could stick. They were untouchable, but maybe it would be too politically toxic to be linked to the Marked Ones.

The officer glanced over to the reporter as she chucked in three. "I'll see your three and raise one," Jay replied. Colleen shook her head. Her brother was too damn honest to bluff. She knew he had something, but the raise of one told her it was weak.

"Didn't say it was for Johnson. I took some of Natalie's information and told the judge it was to get the robots. Said Purt probably did not even know the missing property was there. It will give them a face-saving out to say the place was overrun with squatters."

"Call," Felicity started tossing in the one chip. She laid down her cards: Pair of kings. Jay laid his down: pair of sixes with ace high. The reporter scooped up the pile. He swallowed another Cheese and twisted to his sister.

"I'm coming," Jay shouted.

"Actually," Colleen stated. "You are. I told the captain I needed you to fly us there. She has a squad meeting us at the place. I told them I was rusty with the hover. You are off

108

suspension until the case is over. But Jay, she is meeting us there with a search team."

"She, you talked to Berger and not Mendez?" Jay asked. A slight smirk rose on the corners of his lips. Still, his stomach knotted and twisted, then fell. He was unsure whether to rub his hands together in success or back out, but he'd never do the latter.

With a shrug, Colleen reminded him, "Day shift Jay," but her eyes belied the woman knew she'd defied protocol. Of course, Berger would support her play, but what would happen when Mendez found out. Would he seek retribution? *Nah,* Jay concluded, *he was too much of a straight shooter.* Besides, Colleen appeared whole for the first time in a long while. It was as if she had found her purpose. "Little lady, as soon as Natalie gets back, we are off."

"No time to wait," Colleen said. "Berger has a team, including Natalie, and they will meet us there."

"I brought my badge and gun, so no need to swing by my place. Hell, I've even brought Betsy to fly us there," Jay spoke excitedly, casting his sister a playful gaze. He hungered for the opportunity to get justice for Jan's sake. She was another in a long series of deaths surrounding his life. Payback time, the man thought, tossing the deck of cards on the table and leaping to his feet.

"Who names their quad," Colleen scoffed. "You're such a nerd, bro- I should just call you nerdy."

"Everyone," Jay chuckled, "names their quad. They just don't admit it."

"And you never stop admitting it," Colleen got in the last dig.

Rolling his eyes, "How about her?" Jay asked, pointing to the reporter.

The sister cringed at the thought. She didn't want to deal with this portion. "She can stay here," Colleen insisted.

"Without protection?"

"Hmm," Colleen replied. "Guess we take her, and she waits in the hover."

"Excuse me, ma'am. I'm a member of the free press and often embedded with police teams. I got my press credentials." Her face was pale, sort of jelly yellow.

109

"You're a witness and indeed a target for multiple murders," Colleen retorted.

"Section six o' five of the Federal Press Act of 2049, you got to take me."

"Worst law ever passed," Colleen shouted. It was designed to help stories, primarily those about the genetically enhanced, from being blocked from getting into the papers. Colleen empathized with the reporter's position at the time. The genetically enhanced role and, indeed, lives were so complicated. Both sides saw it as a matter of right and wrong, but neither thought of themselves as either right or wrong. Colleen felt saddened for the Mercury kids with their anxiety disorders and extra-finger. In addition, she and her brother had a strange connection. When it came to genes, she and Jay had a secret around them that even Jay did not know. The officer had promised her great Uncle John and her mother Nicole that she would never tell Jay. "Hide in plain sight," her mother had said. When they were young, her parents, Michael Jay and Nicole Murdoch, would greatly admonish Jay for "showing off" if he did anything that appeared not average. Best Jay died never knowing. Occasionally, she worried Detective Johnson might get close to the truth, but the two had a heart-to-heart two months earlier, and she was sure he'd never dig too deep after the discussion. The officer shook it off. As to the genetically enhanced, most of them mysteriously died off fifteen years ago (surprisingly, neither her nor Jay did), and those who didn't, well, many relocated to the colony on Mars.

The argument went a few rounds. Taking a potential witness to a crime scene gave Colleen the creeps. She even called Berger to prevent it, but in the end, both knew it was the reporter's right.

~

Jay's old black Betsy used four engines like all the hover quads. They circled in each of the corners of the ship. The blades beat the air, and the ship rose. After liftoff, two of the engines rotated, so the edges no longer faced down but toward the back. The machine appeared like a giant bee fluttering towards a flower. The air beat against the glass with soft thumbs like the old automobiles experienced driving on highways. The faint sound, almost imperceptible, was somehow soothing.

A stiff side wind blew a couple of degrees off course. The officer centered, battled the air resistance, and piloted over the city skyscrapers. His fingers stretched off the console to flip the climate control. *I love this quad*, he thought. He remembered when the model first appeared. Of course, he could not afford it new and had to wait for it to be two years old to purchase.

Cool air rushed through the vents. Jay twisted his head to smile at Colleen. She rolled her eye but returned his rounded grin. Their mixed Irish, English, and Native American features were almost identical in design, especially the jaw.

The older stretched out her glove and snapped it over her hand. Iron lines caressed around her steely eyes. It was good to have her back in the game. The ship glided over the cathedral ceilings of an old apartment complex, and they knew they'd reached the docks.

Below, the dark, jagged waters of the river danced. The ship circled back around the waiting warehouse. Like a dead body, the building rotted. Decay was evident, but more importantly, no sign of life emerged. He saw twelve adjacent buildings on the pilot's periphery, but the road coming into the area lay empty.

*Where the hell was their backup,* Jay wondered. He peered at the ship's readings. A low-pressure front was rolling in from the east, and probably some precipitation would accompany it. Indeed, the system suggested an eighty percent chance of rainfall.

No landing tarmac presented itself. Jay pointed toward an old electricity pylon. Coiled wires slithered around its base. Next to it lay a series of plastic tubes to serve as sewer pipes.

"I'll bring the police hover down behind them, and we can walk over," Jay stated. "This way, they don't see us coming."

Machines hummed in the background. The hover's blades whipped and beat the air.

The quad landed on a large cement slab. Jay hated the idea of landing too close to the place. He wanted to be sure they'd have the element of surprise pulling up to the warehouse gates. He pictured arriving first and then proudly kicking in the metal hanger door on the side and storming in with a proud captain, sister, and newswoman all behind him- arresting Renee and her wild lot. The fantasy was excellent, but this was not the direction the raid would take.

Stifling heat sent sweat rolling down officer Jay's face. Captain and others hadn't shown. Jay and his team waited for close to an hour. They even broke radio silence but still nothing.

From the outside, the warehouse appeared like a firetrap— the kind of old low-rent place inhabited by the homeless.

A harsh white arc light shone from an overhead track light. Jay and crew rushed forward to a double paneled white French door. Somehow the place seemed oddly familiar. It was as if Felicity were experiencing déjà vu. The reporter stopped, and Natalie grabbed her hand. "We got to keep going," the officer stated.

"I've seen this place before." The reporter scanned her surroundings and then inspected two large porcelain vases with green scrawled birds in flight embroidered on them. The vases sat on either side with a table between them. They seemed to lose their familiarity up close. The details were undoubtedly novel.

"Have you been here before?"

"No." She twisted her body to inspect a table with a giant black panther statue. Her mind pondered it. *Why did this all seem so familiar?* The sculpture appeared to be gazing out a window with complex white painted wooden blinds. The floor was faux wood with a large white Persian rug.

"Like a dream," Colleen's voice dripped with sarcasm, shaking her head.

"No, but it seems like a place I saw in a picture or something."

"We got to keep moving," Colleen said, and then a light went on Felicity's head when she said it. This place was where Detective Johnson called her. She informed the rookie. "Are you sure?" the officer asked, and she shook her head in affirmation.

"Yeah, you weren't there when I got the call."

They decided to launch into the place without backup. Jay was disappointed because he'd been looking forward to the highly polished black tactical gear helmets with the internal microphones linked to the central computer system and hot white strobe lights. "It's okay," Colleen offered, "I'll make some Mexican food- chicken and bean burritos after this is over."

The brother nodded and assessed the front. "Break the glass doors?" Jay asked, peering inside. "I don't see anyone home."

"Let's avoid the glass," Colleen said. "Less chance for a cut. Around it, the white- looks wood but ...."

"Samsonite," interrupted the news reporter, noticing the luster.

"No metal. See the rusts in the corner." She pointed.

While Jay was sure he could kick the rusty metal door down, Colleen called, "Together on three."

They struck it, and their combined ferocity snapped its hinges and shattered the connecting bolt. It flew back so hard that Jay worried the glass would break from the frame anyway, but it didn't. They charged inside.

The air was funny: cooler than outside with some mold present. The lights came from tiny fluorescent tubes, but the primary source was four large skylights in the ceiling. The place was empty, which jolted Jay with a sense of dread.

Outside he heard the stir of the hovers and the blaring sirens. Hell, Captain Berger was planning to come in with the big show. Well, she'd be quickly disappointed. He went to inspect the far wall of the building. Something about it appeared odd and out of place. He tapped on the wall.

Jay's suspicion of Berger's flair for the big entrance proved true in the next four minutes when four officers in squirrel suits crashed through the ceiling. How the hell would Colleen explain coming up empty? The team's credibility was on the line: nothing except for mold and dust was here.

Colleen strolled to the wall next to him. Unphased by the falling wall of glass from the ceiling. "Do you see it, Jay?"

"I think so," he replied. He tapped the wall twice. It was hollow.

The first squirrel suit in was Natalie. She stood next to Jay. He briefly admitted to her that he loved those tactical helmets before returning to the wall.

The captain entered with six officers in tactical gear behind her. "So, where the hell are the robots?" Her voice was a piercing shrill.

"In a minute, Captain," Colleen stated, and Jay hoped to hell that she was to be proven right. He slapped the wall.

113

Sheetrock cracked under his fist. He grabbed at the hole and ripped, hoping that the owner would not sue the department for property destruction.

After inspecting the rippled edges, Colleen drew out a high-intensity penlight. She flipped it on and peered into the hole. Dust and broken rock fell. The dry smell of plaster filled the air.

Groans came from inside. "Shit, that's Detective Johnson," she screamed and rushed into the hole. Jay tried to grab her and hold her back, in case it was a trap, but she threw his arm off.

Rivulets of dust and debris floated down in his hair. He hated the feeling of dirt on his skin but bore it.

~

The detective was beaten and bruised. It appeared someone worked hard on his face and nose and not in a flattering way. With anxiety written on her face, Natalie rushed to him, grabbed the lapels of his suit coat, and tried to lift him off the concrete curb. Cable bound his arms, and she heard panting. *At least he was still alive*, she thought.

The jacket ripped, and the detective winced in pain. She placed her hands under his arms and raised him by the pits. "They beat me to an inch of my life, sealed me in. Sort of old fashion Caste of Amontillado stuff." He chuckled and then winced from the pain. "I suspected it might be them ripping down the wall."

"Dude," Jay shouted. "If they sealed you in, they weren't coming back to let you out. They were letting you suffocate." Jay went babbling on to the point where he knew Collen would wish he shut the hell up.

"Glad to see you care, Jay," Johnson teased. Even broken, the detective knew how to dig the officer. Jay bristled, but there was an element of truth at the core of his message. When Jay talked, he did so out of concern. It was a nervous tell, and the officer could not deny it.

"Ah, to hell with you, Johnny," the officer replied, and his heavy jawline hung wide, exposing his thick lip.

A chuckle escaped from Johnson. "I figured they'd be pissed enough to do it," Johnny huffed out, while Jay's rant subsided to a low roar.

"Why?" Jay reached over and tried to help the man up.

"Once the information I gave them fails to produce what they want." He tried standing, but the pain caused him to falter. To

114

distract his mind from the chronic throb of agony, he created an alternative acute pain. He bit his lip hard to refocus.

"You gave them bad information?" Natalie asked.

The detective nodded. "If they didn't come back, I hoped I could see the moon in the skylight. From this angle, it was very hard, but it would have made a pleasant death."

From his eyes, Natalie registered the hatred welling up inside the man. *Maybe it gave him the strength to get out?* "I had to give them something. I'm lucky to be still alive." Johnson glanced over to the reporter, and their eyes locked. "Sorry, ma'am, but this is much deeper than you think."

"How so?" This time Captain Berger pressed the issue. She moved closer to the detective. Her eyes screamed, spit it out.

"They plan to release the virus. It is one that those with the genetic marker used to identify the mark ones produce a natural antibody toward, but others don't."

"I'm not following," Felicity added with a shrug.

The detective's eyes narrowed in a mix of pain and anger. He tried to clarify his words. "Imagine this- the virus is lethal to most of the population, but you can purchase the antibodies from the gang if you convert to Purt and pay the price. Dependent people would become docile."

"They could enslave all New Cyber City," the reporter gasped.

"They could tame the world with the way things travel nowadays," the captain announced in muffled words. The captain ordered Felicity removed from the area. Indeed, she was taken into "protective custody" and "held at the station."

# Chapter 8

Innumerable sparrows chirped in the background as an ambulance arrived for Johnson. The scene had all the trappings of a nightmarish daydream. The robotic doctors injected a large twenty-seven-gauge Tuberculin syringe with a fine tip needle around his eye with an anesthetic and placed cotton gauze over the deep gash on his head. Oil, blood, and sweat stained it. Salt from the perspiration stung his eyes. As they carted him inside and placed an intravenous line in his arm, he reassured Felicity not to worry. He'd be working on a plan. She nodded in deep concern and stepped aside to the waiting pale-skinned officer, Asia Thorpe.

His hand grasped the rough aluminon hydraulic rail as they thrust him inside, holding off the robotic doctors just long enough to call a wish of luck to Officer Natalie Ryder. Their eyes locked. Reading the pain on her face, his brow sloped, and he added, "Hey Nat, life is long periods of boredom, day to day but also fun," he smiled at her, and she let out a nervous laugh. The officer remembered a time with him when she was a kid, and they'd all gone to the beach. He'd taken the kids back then on some rides. It was her first time on a roller coaster. He told her life could be both tedious and fun back then.

"I believe it," she responded and stepped closer to his gurney. Her shoulders hunched, forming a tight knot between the blades. He let go of the rail and reached his hand out to tap her arm.

"Occasionally, these periods get punctuated by something horrific and painful," He paused to cough and then continued, "Don't let the pain destroy your life." His mouth sounded hoarse and dry.

A chuckle escaped her lips. She swiped a lock of hair from in front of her face and stepped closer. The inside smelled of menthol, eucalyptus oil, and camphor. Dirt and gravel crushed under her feet as she touched the detective's arm and squeezed his hand, which twitched at her touch.

A dark bruise had formed under the man's left eye. Given his age, anything could turn his situation grave. "You'll do well in the regenerative beds, you- old coot, and before you know it,

116

those stem cells, DNA stimulators, and growth hormone treatments will leave you feeling twenty-five again." This time Johnson laughed.

"True, maybe I'll get some testosterone as well," Johnny chuckled. "Seriously, I hope they have a mechanic to give my arm a once over." He clenched his hand and then opened it. The robot stuck a needle in Johnson's arm, and his eyes rolled back to rest. His body went listless. When the orange and white doors shut, the officer clamped a hand over her mouth because part of the woman worried she'd never see him again. His daughter was her best friend. They'd been close since childhood, and she'd always liked the man despite his periods of Post-traumatic Stress Disorder sponsored withdrawal from the world.

"He's stable for now," the robotic attendant tried to reassure. It Doppler-ed away from the site with screeching sirens, carting him through the New Cyber City sky. Keenly aware of the danger, Natalie whistled softly to herself.

~

True to Berger's promise, Felicity found herself in a cell. The rationale, of course, was a complete lie. Custody served the police. It prevented her from getting the story to her paper. Briefly, her mind searched for who might be still alive to receive her work in the newspaper. The alternate site must be up and running by now. At least, that was her conviction.

The reporter slumped onto the cot in the dusty but highly humid cell and stared the first twenty minutes at the ceiling, saying nothing. Her mind felt as if it had lapsed. Boredom sank in, the words of Johnson echoed in her mind, and she stood. The situation was huge, but it appeared the police were utterly overlooking it! Worse, they were disregarding her. She felt the loss. The emptiness of being ignored was not the same as the pain of the deaths of her colleagues, but they built on each other. A warm tear slid down her cheek.

As she waltzed around her ten-by-ten cell, the newswoman hated different people at different times. At some points, she hated Jay for not sticking up for her. Other points it was the captain for creating an excuse to cage her. Finally, the reporter hated Colleen because the woman had already told her that her husband was returning the next day, and this was the last night Felicity could have stayed at the house. Maybe this whole situation was to give Colleen an out to clean her home in time for her family. *Okay,* she admitted that the last was just paranoia, but it is not uncommon for people to lose it when in a cell.

Glum, the reporter huffed. She'd heard stories of prisoners pacing, like when animals were locked in cages, but now the reality brought it directly home to her.

Three hours after being placed in the cell, Jay showed up. He was apologetic and even handed her a magazine to read, but the reporter knew him to be so straight-laced he'd follow the company line to a tee. *Well, screw him,* she thought, planning to argue her case. "This is all so damn unnecessary. I mean, what the heck Jay."

"The captain is just trying to keep you safe," Jay replied. If he had any empathy for her situation, she could not tell. His face gave nothing away.

"Yeah, while she sits in her office and does nothing," the reporter spat. Her eyes dropped down to her upturned palms. Staring at her hands, she wondered if the dirt covering them would ever come off.

"Nope," Jay answered.

"Well, what is she doing," the newswoman replied, astonished.

"Berger went home," Jay retorted as if almost proud. "It is night shift, and Mendez has taken over."

"What about the virus, Jay?" she asked.

He shrugged, "We are working on it."

"Has anyone alerted Earth Corp?" In the back of the reporter's mind, she wondered if they planned to keep her from here on out and how long that would be. It could take years to catch the Marked Ones. Maybe they place her in witness relocation. The program would force her to give up her identity completely.

"Of course, that is the procedure in a terrorist case," Jay replied. "Mendez himself told us he was on it."

Ambitious and demanding driving, the Scorched Wing procedures made little sense to the reporter. If it were her call, they would be all over the holo-sets of New Cyber City blasting out for tips, but she knew Jay would defend the policy with some bull about causing public panic if she mentioned it. "Ugh!!!" Felicity screamed, threw her hands into the air in desperation, and slumped against the cell wall. Jay flinched. "Well, tell me one thing," the woman continued, "has the lab found anything out about the tattoo?"

"Natalie found the circuit can control the video in the mall and frankly disable scanning of the surveillance drones. But the lab cannot find anything out until they have a sample."

"They do," the woman interjected. "My HR rep."

Confusion flashed over the officer's face. "I'm not following," Jay replied. "Why do you need your HR rep."

"I don't need him, Jay. He's dead," she replied. For a second, Jay stared, confused. "Cohen Shay died in the bombing at my office. He had a tattoo."

"The name is not familiar," Jay said, drawing out his MegaSmart. His fingers tapped the glass screen. He scrolled down the list. "Nobody in the morgue under that name."

"Did they not think of looking at it when he was there and just release him?"

The officer typed further down the screen and then seemed to be searching a different page. "I don't have his name listed amongst the dead. Are you sure he worked that night?"

A sense of fury built in the reporter, but she pushed down her seething nature. It would be no good at this point. He wasn't shunning her. The officer lived in policy and procedure land, where everything was done by the book. The problem was he was the only person who did. "Jay, he was in the room during my...," her voice trailed. She let out a huff and then spat it out with the accompanying sorrow, "my immediate firing when the bomb went off. I saw his body on the ground."

"His wife was in the hospital," Jay replied. "When she was released, we took her...This building," Jay said.

"Yes, Colleen mentioned the woman was involved in the explosion," she replied. "Her husband gave her the information, and she ran with it."

"Hum," Jay replied. "Funny Mendez never mentioned it in the briefing. Unless he did, and I forgot, I usually take copious notes."

"I believe it," Felicity scoffed. Jay chose to ignore her childish outburst. They continued to chat for another fifteen minutes.

~

A rap happened on the door outside the room, and Jay answered. "We got a call from the hospital."

"Yeah," Jay nodded, hoping not to hear more bad news. Inside, his heart waffled and flipped.

"A Detective Johnson wants to video chat with both of you," the guard stated. The two exchanged a wild glance.

"Did he say why?" the officer asked.

"No, just that it was urgent. Captain Mendez is handling the call now. He asked that I check with both of you about how to handle this."

The procedure was straightforward. This action was a call for a prisoner, and the video calls were expensive in those cases. Plus, she lacked a phone account. The administration could take weeks to set up, but Jay decided to hear Johnson out. "I'll take responsibility for the woman in protective custody."

Ten minutes later, they were both in front of the video screen in a room that smelled of detergent and pine cleaner, neither powerful enough to cover the cigarette smell. The captain poured a glass of water for the detainee and handed it to her. She thanked him. Jay offered her a monogrammed cerulean-colored silk napkin to wipe her brow. She took it, removed the grime, sweat, and dirt from the lower holding cells from her face, handed it back to the officer, smoothed her clothes, and sat on a vintage 1903 chrome swivel-cushion replica stool. It possessed the Scorched Wing Division logo on the seat at the table's end.

On the wide seventy-five-inch screen, Johnny lay in his hospital bed. His face was still swollen and bruised—the gash on his head much thinner from the healing beds. Blue-black sensor tape on his skin read his vital signs. The design of the recordings appeared like an odd alien squid trying to eat his neck. "Johnson, you still look horrible," Officer Jay started.

"Well, I looked that way before the attack, so---" Johnny joked. "I think they have me on a gene inducer to speed up my metabolic and healing processes. I finished the mixed hormonal and stem cell cocktail couple of hours ago." Then he moved right into business. "As I told the captain, they are making the virus and preparing it for launch."

"How long?" Jay asked.

"Maybe a couple of days," Johnny replied. "It seemed they were having difficulty calculating how to disperse it as an aerosol."

"Well, at least it gives us some time," Jay replied.

"Very little," Johnny said. His eyes lit up. He'd like a plan, but it mainly was one he knew would be rejected as too risky. Still, it would help give the client faith that he was thinking and planning. Occasionally, he did that because, as he often said, business was business. "Officer Jay," he stated, trying to sound official, while Menendez gazed over his shoulder. "I played a lead and got some information, which I wanted to share."

"Go ahead," Jay replied, pushing his belt up over his stomach and tucking in his shirt as he sat on a thirty-inch stool seat next to the reporter.

"You remember Jackson Newman," Johnny stated.

"The sleazy reporter," Jay snapped but caught Johnny's eyes darting over like he was trying to remind the officer of something. Jay followed the gaze to Felicity. "Not that all reporters are sleazy," he quickly added.

"Jay wears his heart on his sleeve, ma'am. Anyhow," Johnny interrupted. "I got into contact with him when I woke up. I passed out for two hours, and then when I woke, this place fed me the crappiest food."

"Johnson, please get back on task," implored the officer.

"I was getting to it," Johnny rebuked. "After not being able to hold the food down, I remembered lots of things that make me vomit. Newman is one of them, and it hit me- he knows all those underworld types. It is how the man does his business. Figuring I'd had nothing to lose, I called him. We spoke, and he said he'd look into setting up an interview between himself and Renee- you know to get a location."

"Did he get one?" Jay asked.

"No, Renee- well, she refused to meet with him," Johnny said.

"Is this going anywhere, Johnson?" Jay grizzled in frustration.

The detective ran his fingers through his hair and then turned them down the back of his neck. He rubbed the area between the base and shoulder blade. "I'm getting to it. Patience, my overly rigid friend."

"Johnson!" exclaimed Jay. The bellowed word came from his chest. He hated when the detective's thoughts went rogue.

"Back to the story," Johnny huffed. The condescension was evident in his voice. Jay didn't miss it but decided not to respond to it. Johnson liked to tell his stories his way. Jay understood as much and could kick himself for his interruptions. "So, he would not meet with Newman, but the guy played another card. He told Renee that they could use an intermediary reporter. Someone that he knew Renee would want to see. Ms. Felicity." The reporter heard him speaking but decided not to interrupt. No, she was more focused on finding out how to score some coffee in this dive.

"Yeah, he wants to see her kill her," Jay spouted. "Terrible plan if this is heading where I think it is."

"Worse," Johnny replied. "Newman will only let us have the location for a meeting if he has exclusive rights to the entire story. He wants it in writing signed by Ms. Cruickshank."

The demand brought the reporter back to focus. Her eyes grew wide. All this work, all this trauma, and she'd have to give up rights to the story to the tabloid sleaze. "Can you plead with him for a better deal?"

"I tried, believe me," Johnson sighed. The reporter's mind spun and twisted. Briefly, she closed her eyes, and all she saw were the bodies of her co-workers outside the blast door. They'd been her peers, and some were even her friends. *What did she owe them?* Nothing but emotionally everything. Her heart fluttered as her grief rose. The tragedy had linked grief and terror for her since the attack, and she needed to keep pushing them down if she were to stay sane. The words of Howe echoed in her ears: *A good reporter chases down a lead no matter where it goes.* They were the last words he'd said to her.

"Maybe we can arrest him and compel him to give us the location," Jay concluded. Felicity held up a hand to stop the officer from going further. Her heart sank, but she knew what had to be done.

The newswoman swirled her Styrofoam cup of water. Her eyes glazed in the gentle, hypnotic swishing up and back of the liquid. The decision, her decision, had been made by someone else. The sleaze was calling the shots. Maybe it was never her decision to make- a debt to the deceased. She felt unsure of which.

On the other hand, if left to decide, she'd probably head in the same direction even without the guilt. If the last few days taught her anything, it was that the reporter hated feeling helpless. She'd preferred to take the attack to the opponent than all this running. "I'll do it, Mr. Johnson," she exclaimed.

"Now, wait a minute," Jay said. His pleading eyes lingered on the woman, clearly questioning her judgment and sanity. "This is a horrible idea. It puts you right into the hands of a killer."

The captain spoke at this point, "But Jay, maybe you could fly her in and get her out."

"Captain," he replied, "They see a police hover, and she's dead before we even get started."

"She might be dead no matter what we do," Johnson said over the screen, stressing the first word.

"Which is why your plan is horrible, Johnson. This is the typical bullshit you always pull," Jay's insistence and rant seemed unrelenting.

"Jay," the newswoman interrupted. Her eyes bore into him. "I need to do this. I owe it to everyone who worked on the ninety-seventh floor."

"Horseshit," Jay snapped. "Don't give me that crap. I've seen a lot of people die. Many of them were solid friends of mine. They'd never want you to be dead as well. No way would they want you to risk your life for nothing."

"Not for nothing, Jay. It is to stop the unleashing of a deadly virus," the reporter stated.

"Don't let the tears you refuse to shed cloud your vision. You have a life ahead of you. There is no need for this. This division is competent enough to take the Marked Ones down without needing you to throw your life away playing hero."

Not to be intimidated, Felicity stepped closer to Jay, then, deciding otherwise, she spun away. He gasped and twisted back to Johnson on the screen. His disdain was evident in his glare. "Is the game plan really for her to walk right up and passed security and into the bunker or wherever the hell he or she is for a supposed interview?" Jay asked. Johnny nodded on the screen. "You do know how crazy this sounds," he thrust his stubby index finger at the screen and forcefully added.

The reporter giggled. "It does have a sick twist to it. Ironically, I am sure that Mr. Howe would have appreciated this."

"What?" The officer's voice barely contained his fury. Felicity worried if this was more about his dead partner than her.

"Him – firing me and now me walking into a place where I could get killed to make things right for him?"

Officer Jay's anger swelled. This agreement was not what he had in mind at all. The risk was far too significant, and he could not see why the captain even entertained the idea. "Captain, I like to request a psychological exam for Miss Cruickshank," Jay replied. His request would delay the operation until the exam was completed, and he knew it.

"Jay, no," Felicity stated, holding out her hand in a stop gesture. *Why is he doing this?* She thought. *I may not be doing the right thing, but it's still my decision!*

"It's okay if she gets the eval. I am stuck here for at least twelve more hours anyway," Johnson stated.

"Why is that?" Jay asked.

"I'm under observation," the old gumshoe replied.

"You can't just walk out?" This time it was the captain asking the question.

"I tried to sign out against medical advice, and the doctor placed an order that if I did, he would personally sign a psychiatric commitment paper for me. Hell, he'd lock me up for thirty days," Johnson informed.

"Could you fight that in mental health court?" the captain replied.

"I could, but I did take a bit of a head injury. Not the first time either. Jay, you remember the mites," Johnny replied. Jay nodded, remembering their encounter with the parasites that landed from space.

"Sorry to hear," the captain replied, and Jay did a mental double-take. It was unlike the captain to ever be interested in a person outside the force's life. Maybe Johnny had been detained so many times that he'd somehow become part of the law enforcement team, but the officer felt skeptical.

The group talked about the plan for ten minutes longer. Felicity would receive the psychological exam, but the woman knew she'd go no matter what it revealed. In the end, Jay decided it best not to fly in the police quad but to take his own. Betsy would at least offer them the cover of not standing out as a police quad.

The officer straightened up. "If I am going undercover," Jay huffed. "I'll change into my civilian..." He didn't state the last words but added, "I need to get a diagnostic on Betsy."

"Who?" The captain asked.

"My quad," Jay replied. He shot an evil glance at the reporter. She saw the blackened hatred in his eyes. *Did he think she'd just chosen Johnson over him?*

For a minute, Felicity thought, *if he is mad, well, two can play at that, I'll be mad as well,* her mouth opened to speak, but then she decided to let it pass. Life was too short to fill it with anger, especially at someone who cared about her as much as Jay did.

Over the next twenty minutes, they worked out the plan's details. Felicity's job: get Renee to incriminate himself on tape. The problem, of course, was that he had no intention of granting the reporter an interview. He'd planned to kill her and would probably have her recording devices taken. The solution was a second recording device, which appeared like a small fly. She would palm it and toss it off to her side after she was in the room with him before they searched her. The device would broadcast the information to the police and store a backup. Once the gang leader incriminated herself, the police would storm in and arrest them. Two quads, each with three highly trained strike team members, would serve as backup. They agreed primary group would be Jay and Felicity. When Felicity was inside, Jay would search for an alternative entrance to the location.

After agreeing to meet, Newman sent Johnson the location. Jay immediately suggested an all-out frontal assault as an alternative. Johnny reminded the group that the virus might not be on-site, and the attack might give them an incentive to release it immediately. Even Jay admitted that could get horrible. The team immediately drew up the building specifications on record from the Earth Corps computer systems. The location proved to be on the old docks near the east river. Johnny stated he knew the location of the building and an entry point not on the plan. After the detective's observation period ended, Natalie volunteered to pick him up from the hospital and bring him with her team, which strike leader Elise Thompson led. This arrangement put Johnson at ease because he trusted the woman.

The assault teams and Officer Jay would wear full body armor, including Natalie, as she would be on the scene, and it was police procedure. They'd have no armor from Johnson, and it seemed impossible for the reporter to be wearing armor for an interview. It didn't matter, as all realized that the gang would be firing headshots if it came to shoot.

As Jay left the room, he stopped Felicity in the hall. "Hey," he said.

"Hey," she replied.

A long pause ensued, and she finally broke the silence. "Natalie seemed happy. She thought she would look great in the onyx-colored hard shell front and back panels riveted with foam inside and nylon straps. "

"Yeah," Jay replied. But she looks great in pretty much everything."

"I know," Felicity replied.

"You'll look great too," Jay quickly added, as if he should have added it. "Now, I'll be the hardest to fit, especially under my street clothes." Another long silence ensued. "I know this will probably come out all wrong," he said. His hand went up to his eyebrows and rubbed them.

"Just say it, Jay," offered Felicity. "And we can go from there."

"I know what it can be like to hate. Sometimes I feel like I have a hate-on for the whole world," Jay paused to take a deep breath. His words were mixed and messy. His tongue had twisted on him. The phrases he used were not how he intended to say them and definitely not how it sounded in his head, so he rushed the next part, "What I mean to say is, no matter how many of those gang bastards we arrest or kill, it will not bring your friends back."

A wave of grief flooded over Felicity, and she wanted to run off and cry. She twisted away. "I know," she replied. She glanced to each side to communicate this was the wrong time to discuss this.

"I just wanted to say I am sorry for that," he offered.

"Then why did you sandbag me with this evaluation," her words were harsh, and she knew it. *Why could she just let Jay comfort her?* More than anything, she wanted to run into his arms and let him comfort her, but now was not the time to break down.

126

"I guess," Jay added. Damn, where had all his training in trauma and grief gone? I've failed at the basics, he thought. He breathed. "I want to be sure; we are not setting you up for something wrong," he added.

Was he trying to mess her up before her psychiatric evaluation now? No, Jay was not a person to do such things. *He is trying to be genuine*, she thought. "Thank you," she said, and they headed off to meet the others in the fitting room.

~

Two hours later, a psychiatrist entered the reporter's cell. The mid-forties woman was dressed in a Cardigan Navy blue suit made from chinos cloth. The skirt was long and had a zipper on its side.

Felicity wished that the psychiatrist, who was conducting her evaluation, understood her reasoning and decision. She was sure it sounded reasonable.

"Hello, Ms. Cruickshank. I am Dr. Stephanie Long. I am the department psychiatrist."

"Hello, Doctor," Felicity stated. Her nerves danced in her gut. *Just be honest,* she told herself. The two shook hands.

"I'll be asking you some questions. The topics will vary. Some will be to assess your focus, memory, and awareness of yourself and your world. They attempt to understand if your cognitive machinery and thought processes are intact. Others will be aimed at understanding your social and emotional functioning at this point. We understand that you recently lost a bunch of co-workers, and we want to make sure that your relationships with them are not clouding your judgment."

"I understand, doctor," the reporter stated. "But I can assure you this is no backdoor suicide attempt."

"Now, I hadn't mentioned that, but I think it is a good place to start. Tell me about how you decided to join this little expedition to catch – was the person's name- Renee."

"It is," she stated. A drop of sweat prepared to roll down her nose.

"And he is allegedly the man who arranged for your building to be bombed."

"Not just the building but the police, and I suspect I was the target," the reporter replied. "Also, I have reason to suspect Renee is a woman." Unrelenting questions followed. Sweat from pressure and painful words rolled down Felicity's forehead and over her face in the beginning. The reporter and the psychiatrist talked for over an hour. During that time, they reviewed all the case events, focusing on her emotional reactions and pains.

At several points, Felicity felt like crying. She held it back for fear that the evaluator would use it against her, but when the evaluator said, "It sounds like a ton for anyone to deal with," Felicity let the wet works flow. There was practical stuff, like her relationship with her sister and parents and how she slept and ate the last few days. Inside, felt she was blowing the interview, but she pushed it away. Several memory tests included remembering four words for five minutes, counting from one hundred by sevens, and spelling common words backward. She guessed these were efforts to understand her ability to focus and concentrate.

Some of the most challenging questions were about Jay and how he always made her feel like she belonged, and now the reporter felt like she'd been betraying him. Unease came over the reporter. When the discussion ended, Dr. Long lifted her iPad, where she typed notes and videotaped the interview. She smiled and said, "I need to review my data and will let the captain know in an hour."

"Did I pass?" Felicity asked, almost dreading hearing the answer. Her mind worried briefly and reflected on Catch Twenty-Two's book, which she was required to read in college. Was this whole thing a waste of time to justify some preset outcome? Her heart pounded harder.

The psychiatrist smiled. "Don't see this as something you needed to pass. It is about learning about you and your competence to make this decision. If you don't do well, it might be the best thing. The mission sounds risky."

"I think it should be my right to make such decisions. So, am I going to get green-lighted?"

The psychiatrist leaned back in her chair, causing the back to stretch. "Won't know until I look over the results." The reporter saw the rejection stamp slamming on the file in red letters in her mind.

An old punk song from the Germs *Lexicon Devil* screamed in her head. The words were indistinguishable from the loud screeching guitar. The music soared, and all she could make out was, "Give me this, give me that.". She remembered an interview

128

with Darby, the lead singer for the band, and how he'd discussed that part of him wanted to get hurt when he was on stage. Maybe something in her felt the same way. Either way, she wanted out of the cell. If she were to go down, it would be fighting for what she knew was right.

~

Still suffering from the shock that shrink approved the reporter for the mission, Jay idled Betsy up. With a roar, the power surged and choked in the engine. It whined and spat. At least the mechanic team for the department ensured it would not stall out. It lifted first and caught the night wind to its back, propelling it forward. Felicity was the bait. Jay was to set his hover down, and she was to enter the building while the officer would try to make his way to the back.

Captain Mendez ordered Natalie to the hospital with Officer Elise Thompson, a woman who'd had a history for her no-nonsense approach to the streets, and Officer Asia Thorpe, who functioned as a standard member of the strike force. Being the rookie, Natalie would fly and only enter the building if needed. As part of department protocol, Johnson would not enter the building either. His function was to show the entrance and then remain an observer.

Once there, she waited for Johnson to complete his discharge paperwork. Under Johnson's eye still lay smudged with a bruise. After, they escorted Detective Johnson to join up with other hoverquad of officers. He'd show them the entrance, which he swore was hidden and only he could find. They'd enter for an assault at the site. The private detective clicked himself in with his seat belt. They were closer to belay lines with harnesses for repelling on the hovers than traditional belts.

~

The aerial view of New Cyber City's vast skyline was a mix of glass, steel, and colored lights projected out like circuits on a computer motherboard. The bridge connected vast stretches of sprawling buildings off into the distance. The visually stunning newly built Haastings structure towered as the city's apex, a replacement for the tower destroyed nearly a year and a half earlier. The city had yet to complete the project. Felicity stared at the layered slipstream and stacked buildings as if looking at the surface of computer chips, complete with flashing electrical jumps from path to path. The patterned skyline of steel and glass was a testament to human achievement, both good and evil. A quarter of the way there, Jay snaked his private quad down into the lanes between the city streets.

A fog rolled in from the vast river next to the city. Its colloniid properties splattered the light, except for the harshest neon, which cut directly through and reflected. They dove within the darkened patches of sky cut with neon green spotlights circling above. Every bit of Jay hated this plan, and Felicity knew it. He remained stoic through most of the trip, trying to put on a strong face, but when he hit a hard lean to circle wide the corner of Front Street and then ran a red light flying through water street, she knew he was furious.

The tension in the quad settled in her stomach, so the reporter whipped out her fast and loose persona. "We're making a great time," she chirped, trying to help relieve the tension. It did not. In some ways, she'd be glad the flight was over to be away from Jay- even though being with Renee seemed like a more deadly alternative.

The officer breathed profoundly and just said, "' Yeah." Regardless of the situation, she knew that Jay was worried for her safety and the group.

After muttering a swear to herself, the reporter regrouped. "At least the captain sent us two police quads as backup," Felicity replied, with anxious bile resting in her throat. Her pulse throbbed in her ears. "I get them to open the door. When I see Renee there, I give the signal, and they storm into the building. It could not be easier." Jay's impassive face gave nothing away. He said nothing, and it seemed clear his anger petrified his face. Instead, he chose to lift the ridges on the air vents. It sent the cool, climate-controlled air into his face.

Green laser lights pierced in an arc through the night sky. They cut past the fog and appeared to shine on the blue-grey moon. Giant billboards close to a billion pixels played a video of the most wanted with cut-away shots of their victims, alternating with advertisements from corporate sponsors. Massive holographic images of geisha girls dancing in the sky

From a distance, rows of metal cranes for unloading freight ships lined the riverside. A trimaran-designed transport ship with

130

three hulls of cargo rested against one of the loading bays. Heavy ropes attached it to horn cleats.

It rained a fine drizzle, making the trip even more unpleasant for Jay. He glanced down at the controls and gauges. He caught sight of his backup: the two other quads behind him on radar, and then the two blips disappeared. The officer cringed and then quickly recovered, trying to put a good spin on it. Finally, he spoke, "We have radio silence with the police quads, they probably wanted to fly in low below possible radar or scanners, but I am sure they will arrive soon." The officer's voice lacked its typical hopefulness. "You need to train the fly."

Natalie drew out the tiny recording device from her pants pocket and spoke into it. Her voice imprint pattern allowed the machine to pick up the frequency of voices so that they could home in on and the background sounds minimized. This feature helped when recording from a distance.

The hydraulic door hissed and rose. "Let's get'em," Jay insisted as they shuffled from the hover. His voice perked up more than the entire trip over, and Felicity knew this was performance time: Time for her to take the deadly plunge. She grabbed Jay's arm and squeezed it tight. His shifting moodiness wasn't helping. She exited the ship first. He shut off the quad's lights, strapped on his assault helmet, placed in the earpiece to listen and record the conversation, and waited until she reached the building. "Computer power down," was the last thing Felicity heard him say. The air still smelled of heated asphalt and sewage, even though the sun had gone down hours earlier.

Outside, humidified heat made the air lay thick on the skin. The rattling hover's engines sloshed as it landed, blowing up the dust on the ground. The pier's stench wreaked so strongly that Felicity's gag reflex kicked in, and chunks of her prison lunch swirled in her mouth.

Sweat sheened her face. Her finger twisted in her Paisley Underground blonde hair. It looped so tight the hair cut off her circulation, and the finger blued, becoming cold. Jay's hard eyes stared at her. "What?" she questioned.

"Your finger," he said, pointing.

"Oh," she said, as if unaware and unwrapped the knot. The one in her stomach would be much harder to unwrap.

With less than six telephone poles from the building, there is no time for her to back out now. The stiffness in the back of her neck forced her jawline to tighten.

The rain pooled in her hair and ripped from her face. The area around the bunker was littered with garbage, beer bottles, food, cans, cigarette butts, and plastic bags. *The gang members are a bunch of pigs,* she thought. The titanium Kwanza-shaped bunker was surrounded by an electric fence with razor wire at the top. She heard the fence sizzle long before reaching the gate. A sentry was placed on either side to keep unwanted visitors out. Their clothing was black with a patch that read "security" on the side. They appeared more like nightclub bouncers than the real police. With hands up, Felicity approached the bunker guards. Closed-circuit cameras rotated on either side of the fence. Tiny drones hovered over the area, scanning the grounds, and she was confident the concrete beneath her feet contained sensors to monitor for approaching forces.

The reporter drew out her press pass as she approached the guards. Her hands visibly shook. "Renee is expecting me," she stated. "I'm Felicity Cruikshank for an interview." Inside, the woman hoped Renee had not left orders for the guards to shoot her on-site. Detective Johnson believed that Renee was genuinely interested in meeting her before blowing her head off.

"Face the camera," The guard replied, and the reporter did as instructed. It scanned her up and down. The newswoman caught sight of a drone drawing closer. She figured to shoot if Felicity was a fake. Satisfied with her identity and approval, the guard tapped an earpiece and replied, "She is expecting you." The drone withdrew.

*So, Renee is a woman*, Felicity thought. She'd been right all along.

Jay watched her with a pair of binoculars with infrared telescopic lenses from a distance. Once inside, Jay planned to flip on the recorder for the bug in case they searched her with an electronic detecting device and then try to slip around to find the two police hovers and Johnson to get inside.

~

Transversing the New Cyber City sky from the hospital, the twenty-four-block trip to the docks took about ten minutes. Splintered images flashed past the view screens. The climate control system hissed, sending chilled pine-scented air through the quad. A yellow-tinged pink glow shone from the streets, appearing like a faint stain on the inhabitants.

Asia and Elise sat in the back in brown mylar upholstered console chairs bolted to the ground, rehearsing their attack plan. The scene surprised Johnny, who listened to their conversation, with how much of a tender soul Thompson was. He'd always pegged her for a bit of a hard ass. Having never worked with her before, he realized it was all her image. The woman sounded like an old granola bar eater who binged on probiotic tablets. The old gumshoe let the woman's words wash off him, casting his thoughts inward.

In the passenger seat, Johnny sat next to the pilot, Natalie. His eyes stared off into the new Cyber City skyline. He'd realized during the call; that he'd spent most of his life in the city with only two disastrous reprieves. The first was his time as a child in Key West, which ended in the death of his parents, and the second was the third Iraq war, which cost him his arm. Since his losses, he felt more attuned to the darkness in those surrounding him. Indeed, the darkness of the shift captain worried him the most. While he couldn't place his finger on it, he felt something wrong. Maybe it was because of the lack of hassle over the plan. At first, Johnny believed it was because given the threat level combined with no alternative strategy to find the gang and bring them in. In the end, the man caved all too quickly. Maybe the detective just wasn't used to people agreeing with him, especially when the potential for casualties was high. Johnson wasn't so sure now. Perhaps it was inevitable, but he found himself very uncomfortable.

In the distance, he heard Natalie asking him about his son, Joe. Maybe she was trying to settle him, but the words achieved the opposite effect. The woman bragged about how handsome Joe had become, having seen him about a year ago when she visited Katrina (his daughter). Johnny wouldn't know. He'd not seen Joe since the boy entered Earth Corps. Separations felt like a natural part of life for him. Both his kids were adults now, and he regretted not having been there for them while they were little. He still ate at the gumshoe. Instead, he chose to make a polite joke about the Kat-Nat combination, as he used to call them.

133

The police quad rumbled, but Natalie chatted casually about the air turbulence. Her eyes crawled over the control panel, and she held the cyclic control tightly. With one hand, she reached and flipped a small switch on the side panel into the upright position. It snapped loudly into place. She pried more about Joe. *Maybe she's interested in the boy,* the detective thought. He watched her animated gestures while discussing her time with the boy. *Yeah, interest was a real possibility.*

From the back, Elisa wondered next to Natalie's chair. "Everything is going well up here," she asked. Her stud posts, entirely within department regulations as cultural expression, flashed from her ears, catching the detective's eyes.

"Ship is a little sluggish, but I got it under control," Natalie replied.

"Good," Elisa stated. The woman nodded and stared out the front windshield made from tempered glass, argon, and high-impact plastic. "We should be there in ten." Her hand rested on Natalie's shoulder, "right?"

"Yes, ma'am," the officer replied.

While sitting in the quad, Johnson's mind rolled over the building's entrance. Located in a small shop about a block up the road, he'd seen it used as an escape route on a previous job. They'd have to go through the tunnel and hoped for only a few guards to be present. The less, the better. It could get rough. *It's just another case on the docks*, he mumbled to himself, but his mind rolled back to Chin's buffet and the Eddie Whyte affair. He'd felt sure he would not survive the night that time, and for his life, Johnny could not figure out how he did. The image of Chin's crab-eaten body fished out of the mouth of the river some fifty miles down still haunted him. His tongue wetted his lips.

A burst of noise ripped through the ship as the crash alarm blared. Johnny snapped out of his self-reflective daze and analyzed the pilot. "What's going on, rookie?" shouted Officer Elisa. The ship bounced and shook. It threw Elisa, who was standing close to Johnson's lap. Natalie glanced at Elise and Johnny. She shrilly screamed, "It's jammed. We're going down!"

"What?" Asia called outwardly agitated from the back. The other two gazed in horror.

"Cyclic control is not communicating with the rotary blades," Natalie called. "I think it's jammed. Damn, I got no control of this thing."

Johnny barely got off a scream before the quad smashed hard into the asphalt lot and on the concrete sidewalk. The ship scraped along the ground, flipped, and rolled. It hit hard. Metal twisted, and the tempered glass shattered. The detective saw Thompson chuck forward, felt his neck swerve, the crash bags deployed, and then blacked out.

~

In her old, updated, and modernized colonial, Colleen cleaned under red and blue track light illuminations. Dusting pictures and shelves, the officer danced with excitement over her family's return. While Felicity was a great guest, the reporter was still an intruder, and the officer felt glad to have her house back. Gary Jules's Tears for Fear's Mad World cover sang out while she swirled a duster to the beat. She planned to polish the wood later, so when Steve got home with Maska, they'd find a perfectly sparkling house with no visitor's presence.

She stripped the bed and placed an embroidered silk spread on it to welcome her husband home. Her mind flipped back to when they dated. Often their interchanges were a scrappy mix of rephrased lines from ghastly old noir movies and detective television shows. While the man was mired with many faults, Colleen loved him deeply between the moments of fury about him.

A rapid succession of three rhythmic knocks struck the door. Colleen stopped cleaning the room and got up to answer. She figured her husband Steve and son Maska had arrived home early.

"Ms. Colleen Jay-Yazzie?" the young man asked. His crisp blue eyes shined, but his voice was toneless, and he stood overly close.

She nodded at him. "Yes," Colleen stammered. Her cheeks grew warm, and she was sure they were pink. Once, when he was away, her husband had flowers sent to their home. She hoped it was nothing like that but would not be upset if it were. His heart had proven to be steadfast on many occasions. Indeed, even for this trip, he'd called her every day to check in and discuss the day. She'd imagined his bright smile.

"Captain sent us, ma'am. I'm with the twenty-second precinct. I have come to escort you and your brother in for questioning." Colleen felt her stomach twinge. His face was unfamiliar, but the department was enormous, and the precinct was other than the Scorched Wing. Yet, he did not call her "officer," which struck her odd.

"What's this about?" She instinctively questioned, curling her hand into a fist and placing it on her hip.

"Captain says he needs to talk to you regarding a reporter – a Felicity Cruickshank. She's gone missing, and there are elements of her story not checking out."

"Why do they need me, and why not a damn video conference? My family is on its way home."

"I'm sorry, ma'am. I just follow the captain's orders. Making them is way above my pay grade."

Colleen eyed the man suspiciously. "What is your name?" The woman studied his face.

"Officer Davis," the young man said. Something seemed wrong. Sweat rolled from his temples like a person in the early signs of a juice withdrawal.

Colleen said in a low tone. "May I see your verification ID, please? I plan to call him and give him a piece of my mind."

The man grinned toothily and reached toward his shirt but then shot into her in a blitz attack. Overwhelmed, she tried to step back. His fists pounded on her face causing her to stumble. Knocking her into the house, she crashed on the floor, sobbing and confused. He reached into his pocket and yanked out a laser knife. Her heart pounded in her ears, and she knew he intended to end her life.

Battle screams tore out as Colleen leaped and ridge-handed the man. Her strike knocked him back three feet, causing him to slap the wall. He exploded with anger and punched her hard. Years on the force combined with good genetics helped Colleen to defend herself. Thankful of her genetic augmentation, she caught his wrist, spun the man, and flipped him to the ground, but as she did so- two other young men dashed up her steps. With cat-like reflexes, she twisted around the second assailant and, from behind, snapped his neck. The body fell to the floor. The third arrived, her palm struck him in the nose, and blood burst out. She dashed into the living room.

"I'll get her," supposed Office Davis called, marching up the stairs. "You get the loser's body out of here and join me."

"Boss, she stronger and quicker than we'd been told," the man insisted.

"Just luck," the leader Davis protested. "Middle-aged cop ain't taking us down." She round-off on the table to its tile side. He rushed forward to cut her off.

"Computer call the po..." she screamed, but before she'd finished the statement, the second man had cut the electric wire to the machine, and it squeaked off. Her hand managed to catch the light switch and shift it off.

Even though the fake officer was much younger, Colleen felt sure she could take him one on one. Far from frail, his arrogance that he was male and younger would serve as his downfall. But there were two, and they were armed.

Davis turned on the lights. They flickered, and their light vanished. "Idiot," the voice called out. "We were supposed to get her in the car and kill her by the river, so no friggin' body."

"Not a problem," the second voice replied with a tiny hiss as he sucked air back in at the end.

Terrified that this stranger might kill her, she darted to the stairs to the second floor.

~

Occasional electrical flashes lit up the inside of the quad. The zaps echoed out. The officer's eyes focused as she escaped consciousness. Her head hurt. Groggily, Natalie felt something heave on top of her and tried to roll it off. It was too heavy. She felt trapped. A thought broke her mind: there was no escape, and rescue could be hours away. The officer gulped some air and coughed, then reached down and unlatched her harness, but it did not help.

A fog rested over her mind. Her head turned in in the pale glow from the ship's outside. She saw Elisa. The woman's body lay still near the controls. Natalie called over, and there was no response. Parts of the body were twisted, unnatural. Natalie prided herself on being a trained professional. She'd been top of her class in basic training at the police academy. Even though she was still a rookie, she'd won awards from the department for handling difficult situations, many of which were life and death matters. But even with her iron background, the week's events

137

had gotten to her. It was as if the software in her head glitched, causing her mind to fail. She found herself screaming and felt as if she had lost her mind.

Trapped, Natalie struggled. Panic clawed its way into the woman's mind replacing all else. She felt a hand rip the control panel off her, pushing away the cyclic control. A bloody Detective Johnson stared down at her. His eyes were unfocused, and sweat dripped from his far head. "I got you," he said. "Are you able to breathe?"

Her ears grew cloudy, and his voice sounded muffled, but the woman could make out the request. She drew in four deep breaths, which calmed her. "Yeah," she finally whispered. Her left leg felt heavy. It hurt but not intensely so. She figured it out for bruised and maybe a pulled muscle. Then her sense of odors cleared. "What the hell is that smell?" she asked.

"We are about two blocks from the sewage collection plant," Johnson informed. The light briefly flickered on and then just as quickly failed again. "Quad's power grid is unstable- seen the lights flicker a few times when I woke, and you were out."

The rookie's eyes scanned the darkened ship. Electrical cable cords hung like octopus tentacles from broken parts of the ceiling, and she concluded it best if the power remained out instead of "live "electric wires at random points, lighting up. The latter offered the possibility of electrocution. "Incredibly, we are still alive," Natalie insisted.

"Not all of us," the soft-spoken words from Johnson struck her like a bus. She glanced around; Asia's body had been severed in half. Guts spilled all over the metal catwalk in the back of the hover. The initial reaction was a desire to vomit. She'd know the woman, friendly and sweet. With four kids, she'd always been looking around for overtime and if people wanted off their shifts. She wanted to heave, and tears welled up, but this was a mission, and there was no time to cry now. She'd have plenty of time to grieve if they were successful when it was all done. If it failed, well, she would be addicted to the antigens from the gang like everyone else, so her grieving would have to be part-time between "Jonesin" for the crap. *Focus*, she demanded of herself. "Oh hell." Felicity sighed, then realized they were trapped, but others counted on them to complete the mission.

138

Natalie stumbled back a step. Johnny reached out, unsure if the kid had lost her balance. She waved him off. "Exit?" Her voice pleaded.

"The mercury switch, which triggers the hydraulic for the doors, is down," Johnson sighed and placed his hand on her shoulders. "We need to crawl out," he insisted and then pointed to the shattered front window. "It's safe. Don't worry – not jagged."

"Okay," she replied.

"What took us down?" he asked.

"I don't know. It was like the controls all jammed- it was like we were being jammed. Even our GPS went," she offered.

"Possible. Maybe they suspected we were coming?"

"How could they?" Natalie asked. "Patrols fly over this section of the docks almost hourly."

"And yet, just as we are heading for a raid, three hovers go down," Johnny replied.

"You think Jay went down as well?"

"I don't know. Was thinking of trying him to see if we should abort the mission but radio silence and all?"

"What makes you think that they made it?"

"No real reason," Johnson offered. "It was just his old quad was still joystick driven and might have been harder to jam."

"Well, if both of us are down, he should abort," she replied.

"We could give away his position if he did not crash, putting both his and Felicity's lives at risk. Besides, I think our comm gear is down. I need to check and see if my MegaSmart works." Drawing it from his pocket, he tapped on the light function. The cracked phone screen glowed. "It looks like I got two bars."

The quad groaned, and a large piece of metal collapsed from the roof. "Let's get out first," Natalie offered. The gumshoe nodded in agreement.

The reporter climbed through the broken window first. Her mind was partly on the task and partly on the company they had just lost. Yet, inside, she felt like she had forgotten something.

On the other side, she drew herself up by grabbing the end of the quad. Johnny was correct, the glass wasn't sharp, but the outside metal caught her hand and left a gash. Blood trickled down. She grabbed it tight, out of reflex, and then held it to apply pressure. While doing so, her eyes caught movement in the shadows.

139

Steam rose from the grate about twenty-five feet ahead. Voices approached from the distance. *Maybe they'd seen the police quad down, and we're coming to render help.* Her heart pattered with a sense of hope, which quickly dissolved.

A sense of shock encompassed her. The three approaching her were the flirt who liked Carver with the two punk-rockers, which helped provide for her escape. Flirt assessed her. The woman's vengeful eyes glistened as she flipped open a jagged blade.

Natalie huffed. She had no intention of dying.

~

At the top of the steps, she curved through the short hallway and entered the den. The heavy pounding of feet on steps told her one pursued and was close. He moved like the rolling thunder of an approaching storm. She ducked into the closet in the room.

Terrified, Colleen felt weak and shaky from her assault. Blood spewed from her nose. She searched her pocket for her Megasmart phone, but it was missing. She figured that she must have left it on the sink in the bathroom. Age was always making her forget things. Her heart drummed. Sweat trickled as she crouched in the closet and heard him approach.

With each step, her fear rose. Icy sweat rolled over her neck and down her back. Her hands trembled. *She reassured herself, just two of them, probably juice users- I can do this. I have fought worse. I'm just out of practice and taken off guard because they are at my home. I can control the panic. How did they get my address?* Her mind rolled in circles, but she felt her reasoning powers returning. She stared up at the dropped ceiling. She grabbed her palm to stop it from shaking. The sounds grew closer. The copper taste of blood rolled into her mouth.

A chilled shiver coursed up her spine, but she let it flow through. Colleen held her breath, weighed her odds, and stiffened. She wiped away the blood on her upper lip with her left palm. Her eyes darted the area searching for something to use as a weapon in her fight. They rose to the ceiling, and she wondered if it were possible to hide in the above tiles. She hoped they'd support her weight if she laid flat on them. She wondered.

Tapping the laser knife on the walls, Davis wandered through the rooms. The electrical scratch of the searching laser

140

was meant to frighten his victim. The muffled footfalls reached the next room. The moments of escape ticked away.

The officer closed her eyes and pressed the back of her head to the wall. Jan's face appeared. "Spirit, this is no time," the woman mumbled to herself, but the spirit's lips mumbled words. She felt unclear about the meaning. She closed her eyes again and, this time focused harder.

The words came in clearer this time. "Live! Your family needs you," it said. The message brought a sense of power to Colleen, but she found their direction less informative and could not figure out anything to speak to the spirit. She pursed her lips tight. Unsure what to do, Colleen experienced a proverbial light-bulb moment. Her hand darted toward the top of the closet, finding nothing but dust as the woman searched, hoping her husband's poop knife was still hidden.

When she was a child, her mother had brought her to Revival: an old nightclub. She'd watched a holo- version of a band from the late 1990s called Huskerdoo. It was her first punk show, and she'd remembered the energy. The kids pushed off each other in the "pit" while others flew in the air, jumping overhead. Times like these, she drew on how she'd felt then, the violence combined with the sense of belongingness to give herself strength. The memory caused a wave of energy to flow through her, and she felt her genetically altered muscles surge.

Footfalls on the landing made Colleen aware that the fake police officer had left her boy's room and that he'd be in the same room next. Her stomach dropped, and then she gritted her teeth in determination. The muscles around her eyes tensed. She could have used some water; her tongue lipped her lips. The dull pointed poop knife lay in the box. Her hands wrapped around the dark wooden handle. She'd only have one shot to pull this off.

# Chapter 9

Electronically controlled metal bolts snapped back, and Felicity entered the small titanium Kwanza-shaped bunker. Entering the corridor, she was momentarily blinded as a hot white spotlight pierced her eyes. She teared up from the pain and raised her left arm to cover the light. Pretending to swat a fly, Felicity flung the bug on the floor, hoping it was in a good spot.

Once past the door, the lights dimmed to a pink neon-soaked room with a heavy metal grated floor. It was like strolling on an iron catwalk. The atmosphere was business-like, and the entrance hall was lined with computer systems and gang members working on inputting. The gang accumulated immense amounts of data. *Probably tracking member activity,* Felicity thought, but she'd no way of knowing for sure.

The room itself rose about twenty feet high. A mezzanine-level catwalk jetted out about halfway to the ceiling, more like a small balcony. A set of stairs led up to it. Below it, to the other side at her level, appeared to be a lounge-type area with couches and a table.

A burly man waltzed up to her. Halogen lights glowed behind him and told her to spread her arms out. She did, and he frisked her. As expected, he found her recording device. She protested as the man took it and slammed it into the floor. His foot hit on the device and cracked it open. "Hey, I needed that for my interview," she protested, but when the man gazed at her, the reporter quickly added, "I guess the interview is one done off the record." He reached over to her, grabbed her shoulder, and spun her around. Her body jerked, and she protested the harshness of the treatment. The goon pushed her forward, and she headed down the path.

Inside, a long black-haired woman with a fashionably torn and frayed at the edges, a black denim jacket, and an athletic red tailor-made, form-fitting tank-top sat in a black glass chair. Her tanned arms and legs were so muscular that the news reporter mistook her for a male. Her fingers, nails covered in black polish, emerged from a part of cut-off denim gloves. Behind her, two thugs stood with old military-style light-ion-blasters (LIB-10s) pointed at Felicity. They motioned for the woman to sit.

The most striking feature of the woman was her deep red eyes. As the chisel-jawed lady did not appear to be an albino, Felicity assumed they must be contact lenses. Her red tank top and mascara black eyeshadow heightened the intensity of her eyes.

"Am I to presume you're Renee," the reporter graciously asked.

"It would be an accurate assumption," the woman replied. The muscly dame delicately nibbled on a hamburger with a spork and knife. Since beef was scarce in these times, it was almost a miracle that people could get their hands on food such as steak and hamburgers. Even the rich had to switch to a poultry diet to cut carbon emissions, so Felicity couldn't fault the woman for trying to savor the taste.

The newswoman scanned the room, causing her eyes to linger on the sight next door. A crew worked by the computer plugged in through neural links.

"Looks like your people are collecting a lot of data," Felicity inquired, shifting her gaze to Renee.

Renee peered up from her meal, "Workers are nothing more than semi-efficient chips in a huge data-processing mechanism."

"I see," Felicity responded. "About our interview, it seems one of your thugs smashed my recording device, so I'll have to take notes. The woman drew out an electronic pencil. Do you have a mobile writing pad I can use?"

"Please have a seat," Renee said. "But quickly added, you do know I am not going to give you an interview, right?"

The reporter's eyes widened. "Oh, I am not that naive," she stated. In the far corner was a purple studio couch. The journalist took a seat but emotionally felt like she was in horrible shape. The newswoman grabbed one of the hideously mismatched red throw pillows and laid it over her lap. She hadn't felt this sick since watching movies at Colleen's house.

"So, why'd you come?" the gang leader gruffly replied. She'd finished the burger and washed it down with some water from a natural Canadian spring. After several gulps, the woman pulled out a box of German dark chocolate and unlaced the ribbon around the box. She snagged a piece and chucked it into her mouth. It felt strange to watch the gang leader eat, and the whole experience put Felicity off-kilter.

*It really must suck to be her boyfriend,* Felicity thought. *This girl is living lavishly.*

"What?" The reporter finally replied after she stopped drooling over Renee's meal. It was a lame effort to buy time. The lameness of this plan was just starting to hit her. Indeed the project was a long shot from its start.

"Why ya here, Cruickshank?" The woman with the jacket over her athletic build asked politely but sly. She crossed her legs, exposing the rubbery soles of her lace-up Dr. Martens Hazil Combat boots. As leather was scarce, even many wealthy people did not possess the material. Felicity nearly gasped audibly. Suddenly, the gang leader became more specific. "If you know I plan to kill you, why fly here?"

*I should have taken the job on the stock exchange;* Felicity thought at least there she would have had a shot at such fine material like the boots. "Maybe I was curious? It killed the cat, you know?" Felicity's attempt to be coy fell on deaf ears, so she added, "Come on, aren't you curious about me? I like to get to know you better."

"If you think you're stalling," the gang leader stated. "I think it's only fair to tell you. We shot down both of the police quads, backing you up. Your police buds are deader than doornails, and while my guards are still trying to locate your copper friend, it Is only a matter of time before I have his head hanging from one of my copper hooks."

"Well," Felicity gulped, hoping the matter was not true. "It seems you have time to chat then. I have a bunch of matters I am interested in. Like how you knew I would have back up."

"I suspected as much, and I have my sources," the woman replied.

Felicity recognized the sociopath was a braggart, so she tried to get the woman started. "Would those sources be on the force?"

"Maybe they are, maybe they're not," the coy reply told the newswoman. The gang leader stretched in her chair and yawned.

*Bitch,* Felicity thought. *How bout some respect here!*

"So is the way you got these sources from your affiliation with Purt?" The woman figured it best to lead with the shocking to see how much Renee knew. The woman chuckled, and the reporter realized it was no surprise that she'd figured out the connection.

~

Natalie scowled at the three. "Freeze and drop your weapons," she stated. Her cold eyes hardened as her hand slid toward the ion blaster slung to her hip. The opposition laughed. Behind her, Natalie heard Johnson grunt trying to slither through the broken windshield.

Even though she wore body armor, the officer was sure her opponents would be taking headshots and thus bypassing her defenses. The gang members widened, one falling slightly behind and the others separating by about four paces, making it hard to hit them all at once. "Brash," the flirty woman she'd seen at the mall said and continued her march. The officer restated her command. This time, her eyes shifted and contacted each one directly. The two punks next to the flirt breathed heavily. One hand twitched by his pistol. A sad smile crossed the second punk's lips. His eyes seemed to plead for her to give up. Outnumbered, they'd planned to kill Natalie. Behind, Johnson continued to struggle. He would be an easy kill once she was gone, and poor Felicity would be left with Renee on her own.

"It would be a lot easier if you listened," the rookie started licking her lips while her hand itched and her muscles tightened. Her fingers hovered an inch from her holstered gun. *Could she kill them?* She winked at one of the males.

"Three can kill a lot quicker than one," the flirt coarsely sighed, then cast the knife while the other two went to draw their guns. Natalie drew, aimed, bit her lip, and fired four times. She knocked the blade from the air. All three body's hit the ground after her pistol was already holstered.

Her body twisted back to the detective. "Damn, your quick," Johnson stated, finally heaving himself out of the wreckage.

"I was trained by the best," she stated, and Johnny felt a sense of pride.

The communication link crackled. Startled, Natalie pressed the button. Jay's voice emerged from the other end of the line. He'd broken radio silence.

"Jay," Natalie stated. "Is that you?" Johnson stared at her like who else would it be, but her face crinkled, and he knew it as a get-lost expression.

"Yeah, it is me," Jay replied, and the detective rolled his eyes. An idiot question and a moronic answer. "I'd been trying to reach you on the helmet communication system." The words crushed Natalie. In her haste to leave the quad, she'd left the assault helmet behind. As if sensing something was wrong, Jay added, "I am glad you guys are okay. You missed our meeting point. Has Johnson given the coordinates for the entrance to Elise?"

Natalie rocked back on her foot and twisted on the heel so that her face was away from Johnson. "She didn't make it," the officer stated, and her voice crackled enough that Johnny realized she was shedding tears.

A five-second pause followed, "And Johnson?" the beat cop broke the silence. Natalie handed the communication link to the detective.

"I made it, Jay-Jay," Johnny said, bringing a bit of upbeat to the conversation.

"For the record, this plan sucked," Jay replied. His husky voice boomed. "It is crap like this...."

"Later, Jay," the detective said. "They might have intercepted the line."

"Where is my entrance?"

"It is located in the basement of the sewage plant," Johnny stated. "It is the large tube. First, make sure you shut it down and then walk through."

"Understood, you guys just wait there, and I'll get you both when the mission is done,"

"No," Johnny huffed. "My plan, and I'll see you inside."

"No sense in you getting Natalie killed."

"I don't plan to. Nat will wait with the quad."

"I will not," she insisted. "I am an officer, damn it, I'm going in."

"Jay ordered her to wait," Johnny stated. His voice was slow and deliberate. "and I'll see you inside."

"Johnny, why don't we meet up at the sewage treatment plant and go in together."

"I plan to go through the pipe in the small stake shop restaurant across the street from the treatment plant."

"Wait, why don't I go through there?"

"I figured our odds better if we went from two angles."

"No, you didn't want me walking through the sludge and waste while you travel through an underground tunnel."

"No, I am systematically trying to increase the odds-"

His comment sounded flimsy. "Then you go through the treatment plant,"

"Jay, you are messing up the plan," Johnny tried but could not suppress the giggle. Natalie grabbed the communication link.

"Jay," Natalie interrupted. "Should we call in for backup?"

"Not yet," Jay replied. 'The problem is the same: a frontal assault would give them the incentive to release the virus. We need to minimize the risk by getting inside and finding the virus if it is even on-site, and now getting Felicity out. If it is onsite and we can open the front door, we could radio in the assault. Listen, rookie, Johnny is right...."

"Jay, meet us both at the steak place," she cut him off. "This is taking too much comm time, shutting down." She clicked off before the officer could order her not to go.

Her eyes fell on Johnson. "What?" he asked.

"You know what," she replied. "This is serious business, and you were making fun of him."

"I was increasing-"

"Don't!" she interrupted. Johnson went to explain, and she cut him off with a "Just don't."

~

"I got to ask again," the gang leader called. "Knowing I planned to kill you, why did you come here? Are you suicidal? Did you realize the end was inevitable, so you figured you would come and see your executioner?" The words struck the reporter hard. Maybe a part of her wanted to die. Fear of her sister being yanked into this gang sunk into her, and she vowed against it, but the reporter decided to play it cool.

"Not here for anything, just to discuss something," Felicity replied while raising her hands." Since I will be killed, maybe you can enlighten me. I must admit part of little ole me wants to die knowing."

"What?"

"A couple of things, the first is about your plan to infect the entire megalopolis."

A man waltzed over and whispered something in Renee's ear. He placed the fly Felicity had thrown on the table. Renee smiled. "I believe this is your toy," she stated. Her fist came down hard and broke the electronics. "We scan for integrated circuit technology, and frankly, your little toss at the entrance was watched on our video camera."

The newswoman's heart sank. Even if she got information now, it would be her word against Renee's. He probably even had people on his payroll in the force to block her, but maybe this could work in her favor.

"It's kinda funny your team went for a literal bug design to throw us off, but frankly, the instrument failed on multiple levels. "

"So, you were enrapturing me with a tale about the virus." She leaned in and placed her hand under her chin.

"You know about the virus?" Renee fake surprise, not even a well-done fake. She seemed more flattered, ready to wax poetic about her grand achievement. "Of course, you would- such a good reporter. It is made from our blood, you know."

"Really?" The reporter asked, forcing her eyes to widen like she had a deep interest.

"Yes, and our genes are the only ones that produce the antibody."

"So, what's the plan to infect everyone?"

With a toss of her hair, the gang leader grinned toothily and excitedly. "Airborne with a dispersal canister, of course, and then they will need us to survive. They may not listen to save themselves, but I find people will do a lot to save their children. But don't worry, your sister will be part of it. She will produce blood to save the city and increase our power."

The newswoman grunted in disgust, fighting hard to contain herself. "It's almost in final form," Renee stated, waving to the giant vats behind her. They appeared as the type one would find in a cheap winery. "Once it gets that way, we will release it. It is a nasty little creature. A virus infects human bodies and mutates them to the point where they can either die or receive the antidote, but the antidote is the proteins coded for from the genetic markers found in my group."

The news reporter's gut instinct was to ask if Renee initially ordered the virus to be designed to dump into the water supply. Since they purchased a bunker so close to the water treatment plant, it would make sense, but she knew the gang leader would never admit to failure. "Viruses tend to mutate," Felicity cautioned. "This can be bad for you as well."

~

On the tiny earpiece he wore, Jay had followed the conversation of the ruthless, amoral gang leader. He'd heard the fly pick up, and then there was a loud crack and nothingness.

With fist-clenching anger, the officer knew things had taken a horrible turn. Briefly, he pondered just going in gun blazing but figured he would be dead at the door, or worse, and his assault triggered the gang to release the virus. The complex security systems were immense and vast. He needed to meet up with Ryder quickly and execute their assault.

Heart thumping in his chest, the officer thought he should be able to see the building, but the fog was thick. He worried the gang might have patrols out at this distance. Steeling himself for the journey ahead, he raised his chin, breathed, and pushed on.

~

The door flung wide, and Colleen stabbed with all her might. It quickly pierced Davis's skin, blood gushed out, covering her hand, and she jerked the knife up. Her anger blistered and exploded with all the strength she could muster. Davis's eyes glanced down as blood dripped out his mouth.

All Davis found was a poop knife to his stomach. He gagged for breath, blood pouring out. His eyes rolled back in anguish, and he collapsed his weight on the blade. With blood-covered hands, Colleen yanked the knife back, catching it under the man's rib. But with one last effort, the fake officer heaved his small laser-bladed weapon and stabbed the older woman.

Agony exploded as Colleen tore through her abdominal flesh. In her pain, she dragged her knife. The crack of his rib echoed, and then she thrust forward again. Davis's face twisted in pain, and he fell to the ground, striking his head on a stand-up combination washer and dryer.

Officer Davis's blue eyes widened as he lay there. Colleen twisted, plucking the keys to the quad from her pocket, but the loss of her blood sent her crumpling to the ground. Immediately,

149

her mind whirred, assessing her situation. *Where was her last assailant?*

Colleen tried to reposition herself so no more blood would spill. Her life essence was draining from her. She briefly thought of Mount Pocono and how she'd hoped to see it one day. The dire situation turned even bleaker.

"Computer," she murmured, hoping the smart house would pick up on her voice. The assassins had cut the machine's wire. The woman crawled slowly over the floor to hit the touch glass panel to the backup system. With each inch, her blood painted the rug.   She reached the control board for the smart houseback up system. "Computer," the machine chirped and whirled.  "Call 911 and tell them it's an emergency. I've been stabbed."

"Ok, placing a call to emergency services now," the computer replied.

*Just make it quick,* Colleen grumbled, clutching her wound. Pain shot through her system.

~

The woman waved her hand dismissively. Her fingernails were long, sharp, and perfectly sculpted. "If it backfires, well, then so much for the world and my retirement plan. Sometimes, you got to take a risk, kid."

*Anarchistic bitch,* Felicity thought. Her eyes locked on the woman, assessing every possible point to strike at Renee. Part of her wanted to gouge the woman's eyes out with her thumbs. All her grief and sadness had rolled into hate. The situation had transformed. Her motivation changed with it. This was more than justice for her friends. It was vengeance, pure and simple. Frankly, she was ok with that. She scanned the woman for weakness and an opportunity to leap on her and bury her nails into Renee's eyes. She weighed these thoughts with the need to buy Jay time. If she were to leap forward and was killed, he would have no way of knowing or getting in.

Surely, he'd be trying to get inside. Maybe he would get lucky and find the entrance Detective Johnson had said existed. Her heart sank, thinking that Johnson and Natalie Ryder were dead. All those courageous police officers were down. Her face darkened. *Would Renee win?* No one was left to stop her. No one was left to protect Felicity. No one was left to defend her sister,

150

who would be trapped forever, producing antibodies for the masses. "I have another question." The gang leader took a slow sip of her water, and the reporter suspected it was deliberate to buy time and make her wait. Waiting was all the reporter had, buy time and hope for an opening. No big deal, let the evil bitch brag.

Cherry red lipstick stained the mouth of the glass as she lowered it. "Lemme guess. Our ties to good ol' Purt?" It was clear that Renee was getting something from this encounter: some little thrill. Maybe she served as good entertainment value. The reporter considered asking the woman about her relationship with Jackson Newman but did not want to spoil any momentum keeping her talking. No, she needed to keep the entertainment value high. Her life depended on it and maybe the life of her sister. The news reporter wanted to stay focused on the one subject she suspected always held Renee's attention: Renee.

"Yes, Renee. Your ties to Purt." The gang leader yanked out a pair of Japanese sunglasses: the expensive kind made from polarized plastic, designed to change shade with varying light. The sunglasses had a garnet-red tint because of how bright-lit the room was. *Bet they run from pink to burgundy*, the newswoman thought. *It is just like the freak to want to see the world through rose color glasses one minute and blood red the next.*

Felicity got the feeling the gang leader was trying to impress her. Maybe this was a way of showing off. Perhaps she'd let her live if the reporter promised to let the rest of the world know what an expensive life the Marked Ones led. The glasses appeared far too big for Renee's eyes and placed awkwardly on her face. Felicity wondered if the woman could see anything through the deepest red.

"What aspect of it?" Renee leaned back and put her hands behind her head, kicking up her legs on a chair. The reporter felt that the gang leader acted like this moment was an interview on an old-fashioned radio program. The callousness further enraged Felicity, but she hoped her poker face held up and kept the psychopath from knowing.

The gang leader smirked and motioned for Felicity to go on. "I just don't understand why you're in this partnership with them," Felicity said.

"It's just a business arrangement."

"But you run juice, and they fight it."

151

"Two sides of the same coin. Don't be naive." She deliberately chose her words to be as irritating as possible. The tone conveyed most of the mocking message. She'd seen Felicity as naive and mentally weak.

"How so?"

"Simple. I get money, and we liberate the world of blind temptation to sin!" Renee exclaimed. "Personally, I'd rather be sipping a margarita in the Cayman, but until that time, this is the job. I take pride in my work."

"Now you sound like one of them," Felicity countered, and then her eyes caught sight of the tattoo on the hand. Of course, she was a cross-over with them. Her mind thought of Jan. Just days before, the woman dominated the concrete jungle and told her partner she'd give her life for a friend, and then she did. It wasn't fair, and this bitch was behind it.

"But you are fully aware Purt is manipulating you to keep the juice on the streets. Right?" Felicity continued. "And why would they do it?"

The woman took her feet from the chair, placed them back on the floor, and swiveled toward the reporter, obnoxiously close. "Honestly, it's something I don't know. But it seems like they do it to get more lifelong followers- "

"Heh, that makes sense, but Purt doesn't do that. Besides, I don't think people are that naïve to join Purt like that."

"That's what I thought at first, but Purt gives them meaning. It looks at them and tells them they are core to the future of this world. And why would they rebel against that, especially from the group that saved their lives from the horrible addiction? It seems you have overestimated people's willpower." Felicity swallowed and frowned as Renee stood up. She wore black patterned shorts with a belt on top. The tough girl took off her gloves, revealing a tattoo like her HR representatives. How deep was Cohen Shay involved with The Marked Ones? Renee slapped her hands on the table.

"You know, I thought you'd be here to beg that your sister doesn't join the gang. I can see you now. You are begging on your knees, pleading for poor Susan could be exempt from joining, to which I'd smack you down with a big powerful 'No.'" Renee cackled, drawing out her hand motions to elaborate. "But maybe you are starting to realize it is for the best. Your sister will become a master. As with all the Marked Ones, she is a post-human being queen of this dying society."

"You are already trying to recruit her?!" Disgust piled in Felicity, and she felt her cheeks heating up with anger. At whatever cost, she had to protect Susan from this group.

"She is almost of age. The gene becomes expressed in the teen years post-puberty. She's got a long waiting list, though. There's your sister, the Dennis kid, some chick named Addison. There are many more marked, but my going on would bore you, wouldn't it?"

"Can't disagree," scoffed the newswoman, and then she felt like she'd blown her stalling attempt. She might as well just said, *Kill me. You are so dull.*

Catching hold of herself, the gang leader drew back, stopped her bragging rant, and recomposed herself. "Anyhow, your sister is the future, honey," the gang leader's voice dropped to a sickly-sweet tone. "You are the present. I thought that maybe you join us. When your sister joins, her blood could go to you, and in return, you would write us charming stories. Hell, we pay you a ton more than you are making now."

*So that's why I'm not dead,* Felicity thought. *They want to recruit me with the "better rich than dead" selling points.* She inhaled. Her father had made a similar offer to come and work for him on the stock market. He'd promised her a life of wealth, and she'd chosen to struggle instead, and where did it get her- nowhere. They were even going to fire her from the job. Renee was a total psychopath, but at least she was a wealthy one. Felicity was a dweeb at best. The thoughts were painful, and they rolled in her head, but in the end, she found solace in the fact that she needed to be her own woman: not one owned by her daddy or this gang of fools. "Look, if this was also what you wanted to get out of this little talk, it's not happening."

Renee sat back down on the glass chair. Her plucked, shaped, thin eyebrows arched. She put her combat gloves back on and motioned for the journalist to continue as she twirled her hair.

All at once, it hit the reporter that Purt's leadership would not be immune to the virus. This scenario was a double-cross. She knew the woman would love to brag about it and probably be in the throes of ecstasy just to get her position known. Talk about entertainment value. Clearly, she had to play the card. "Does your business partner," Felicity asked, "know you will release the virus?"

"Why?"

"It seems to me," Felicity said, "This would be a wonderful coo for you." Renee shook her head, and the woman could barely contain herself with pride in her achievement. "I mean, here you are playing second fiddle, but they aren't immune, so they will become dependent on you." A sly smile crossed the gang leader's lips. "What a coop," the reporter continued.

"That wasn't even remotely the point of this conversation. I need you to focus here! Your life is at stake if you don't accept my offer," the news reporter struck a nerve. The gang leader revealed her slyness.

"So, got the double-cross going on and..."

"I never said anything like...."

"Ok. One last thing, I figure you stole some robots. Do you know anything regarding these deals?"

"Nah. Talk to my right-hand man, Cohen Shay, if you want to find out about that crap. He does all the arrangements."

Cohen? He did work for the *Marked Ones*. "Cohen? But he joined the choir invisible!" Felicity exclaimed, suspicious and wanting to know more. The gang leader waved a hand, and the reporter's HR representative emerged from the back—a wave of betrayal crushed over Felicity.

"Ha, what a classy euphemism, but no, he ain't dead." Renee slyly laughed. She reached out her hand, and Cohen took it. The gang leader squeezed twice and glanced at Cohen (both for Felicity's benefit), "He's important to me. He is vital to the future of New Cyber City. He helps me make all of the gang-related decisions."

"You bastard," Felicity mumbled, glaring at Cohen. It seemed he took notice and turned to face her.

~

The HADO competition produced a second-place trophy for Maska. He talked incessantly about the competition all the way home in the aqua-marine quad.  About a half-hour before arriving home, Steven tried to phone his wife, but she didn't answer the phone. He called the computer at the house, but the system seemed off. Knowing his wife, he figured she was cleaning the

154

house before their arrival and had unplugged the smart computer system to take it apart to wipe down the touch glass.

When the quad landed in the driveway of the old colonial home, Steve and the boy unloaded the computer gear and waltzed up the steps of the house. With a jovial tone, the father teased his son about one of his mistakes, which left the boy diving out of the way of a virtual reality fireball.

When Steven arrived, the front door was ajar. Concern grew inside the old cop. Jay wished for his ion blaster back, drawing an old service laser from his pocket.

The pathway leading to the steps was a typical solar floor that met a concrete pavement. Steve called his wife "Colleen...Colleen...!" as he reached the top step. No response. An old song played from his home. His eyes cast a glance inside. For a man his age, Steven moved with solid muscles.

He called inside and with no answer, worried his wife had left the house suddenly or just forgotten to close the door. Their neighborhood was safe, but still, leaving the door wide open was an invitation for trouble in the city. *Where would she have gone?* The front door opened straight into the living room. The walls to the room were papered a French lace doily white color. An old-fashioned gas fireplace rimmed with heavy white occupied the middle of the southern barrier. The flames were not lit.

When Colleen was home, she typically kept the fireplace burning at night, even though the area's heat never fell much below seventy. She told Steven once it reminded her of when they were first married before the kid. She remembered they moved from the reservation, where Colleen had spent many years. It was a time before Manhattan flooded from rising sea levels, and they were forced to vacate the place and move into New Cyber City.

~

In the distance was the domed top of the steak place. It rested shortly before the five-chamber sewage treatment plant— each chamber basin was designed to handle a different process from anaerobic to the pump-out chamber. The churning bins hummed and swirled. Jay had always thought he would visit the plant someday, preferably with a child of his own, but now the prospects of such an endeavor seemed so far away. He'd just be happy to make it through the night in one piece.

Moths fluttered around the streetlamp on the walkway by the dock. During the day, they used sunlight to guide their flight patterns. At night the dull bluish-white lights solar lights hypnotized them into a form of entrapment by convincing them that they were flying toward the sun. The officer approached the building, hoping this raid was not a similar fool's errand created by an illusion of the light of finding the truth and bringing justice.

The place was primarily a single-room building made from cheap Taiwanese aluminum alloy tinted a sloppy sun-washed brownish orange. The officer hurried toward the building. As he approached, he heard a faint scurry. He spun toward the sound. Through the fog, two figures came. His finger waited on the trigger. If they fired, he was a clear target. The officer needed to beat them to the shot.

"Stand your ground, or I'll shoot," he called.

"It's us, Jay," a female voice called back, "Johnson and Ryder."

Jay locked eyes with both, staring them down. "What the hell? You could have given me a heart attack." He slumped back against the building wall.

"Sorry," Natalie replied. "You were just as much a blur to us as we were to you. If I wasn't sure I could outdraw whoever it was, I might have fired."

"Well, thanks for not firing then." His voice oozed with sarcasm.

"We need to get inside," Johnson stated.

"Does someone live here?" Officer Ryder asked.

"Nah, who would move into a place like this," Jay replied with an edge of derision in his voice. Natalie traced a finger over the bridge of her nose and ignored the sarcastic tone.

"People live at these places because they are out of options," Natalie offered. If the detective could be a pompous ass, she saw Jay could be equally as bad.

"Homeless doesn't have standards," Johnson replied. "But truthfully, the place is still open. The owner moved to Florida about a year ago after – well, let's just say he needed to get out of the city. Now, he has his cousin come in and open on big events at the dock."

They'd come to the shop. It was locked, but the detective used the cables on his bionic arm to make short work of the

156

electronic combination. Then he reconnected the wires back to his Smith and Wesson, so his targeting computer could better guide his shots. Soon, they were inside and staring at an empty joint.

"Where's the entrance Johnny?" the officer asked.

"In the back," he replied, leaping over the counter, and yanking up the floorboard. A thick metal door with a handle on it rested there. "Old bomb shelter a past owner cut into the sewer lines. I guess he figured it for an escape tunnel if the Russians dropped the big one. He'd have access to the shelter, and after a couple of months, when the food ran out, he could explore the underground without ever having to come to the surface to seek out food." He grabbed the solid metal handle of the floorboard. His arms strained. It was bolted shut, and the other two stared at him skeptically.

With his bionic, Johnson tightened the grip on the handle. "Pray it won't snap," he called. "Or that my back doesn't give out. I got to be careful to use all arm and no, rest of me." He positioned his feet as if sitting and held his arms as if curling weights on the floor. He tugged. His face reddened and strained. His hands shook. Nothing.

The detective drew back as Jay went off into a rant. Natalie searched the counter area, determined to find a key. "Jay," Johnson said. "Why don't you help her?"

The officer rushed to the rookie's side, desperately searching the boxes. He even threw open the lid on an outdated standing freezer, possibly forty years old, exposing aged faux steak. The freezer was still running.

For his part, the detective took three deep breaths and prepared himself. He cleared his mind, ready to try again. Focusing on the hydraulic lifts in his circuit panels, he reassured himself that this was doable. His whole body shook as he tried again. As his hand drew back, the sound of the metal crumpling under his pressure-filled the room. The panel twisted and groaned.

The hatch snapped open to the old bomb shelter below. They exchanged nods. At the end of the bomb shelter sat a watertight sliding bulkhead door. Manually actuated, Johnny grabbed a shaft and heaved the chain drive, rotating three gears until the door slid away. The area was pitch black, but the detective reached toward the wall and tugged at a chain. They

157

heard a click, and a red light came. Twenty feet later, they'd reached a metal fence. A chain with locked secured the passage. "Now what?" Jay asked.

The old detective reached toward the pressurized lock. He grabbed it into his bionic and squeezed. The crunching sounds of metal and then a pop happened almost simultaneously. In front of them was another ladder leading down. "It takes us to the sewer tunnels," Johnson commented. "So, you see, we were all heading into the muck." Down twelve rungs, the old detective leaped off and into a puddle. His feet splashed, and he whipped out his MegaSmart to light the way with its blue-white glow.

The rookie came down next, sure that at least a hundred rats would circle her at the bottom, ready to devour her. She was disappointed only to see one scurrying in the distance. The sounds of water trickling into the sewer pipe echoed in the distance.

About one hundred yards into the tunnel, they came to a large tube. "We need to climb up this," Johnson said.

~

"Now, how the hell did that happen?" Felicity questioned, confused and feeling like she was in a ghastly plot twist like one of the movies at Colleen's house- only there was no love story here.

"The glass was bomb-resistant, and I took for cover by a pretty bomb-resistant desk. I guess your place was built for blasts like that, huh?" The two guards set their guns down as Renee repositioned herself, displaying her black combat boots. The laid-back leader looked like she was lying sideways on the chair. Felicity noted the gang leader's charismatic and easy-going nature. This girl was like a Venus flytrap, very alluring but extremely dangerous. No wonder she had so many people on her side.

With so much to tell, Renee appeared just horrible at telling it. "He's vital?" The reporter wanted nothing more than to grab his sick smiling face and stuff it in a toilet until he drowned.

"Of course, sweetie. All the *Marked Ones* are."

"Because of the virus?" The reporter's mind worked the angles, seeking the play.

"Yes, but also because they like to use people already on the inside," Cohen added. "I'd worked at that paper for ten years, and what did I have to show? A small retirement pension would leave my wife and me eating cat food."

The reporter tried to get up, but one of the goons shoved her back hard into the sofa. "You're sick." The reporter spat, and the cold gang leader only grinned a toothy smile. She waved away the HR representative.

"Now um…Since you refused my very kind and generous offer, I'm gonna have my guards shoot you in the stomach. The shot will put a hole in you big enough for a cantaloupe. It will be unbearable, but I will enjoy watching you crawl in agony for the last few minutes of your life…."She paused to compose herself and think of something more wicked, "Plan to even laugh through your torment."

The words made Felicity cringe, and a string of curses caught in her throat. The guards raised their weapons, waiting for the command to fire. Terror filled Felicity's eyes, and as she wiped it away, she saw a movement high in the dark corner of the steal grate above. "As a dying woman, grant me the honor of one last question."

"Why?" The impertinence in the gang leader's voice was unmistakable. She struggled to maintain Renee's gaze.

"Humor me so that I may die in peace."

"I have no concern for your peace," the gang leader scathed, but the reporter gave her sweetest glance. "Fine, but I plan to torture you worse for it."

"Can the tattoos be modified?"

"They are tattoos, so you can add them," Renee scoffed.

"It would change the circuit panel," the reporter pressed the lead. This was what her editor wanted- a reporter who was daring enough even in death to chase down the truth. No playing it safe, and this was who she'd chosen to become. The gang leader sneered.

Ignoring mocking or taking it as confirmation, Felicity asked, "Why did you steal the robots?" The newswoman suspected the answer but wanted to see if the woman would confirm.

The gang leader appeared amazed. "None of your damn business, and you are out of questions, dearie," Renee gruffly shouted, and to the guards coldly added, "Kill her."

159

Felicity was unable to keep a hint of a grin from her cheeks. She'd been expecting this and hoped it would trigger her back- up into action.

As the order was given, the guards were struck from behind and flopped into a tumble. Behind them stood Johnson, Ryder, and Jay high up on the mezzanine level of the catwalk. "Get them," the gang leader called, pointing at them for the room full of her members. Guns poured out, firing bullets and laser blasts in the general direction of the newswoman's support. Pressed to the wall, Johnny fought hard. His targeting computer hit with fantastic accuracy.

As if unconcerned by the chaos around her, Renee rose from her chair and toward Felicity. The reporter questioned if the woman believed herself invincible or if this was just an act to rally her troops. Laser blasts crashed all around as new guards rushed toward their leader.

An old-fashioned stiletto knife popped out, and Renee leaped into action against the reporter. "I'm gonna stick you, baby, like a pin into a bug." She danced and jived with a huge smile covering her face. "Stabby, stabby, stabby." The words belied a joy for which the gang leader longed. She thrust out the knife toward the reporter's sternum. The reporter leaped back. Renee slashed from side to side, hoping to slice open the abdominal cavity. Felicity grasped her wrist with her right hand and her elbow with her left. The reporter glided, smooth as flowing water, to the side. Her strike on the elbow strained the ligament enough that Renee screamed in pain and then giggled.

The blade fell from the gang leaders' hand and onto the steel catwalk. Lights go on at the end of the corridor. She tucked back. The reporter swiftly kicked in, and it tumbled into the great.

Dumbfounded, the gang leader glanced up. "Now, I will have to punch you in the face and then choke the life out of you," she called. Renee might have been a great gang leader, but the reporter felt her crazy to keep telegraphing her actions in a fight. Maybe the woman was psychotic? They struggle with several punches thrown. Trying to get an excellent strike to gouge Renee's eyes, Felicity moved in. Unfortunately, as she leaped into Renee, she took a punch right to her face, but she managed to get hold of her eyes. Felicity raked her eyes. Blood spouted over the reporter's nails.

Renee landed a blow to Felicity's nose, stunning the reporter and forcing her to back up. The gang leader pushed her advantage with another series of punches, but her success was short-lived.

A reign of laser blasts from Johnny, Jay, and Natalie hailed on the metal deck. They struck gang members rushing forward to fire back.

Falling back to a boxing stance, Felicity prepared to defend herself. She efficiently dodged the first punch but then received a rapid flurry of strikes against her. The reporter batted them away, and the gang leader stepped back with a bit of uncertainty in her eyes. She screamed and launched herself.

A punch knocked Felicity off balance, but Renee slipped, and the reporter threw a fist right at the gang leader's face. The leader's head snapped back, and blood trickled from her nose. She launched a series of punches at the reporter. Felicity ducked and then rolled under the table. As she did so, her leg swept Renee off balance. The gang leader looked up from the metal floor, watching the reporter bolt.

Two brutish guards fired but missed as Felicity made a serpentined break for the exit. Closing the door frantically, the journalist ran around behind the bunker to take cover. She knew the guards weren't that stupid and quietly snuck over to the nearest spot to hide. The girl held her breath as she saw the two guards patrolling the bunker. Once she was sure they were gone, she dashed and didn't look back.

The savage guards howled and dashed onto the landing.

~

The dying officer heaved herself over the cooling body of the fake Officer Davis. His blood mingled with her own. Suppressing the urge to vomit, she grabbed his laser knife and went limp. "Computer, Billie Holiday, *I'll be seeing you,*" she called, wondering where the police were. The smart house complied.

Up the stairs rushed, the second, and into the bathroom. Colleen held her breath and waited. Retching sounds followed. Clearly, this junky was not up to the task of killing. *Don't come to slaughter unless you plan to fight,* she thought. They drew first blood.

161

His ragged breaths approached. If Colleen passed out, there would be no tomorrow. For a moment, the idea of peace and passing felt inevitable. She felt her strength fading. Then a horrifying thought beat in her brain. She'd never see Steven again or Maska. Her brain screamed, "No!" Adrenalin pulsed through her system.

Her eyes narrowed, and Colleen battled not to drift into unconsciousness. She focused on the pain to stay awake. She closed her eyes, and Jan's face stared back at her. "I failed you," she told the spirit. "Let my death be quick now!" Disappointment flooded the officer.

"Not yet," the spirit mouthed. Her face was beautiful and fierce. "Get moving." Her eyes opened, but the area around her was darkening. The officer's eyes shut again. The image of Maska's *birth* played in her mind. The officer swore to live at least until his vision quest.

Colleen remembered years before when Uncle John Rutledge joined her prior to her vision quest. A dark black raven circled behind him. "You are destined to have a proud life and a line full of love," he told her, and every ounce of her believed him. He had beat colonization and managed to survive, becoming influential in two cultures: the native one and the common. Colleen's eyes shot open. A hint of mischief played in them.

The man drew closer. Worry beat inside her. *Did she have enough strength to fight back?* His breath touched her skin. She spun and plunged the laser into the side of his head and slashed the poop knife across his throat. His body fell backward and collapsed.

The deep wound made her numb. Each drop of life spilling to the floor served to weaken further. She staggered a few feet more, ready to collapse. With a cold chill, her body shook.

Salty cold water dripped down her face. It rolled into her eyes, causing them to sting. From setting in shock, her body shivered. Her skin seeped fluid as she dragged forward: one hand at a time. Her arm muscles trembled and shook. Her thin bloodless hands moved through the hallway carpet and onto the white tile of the bathroom. She had one desire: to live. With all her strength, she heaved herself over the rough edge.

Trying to raise her head, Colleen felt a wave of dizziness washed through her head. She let her body fall back for the

162

moment. Exhausted, her eyes cast down at her hands. They appeared an ashen color. *I mustn't sleep*, the officer reminded herself. *Sleep is death*. The hard floor pressured her knees. She felt the cold tiles, and her skin ached where blood gushed out. Her body demanded rest, just to close her eyes and sleep, but she knew if she stopped now, she would bleed out and die. Despite the agony, she reached again and carried her weight forward. Her vision blurred from pain.

Close to her mega smartphone, she reached. The tips of her finger touched the phone, and reaching made her gasp from pain. Colleen slipped under her own weight, sobbing on the bathroom floor: unable to hit the button to dial. Her upstairs smelled of mildew and various cleaners. The smell wanted to make her gag.

It was getting hard to breathe. Colleen made one more reach. This time the light on the phone came on, and an old number rang.

Colleen heard people enter the house downstairs: probably looters. Since thieves generally were not killers, a moan escaped her lips. She hoped they would come up to help. Instead, they ran off. It was too much for Colleen, and she sobbed loudly.

A door slammed on her first floor, "Hello," was repeated several times. Colleen felt terror, wondering if this was a savior or her end, but something about the voice sounded familiar.

"Help," Colleen called.

Since childhood, Colleen would stare at the stars. In those days, she would climb on the windowsill and sit on it like a ledge. Their mother would panic seeing it and order her to get down immediately. Terrified, Colleen would fall. Now Colleen dragged herself to the end of the steps with one plan to fall.

Her mind swirled with dizziness. Her peripheral vision shrunk to a blurry black fuzz. In front of her, Jan stood. "Reach for me," the ghost mouthed.

"I can't," Colleen muttered. "So much pain." Her hands trembled.

"Now," the ghost demanded, and Colleen knew she'd have to listen to get her spirit back. The officer reached forward. The apparition drew away, and she tumbled down the steps.

# Chapter 10

The laser and gunfire barrage pushed the three back into the corridor they'd entered. The team ducked close to a slight curve in the wall and alternated coming out to fire. Two at a time in rhythm, with one serving as a backup to the person switching out. "Back to the sewer?' Johnny questioned. The three fired back into the pitch-black tunnel leading to the mezzanine deck.

"Not without Ms. Cruickshank," Jay insisted. His sweating hands clung tightly to his weapon, parallel to his face. He leaped out, fired with Johnny, and then fired a second shot while Johnny shifted back, and Natalie came out firing.

"I think the virus is here. Those vats are filled with it," Johnny offered, and the other two nodded, "but I am not completely sure. I got an idea on how to find out."

"So, how do we get around them and to the vats?" Natalie chimed in. Bullets struck the wall with a clink, and one of them chipped off a bit of the rock from their cover.

"Ask the damn detective," Jay spat. The beat cop's head bobbed from side to side, "this is his plan." Natalie glanced over at Johnny and could see this entire plan was a lie. He'd been bluffing, and now they were all paying the price.

Someone once said the best defense is a potent offense, and Johnson planned to be as offensive as needed. "Look, I planned to get Ms. Cruickshank in with you and your two highly trained police squads. You can't blame me because they got knocked out of the sky."

"It was your job to get them in," Jay barked.

"Think of it, Jay. Police regularly fly over the docks for patrols," Johnson jeered.

"What are you implying? Speak it, plain man," Jay called out.

"I suggest they had information of our plan and our arrival time," Johnson flatly stated.

Being stubborn, Jay said, "Sounds like a conspiracy theory and frankly don't make sense." He let off two rounds of fire into the whole.

"Jay," Natalie offered. She caught sight of a person moving and gunned them down. "I think Johnson is hinting there

164

was an inside tip." The mixed smell of ozone from the lasers and sulfur from the bullets lingered heavily.

The beat cop stood so close to the rookie's side that he saw the tension in her shoulder muscles and the tightness of her neck. "Sure, create a fiction of a cop on the take," Jay yelled. His blaster blazed into the hall. A spin and grind of metal came from down the corridor. "This is going from bad to worse Jay screamed as he caught sight of the eight-foot form with glowing fuchsia eyes.

The Gatling spray from the robot's weapons drenched the corridor, pushing them all close to the wall. The cacophony of the bullet sounds deafening. For every one hundred shots, a tracer let the darkness like a hypersonic firefly skirting through the darkness. "We're trapped," Natalie called. "It was nice...."

"Don't say that shit," Johnson yelled. "I'll draw the fire. I can hit its vision. You and Natalie get back down the tunnel and to the tube. Take it back to the steak joint. I got the reporter." He touched the microchip on his bionic finger. He recalculated the entire processor via Bluetooth communication with an embedded electronic device implanted into his lower cerebellum to gear for rapid-fire. A process Jay knew would exhaust the detective in a matter of minutes.

"Johnson," Jay shouted. "I'll get the girl."

"How romantic, Jay, but my client, and frankly, I'm expecting a huge bonus from her for this." He jumped out in the open. His targeting computer landed three direct hits on the robot visual panel. He tucked and rolled as Jay and Natalie laid down a strong blast striking the robot in the head and arms with multiple shots.

The two were pushed back deeper into the tunnel as Johnny fired at the robot's back, forcing it to turn. The machine was blind, but a spray of bullets would easily find him. He was caught between the proverbial rock and a hard place between the rotating robot and the gang's kill zone.

~

Tumbling down the steps, Colleen hit bottom with a slap. Blood, expelled from her body, coated the step's rug. Her body jerked in an unconditioned response to the brutal hit on the landing. She heard a gasp and caught sight of her husband and son. Her husband had been holding his phone and dropped it immediately and rushed toward her in shocked confusion.

"Maska get my phone," he yelled. Steven managed to reach her and touch her face as the room faded to black. She thought she'd heard him pleading desperately for an emergency to send a quad.

A flood of relief flushed her. A peacefulness came as death began to set into her. As she drifted off, the voice of a pleading Maska begged her to stay. The boy's face shattered the darkness. Not his face but an image of him. Her hand reached out and touched his arm.   He grabbed her hand, and their fingers intertwined. Their palms pressed together.  She needed to fight.

~

They scurried for three hundred feet to the door to the climate-controlled system room. Jay whipped the metal door open, and the two headed to the panel. When they reached it, Jay slid it back, exposing the tube. "You go first," Jay called to Natalie. "I'll follow."

She jumped into the tube and slid down. As she did, Jay called to her. "I need to make sure that Johnson is alright. Get to the bottom and give the officer a down call. I'll get the front door open."

It was too late to stop her own descent. It was stupid to split up because it decreased the odds of survival. She shook her head "no" and screamed up to him, but there was no answer. He'd taken off back to the fight. Damn, she should have known he wouldn't let Johnson go. It was s horrible mistake in the fog of war.

Within seconds, she reached the bottom of the tube. She almost lost it over the failure of her team to include her in the decisions. She hated this rampant testosterone shit when it emerged. Natalie checked her MegaSmart, no bars, but she reached for her short-ranged comm link. Maybe she'd catch other officers in the area. She'd be forced back to the steak place if all else failed.   One thing was sure: she once again found herself alone and up to her ankles in sewer muck.

~

Instinct forced Johnson to collapse to the floor. He covered his head. The blinded robot dropped his arm and fired where Johnson's shot came from- directly into the crowd. A burst of light and shrieks of dying brought his mind back to the war. Tears

166

flooded his eyes, and he pushed tighter to the ground. A bullet whizzed past his shoulder, scraping his back. Another sliced by the back of his neck. He spent all his energy trying to contain himself and ensure that he did not raise his head.

Laser light flashed and danced. The corridor lightened, darkened, lightened, and darkened again. Screams of pain and terror rose over even the loud sounds of gunfire.

Within two minutes, it was over as the robot exploded. It took Johnson another two full minutes before he braved to rise and tuck his shirt into his pants. Tears still streamed down his face. Bodies flooded the corridor. He saw gang members groaning on the ground in total pain, and the detective shivered from the fright of so much carnage, lying barely visible in the dark. Just outlined silhouettes from the neon room.

The emotionality weighed on him as he stumbled in pain from the graze he'd received from the bullet. And then his eyes caught sight of hopelessness. Three more robots were advancing up the stairs.

Blinding white pain coursed through his neck and back from the wounds. Blood stained his shirt. His heart sank, but he darted toward the opposite end of the mezzanine. He had to find his client.

~

The burst of action had Officer Jay feeling energized. The adrenaline rush brought strange thoughts to his head and an invincible numbness to his body. Maybe he was ready to die, going out saving a civilian and taking down one of the deadliest gangs in New Cyber City. There was no better way to go. His brain flashed on a police plack on the wall by this spot, honoring his death.

Jay certainly was much older now than his father was when he'd passed. Unlike his dad, though, he could make a real difference. He proceeded back to catch up with Johnson. The detective had stated the vats were holding the virus. *No,* he corrected himself; *the detective said that the vats contained the virus.* He might have been wrong. The worry of the wrongness infected his thoughts, and a jolt of anxiety coursed through him. Maybe he needed to let himself feel the pressure or at least tug at the thread knotted in his mind.

Jay had ordered Natalie to command the assault without confirmation of the contents. A rookie mistake, and he could have kicked himself for it. It was the kind of mistake that got people killed, and his mind worried in this case. It could have led to millions in the city becoming dependent on the Marked Ones.

Briefly, he felt torn about going back to catch up with her or breaking radio silence with the short-range communication system to back her off from the call. Since he still needed to find Johnson and Felicity, the officer again decided to break radio silence. It did not matter now; the whole encampment knew they were here. The element of surprise was long gone.

With a dull ache in his heart, the officer tapped the communication link. It crackled with static. His heart jumped for a minute. It was nearly impossible for the gang to have known the exact frequency to block. Rapidly, his mind calculated the permutation problem. Given all the radio channel possibilities, the odds were over a million to one against. He chided himself for dealing with trivia when he needed to find the others and get the door opened. Jay reached for his MegaSmart, and to his shock, he'd no bars.

~

Panting, Natalie made it back to the steak shop. Finally, she had bars for her phone. Leaning on the counter, the officer flipped the app to call emergency. She identified herself and then gave the officer down call and information. As regular police quads passed the area, she suspected back up quickly. The officer online remaindered her to wait. She stated it was her plan.

After the call, she logged into the Earth Corps computer system and filed a terrorist action in progress form. As she completed the form, she peered out the shop's door and saw Felicity fleeing, probably back to the quad. Behind her, by one hundred fifty yards, two guards gave chase firing bullets at the reporter. Pop, pop, pop, every three seconds, the sound rang out. The officer called for the shooters to freeze. They did not. Aiming, Natalie fired, killing both men, then she rushed out to catch her and bring her to the steak shop.

The running reporter wasn't slowing down. Natalie worried. She was so panicked that she had not even noticed the reporter. The officer would have to run alongside her and calm her down.

Even though Natalie ran a mile every morning, Felicity was quicker. While Natalie called out repeatedly, it seemed the woman was only getting further and further away. For a nanosecond, Natalie felt selfish as her body experienced joy at running.

~

The ambulance was a blur of lights and sirens as Colleen faded in and out of consciousness. Two medical technicians and an android worked on the officer. Words like "get the i.v." and "prepare the shot" echoed in her ears as they whisked to the emergency room. Her husband held one hand and her son the other.

Huge IV lines pierced her skin and filled her with fluid. Robotic lasers cut into her belly while dissolvable silk stitches sewed the wound closed. One technician said, "We are pouring liquid skin over the stitches to allow it to heal faster, but they may need to cut in again at the hospital." She faded out.

When she came back to consciousness, the officer's lips were chapped and dry. Her belly hurt, but somehow, she felt safe. It was as if the spirit world were riding with her to protect her.

*How the hell did they get her address?* She'd done undercover work for many years, so most of her file was blank with a restrictive access code for even the most basic information. The goal was for her never to be able to be tracked down, and yet, they had.

At least one of them had been a juicer. Colleen doubted anyone on juice could have planned out a strike, and their failed execution proved highlighted what she knew of their limitations. She pondered. She'd handled the hundreds of cases to which they were tied. Was her past catching up to her? Exhaustion set in. She lacked the energy to think this through. The officer's eyes closed. Her mind drifted off again to the darkness of a dream of her uncle handing her a piece of spearmint gum on the day of her spirit walk.

~

With a dead run, Johnson hit the far end of the mezzanine and leaped off toward the marked biological hazard vats. He landed hard, and it knocked the wind from him for a nanosecond. Quickly, he crawled off to the side and shimmied to the ground. Three Marked Ones trampled over each other to reach him.

The targeting computer on his arm raised it, and he fired. The gang members ducked behind the vat. Then they shot out and returned the fire. He saw flashing lights and the remaining guards trying to circle to his other side.

The detective reached his hand to his neck. Blood still trickled out from his near-miss in the hall. The wound smarted, and he felt a bit dizzy. He tightened next to the vat and worried the gang would coordinate its attack from both sides. Two guards ducked behind a vat just to his left. He knew they were planning to circle. He could get the drop on one, but these two plus the three in front would be impossible to kill.

~

Exhaustion finally caused Felicity to stop running, and Natalie drew up next to her. The woman dropped her hands to her knees and took several rapid breaths.

"God, you're quick," Natalie stated. Her voice huffed from the jog but forced low to avoid spooking the reporter—Felicity's eyes caste to her. The reporter sobbed, "I thought I was dead," she mewed and turned away. The policewoman hoped that one good thing emerged through the encounter, that the reporter realized that she wanted to live.

The officer shook her head. "It's almost over," Natalie said. "Johnny and Jay are still inside, and I called in for backup, so I suspect them to arrive in minutes." They stared at each other. Worry and sadness were utterly evident.

A huge flash lit and then disappeared from the heavens. The sky crackled with lightning. New Cyber City was prone to almost nightly thunderstorms. Both knew the downpour would be minutes away.

"The virus is inside," the reporter stated. Her face was pale white, and her eyes haunted by a frantic gaze.

"How do you know?" The newswoman looked around her, checking both sides. Maybe her emotions had overridden her judgment.

"Renee confirmed it," the reporter said. "She indicated it was in the vats- at least some of them."

A worried expression crossed the officer's face. Her jaw slacked. "Damn, I hope we did not trigger a release," Natalie stated. A gentle breeze caressed her face.

A vague sense of sorrow haunted the reporter. "She mentioned it wasn't completed, but I am not sure if she meant the amount needed or something with the virus itself," the reporter replied. "We need to go back."

"What? No, that would be awful. I need to wait for her for our police and Earth Corps backup to arrive," Natalie stated. Another flash of lightning followed by the roll of thunder, and Natalie found herself pressed to want to take shelter. Pleadingly, her hand beckoned to the steak place. The reporter ignored it.

"What happened to our original assault team?" The news reporter stared tensely at the officer.

"The quads crashed," Natalie acknowledged, tilting her head back to the shop to hide from the coming storm.

"Do you know how?"

"Some sort of interference jammed our systems," the officer replied. "Look, it might be best to make this conversation inside the shop. It is where Johnson's entrance to the hut is located."

The reporter liked entering the hut and waltzed next to the reporter. "And if we don't shut that system down, what makes you think additional police or Earth Corp won't crash." Even Natalie saw the newswoman had a point. "Believe me, I won't go back unless absolutely necessary, but Johnson and Jay are in serious trouble if we don't return."

"Look if it is the robots," the officer insisted, tugging at the skin at the base of her chin.

"Not just that, but I know which tank is the correct one," she exaggerated. She had a general idea of the correct tank. "Also, if we kept Renee- the woman implicated Purt. We could take the whole network down." The rookie lived In New Cybercity her whole life, so she completely doubted the last statement. The two decided to head back to make sure the two drums, which Renee pointed to, were not damaged.

~

In the dark, Jay crossed many bodies. Some are still lying on the ground groaning in pain. Some screamed out at him not to let them die. They begged and pleaded for something to ease their pain or for him just to stay with them so they were not scared or die alone. He pushed forward and hoped they would survive

171

long enough for ambulances to arrive. Others were stone cold, like a three-day-old turd.

Panicked, Jay stared. There was nothing he could do. Death seemed assured. It was a moment that he knew he would carry filled with regret. He climbed over them, and one grabbed at his leg. "medical help will be here soon," he called as the guy tried to draw a knife and stab his leg. Jay shot him and then kicked the body off. Some people you just can't help.

Jay saw the neon room at the end of the tunnel and glanced to both sides, but no sign of Johnson. The man only had a roughly fifteen-minute head start on the officer, and the officer hoped he'd see him in the office area of the Kwanza hut.

The room had cleared, and he wondered where all the gang members had gone. His mind briefly worried they'd caught Johnson and had taken him someplace for a very public execution. The officer didn't believe that. Still, this presented one opportunity to open the steel front door. It would allow the backup to arrive and get in as soon as possible.

Parts of the gate broke off, and twisting steel echoed out, followed by a loud crash. His eyes caught sight of Johnson now. Gang member gunfire on the far side had pinned down the detective behind a vat. If he shot, he'd give away his position. His brain calculated the odds. Confident that his actions would provide a distraction and get the gang members to peel off to chase him, he hoped Johnson could hold out until he started the computer.

He hit the metal great. It reminded him of an old-fashioned fire escape, and he started down. He reached the bottom and caught sight of a robot marching toward the stairs.

The officer dove under the bench. He pushed two chairs and shoved one aside while creeping below. The wires hung around him. He knew the computers were right above, but he needed to get closer to the locking mechanism.

In the distance, one gang member stood guard by the steel door. He was huge with twenty-two-inch biceps. Jay prepared to jump him.

~

Up to their ankles in sewer water, Felicity and Natalie trudged through the muck. Each step splashed and weighed the two back as they pushed forward. Rats squeaking, and occasionally, one swimming next to their feet caused flinching.

172

"Are you sure this is the right way?" the reporter asked. The light from her MegaSmart phone was so dim that the two could barely see their hands in front of their faces.

"Yes, this is the way," Natalie stated.

"One hell of a job," the reporter added. "Tell me, is it every day you almost die?"

"No," Natalie replied. "Most days are dull, but then there are days like this punctuated with insanity. Don't get me wrong. I don't want to die. Frankly, the thought terrifies me, and it kind of makes you a bit paranoid. I find myself looking over my shoulder more and more every day, but I like the idea of making a difference. Pension is not so bad either."

"Ah," Felicity said. "I worry I'll eat cat food in my old age. Reporter work doesn't pay much, especially for my pape...." Her words trailed off as her newspaper had been destroyed. One of the hardest things for Felicity was accepting that her reporter career might be a thing of the past.

They reached the tube. "We need to climb up this. Our first time through, Johnny cut the mesh that blocks this off. It takes us to a hatch, just behind the climate control system. Passed that is one door and onto the tunnel to the mezzanine level. You got it?"

"Okay," Felicity replied. They crawled up and slid the hatch aside. The stainless-steel climate-controlled and air purifying unit hummed. Recessed lights covered the room. They crept to the metal door to the corridor.

~

Slouched against the vat, Detective Johnson prepared his last stand. He flipped open the cartridge on his Smith and Wesson and loaded a fresh one. Two hundred blasts left, but he'd never get them all off. Even now, he heard the scurry of gang members surrounding his position. His brain questioned why he'd taken this job. Two years ago, he could have justified it on his financial desperation. Frankly, he needed the work. But lately, business was pouring into his office as his wife helped him meet a wealthier clientele. Maybe that had been it. He prided himself on being his own man, and the idea of being a kept husband failed to sit well with him. To overcome it, recently, he'd taken riskier cases.

But as the detective thought of his situation, he realized that had not been the whole of it. It went deeper, and probably if he admitted it weirder. The deeper was his desire to be involved in

173

the action. Maybe through the war, he'd become an adrenaline junky.

The weirder was simply his disbelief that he was still alive. During the Eddie Whyte case a year and a half back, he stared down at a hopeless situation, and yet, he'd been allowed to walk away for some unknown reason. Inside, he wondered if he had died that night and if this was some odd afterlife he was stuck in. He would never admit that belief to anyone, especially Jay. Even if it was, the situation was far from a bad one. He'd reconciled with his wife, and his daughter was back in his life. A bulb went off in his head, be happy you are alive. Don't squander the universe's chances, he thought and then chuckled, "Damn, Johnson, just like you to self-analyze the answer when it is too late to do anything about it." His hand tightened on the ion cannon.

The footfalls had encircled him. Prepared to meet his maker, he leaped up…

~

Jay tackled the gang member guarding the door. Having the element of surprise, the officer unleashed a flurry of punches. Many struck, and then the gang member blocked a few. The officer's actions drew the attention of other guards, and red lights burst through the room, setting off an alarm. The lights changed, and the sirens honked and screeched. Behind him, the officer heard the gang members returning.

With all the strength he could muster, Jay hauled the man up with one hand and smashed a fist with the other dead into the guard's face. To his surprise, the guy's head flapped back and struck the ground, rendering the man unconscious.

Quickly, Jay placed the man's hand on the panel. A crack of the electronic bolts echoed through the Kwanza hut. With a snap, the door hissed and slid back. Outside, rain fell. It splattered and bounced on the asphalt, making a gentle swooshing sound.

From the front, the guard fired three bullets, which struck Jay straight into his armor at the left shoulder. The officer spun from the impact. Behind him, he caught sight of people advancing from inside, but his priority was the immediate shooter. He raised his blaster and fired his weapon as another bullet caught the armor of his chest. The ion blast set the front guard ablaze, and he tumbled backward. The shot knocked the wind out of Jay, and his vision narrowed, with the periphery turning grey.

A laser blast struck Jay directly in his back, and he tumbled out to the area between the fence and the building. He felt lucky, his body armor had absorbed the shot, but his body still ached from the strikes. His jawline firmed. He steadied himself and hobbled out into the rainy night. A sense of joy captured him as he caught sight of something beautiful.

Night clubs in the twin city across the river illuminated the water. In the reflection, Jay saw the Earth Corps battle cruisers hovering through the air. Then the horror behind him, gang members poured out in their midst and waltzed into robots. Actuators turned and twisting of their metal gears as they pounced.

~

The detective fired at the two guards before him, knowing the blast to his back would end his life. His shots hit and tumbled the two guards. He heard fire from behind him, but he still stood. Quickly he spun around, and on the mezzanine deck, he saw Natalie Ryder. She waved her laser to him. Next to her stood the reporter. The alarms went off, and they entered a room flooded with blinking red lights.

The two women pointed to something at the front of the building and then hurried down the stairs. He headed over the ten yards to greet them at the bottom of the steps. "Jay's at the front," Felicity called. "Guards are almost on him."

The three wound their way around the drums and over the catwalk to get to the front. Kwanza hut had almost wholly emptied with those still alive in hot pursuit of Officer Jay.

~

The Earth Corp ship rocketed through the rainy night sky. A loud boom shattered the ground as it approached at sonic speed, coming up the river, then quickly dropped to subsonic. The massive turbofans blazed while it hurried forward. A sense of pride rose as it appeared the carvery had arrived. It then rolled and then hit by ground fire plummeted.

Sucking in the air, Natalie held her breath. Shock rippled through her. "Please," she mumbled. Her eyes teared up.

Earth Corp ships fell from the sky and crashed into the river. A shower of water spurted into the neon night sky of the river. As the hover ship sank below the water, the group stared in

175

horror. Johnson worried his plan backfired. His heart sank, hoping his son Joe wasn't on the Earth Corps craft.

The news reporter's eyes dart around, "We need to get to the computer and figure out how to bring the defense system down, or the same will happen to the police quads."

They rushed back into the room and reached a computer system. The reporter drew out Natalie's MegaSmart, "Maybe we could get Earth Corps computers to hack it. At the very least, we need to get harbor patrol to see if there were survivors to rescue."

"Earth Corps knows from its tracking what happened to the ship. They must have been emp or jammed because that one shot was insufficient to bring that ship down. We can not get into the Earth Corps system," Johnson stated. He hauled a fine copper wire from his arm. "Let me see if I can shut it down." The detective connected himself to the system.

"Are you going to hack it?"

"Technically, what I do is not hacking," the detective sighed. His lackluster voice suggested he'd given this speech at least a few times before. "Hacking is cutting through the code and finding weaknesses in programs. It is code versus code. I don't even know where to begin doing such a thing."

"Oh," Felicity shot him a soft glance.

"The computer is run but chips. Chips are circuits. Programs shut on and off the energy flow. I sort of just coax the circuits I need to turn on and off electrically. I'll need you to cover me in case something happens. I'll be indisposed for a bit."

~

Initially, the site of the Earth Corp ships caused the gang members to draw back into the hut. Their retreat gave Jay a bit of a lead. Then the Earth Corp ship crashed into the river. Noise from the guards regrouping from behind him caught Jay's attention. The rain pounded on his skin. It soaked his hair.

Hobbling, Jay tried to contact Natalie. The frequency band was jammed. His chest still hurt from the pain of the gunshots, which struck his armor. He fired at the locked gate in front of him. His shots blew a hole in the chain-linked, but the bulk of the fence still stood. He'd have to crawl under the center bar to get through the opening. From the rear, the guards exited the hut to pursue him.

Frustrated, he shot back over his shoulder at the approaching robots. The orange fireball struck the robot, sounding like the slamming of a metal trash can. Despite his heavy breathing, the man bolted forward and through the fence. Reaching the other side, a site of hope appeared in the sky, but Jay was about over with hope.

Blue and red lights flashed in the distance, and Jay had mixed feelings. He wished the police would come but feared they meet the same fate as the assault team and Earth Corps.

~

Johnson's eyes rolled back into his head. The vanilla white of the balls could be seen through his narrow slits. It was as if an unbelievable pain crusted in his skull. Time passed. The instruments converted the data into a holographic chart of the data. He jiggled the machine and another data screen popped up.

A flash of understanding lit his mind: This one wasn't the virus but a giant juice vat.

"Just juice," he called. Max Euwe's quote from the last century, "Strategy requires thought. Tactics require observation," flashed in his brain. He decided to change his tactics.

Felicity stared in shock. She'd never seen one this big. The hologram vanished.

The HR officer emerged from the darkness. The two share a glare. He raised the laser pistol, and the officer stared in shock. Johnson had no clear shot on the Cohen Shay.

Swiftly, his eyes scanned the room. He had one shot- the one vat was the virus, the second was juice, which was which. He tapped three buttons on his bionic arm. It activated the analysis program. The program would take three minutes. He didn't have that long. A blue glow shimmered over the vat, and Johnson picked that one and fired. The juice flowed like the Mississippi River onto the HR representative. The steaming hot chemical brewing in the vat caused him to crumple in agony.

The report approached the detective, and they high five. Cohen Shay lay flipping on the ground by the vat holding the juice. The ruptured tank poured all over his body. The juice ate his nerves raw. A bit of pity for the man struck them both. Death from boiling juice was horrible was to go even if he was nothing but a soulless, black hole. He struggled to speak to Johnson and the reporter. "They stole the robots to understand their mental software better. They'd hoped to create a program from it, which would cause all the robots to ignore their activity. Purt and the Marked Ones would be a blind spot to the police robots." Felicity patted the man's hand. She'd studied him and understood what he must have gone through.

A giant robot rolled into the room. Johnson spun toward it. "Run! Do you hear me?" he called out.

# Chapter 11

Rain fell heavily. A faint smell of smoke lingered in the air. The swarm of gang members approached the area where Jay rushed, but worse, a robot was almost on him. He had never seen a machine quite that menacing. Its guns fell into firing position. It could easily rip him to shreds.

Jay swerved and snaked as the robot fired. Turing a bend out of the direct line of fire, the burn of lactic acid building in his muscles slowed down the officer. He suppressed the ache and glanced over his shoulder as he bolted. A sense of relief emerged as the mechanical human had given up to pursue other targets. He huddled by the corner two blocks later and rechecked his communication band.

The gang members were still jamming him. He struggled to catch his breath, coughed several times, spit, and straightened. His head throbbed, and he expected his blood pressure had skyrocketed from the stress. The rain stung his eyes, and he shook it from his hair.

As he turned the corner, a robot stood four feet in front of him. He knew what to expect and leaped backward. It fired. Jay flushed back on his shoulders and landed on the ground, barely dodging the shots.

In the puddles, Jay screamed and skidded back by kicking his heels on the wet, filthy asphalt, scraping up the muck of water and dirt. Terror in his eyes, he managed to fire a shot right into the angry droid, and the thing exploded. His body racket with dry sobs as the officer lay in the puddle for a few seconds longer. He hated dirt, and now it covered him.

His face stared up at the neon sky while water showers fell over it. It washed away his tears. When he heard the metallic grind of a second robot, he heaved his body from the muddy water. His underwear chaffed his skin around his groin and on the sides of his legs. He needed to stay in front of it until he could get a clear shot.

His eyes bulged as he darted along the dock. He passed several closed shops and warehouses. He needed to reach the river. His body armor had been shredded at the sides from all the rounds it had received. At the riverside, the officer twisted over the metal rail and onto the concrete pier less than two feet in diameter off the water.

The grinding of gears indicated the robot was close. Jay's heart pounded, and he felt the beat in his throat. The robot's targeting computer would quickly register the armor and switch to a headshot between his assault helmet and torso. He had one shot. If he missed it, he'd be dead.

~

To confuse the sensors of the beast, Johnny shot at the sprinkler system setting it off. Water fell and doused the computers, causing them to short and steam. The lights blinked on and off, adding to the cacophony provided by the alarm system.

Chaos flooded the area as gang members seemed more interested in saving their hides than trying to stop the police arrival. This turn of events left Johnson, Facility, and Natalie unencumbered to put some room between themselves and the robot. With its machine gun extended, the heavy footfalls of the robot clanked over the steel grate.

The iron monster appeared to be centering his action on Felicity. Johnny took the opportunity to circle it.

Felicity dove to the floor and crawled, reaching for the nearby broom. It was the least she could do to protect herself. In the background, *Love is Forever* by Leonora played crackling on the nearby speakers. She'd wondered if one of the gang members clicked it on as a joke.

Felicity lunged for the broom and ducked under a table. She waited for the right moment to strike.

~

In a heavy downpour, Jay's mind calculated the best angle, knowing the robot would take the most precise route to launch its attack. He raised his gun. It weighed heavily in his hands. The machine peered over his head and dropped its firing arm as Jay fired.  He had the jump. A barrage of bullets ricocheted.

A shot struck Jay's arm, close to his head. Pain seared through the officer. In the volley, the robot exploded into a fireball. A loud ringing occupied Jay's ears, but he knew things weren't over yet.

Ripping off his shirt, Jay tied off his wound.  He glanced it over. It wasn't more than a scrape, and he counted himself lucky it was not worse. His speed beat the damn thing's targeting computer.

With the clouds passing overhead, the light from the moon reflected off the water. He took a second to enjoy it, catch his breath, and then drag himself back to the dock. He flopped to the other side of the rail and groaned. He felt lucky to have been born strong enough to carry his weight. Happy the rain stopped and hoping it would not start soon again, Jay chuckled.

Hobbling to his feet, Jay strolled back to the Kwanza hut. He heard three guards coming down the road and ducked to the side of the dock. The police were close. Jay needed to hold on until they arrived close enough for him to signal the danger awaiting. He needed to make sure they did not wind up dead like the Earth Corps ship.

~

With rage, the detective's bionic arm struck the machine. It pierced its skin, dug deep into its guts, and yanked out its central processor.  Sparks flew into the air, and electrical energy flow rippled into his bionic arm. Johnny felt them strike and singe his face.  The machine collapsed, and so did the old detective. A small chuckle escaped from between his lips.

Sensing her opportunity, Felicity leaped from under the table and drove the wooden broom into the gears exposed on the robot's neck. It shorted, and the stick broke, but the reporter twisted it deeper and deeper. Each inch released more of her rage. The machine died.

Eyes swollen from tears, Johnny's body felt on fire from pain, but he giggled uncontrollably. His body screamed with pain and the madness of his mixture of laughter, pain, and fright. His laughing of many emotions became so frantic and uncontrolled that his opponents became intimidated.

Sobbing, Johnson dragged himself with his one human arm. Agony rifled through his body, but he never gave up. He reached for his Smith and Wesson. Natalie Ryder rushed to his side and lifted him.

Johnson draped his arm over her shoulders. Natalie tried to laugh week with relief. Her armored body was in front of him, acting as a shield—shots rapidly connected with the armor.

Close to the robot, Felicity felt something flash past her ear. She looked up, and it was a gang member. He held a gun, preparing another shot, but a laser blast from Natalie Ryder hit him. The amazing woman had Johnson in one arm and fired the laser with her free hand. Then she and Johnny turned their attention to the remaining gang members in the room.

The gang members dodged behind vats and dropped under tables as the ion blasts sizzled through the room. They fired back at the two, and Felicity tried to sneak behind them and catch them, but when she glanced up, three were behind her.

Felicity wore thin body armor. At the fitting, the focus was on how to get it past the initial security check when she entered the facility. It was little more than a body stocking, but it was strong enough to stop small-caliber bullets. She hoped they were distracted by the blasts from her colleagues and the falling water from the sprinklers. Still, one high caliber blast and her blood splatter all over the room, mixing with the falling water. Only two hundred feet from the door, she decided it best to take her chances on getting out of the building, at least for now.

~

The first police hover tore through the darkness, and Jay felt surprised that it did not appear to be falling from the sky. He waved for them to pick him up, but they must not have seen him, for they passed by without stopping. The officer had some feelings about that but decided it wasn't worth it. In the distance, he saw at least fifty more cars coming from all city points. The sounds of sirens filled the air.

To distract himself, he focused on the gorgeous riverside condominiums. One of the complexes extended into the water and had boat slips. The ships docked around it were beautiful. Between the yachts and condos, both of which he could never afford. He saw a large motorcycle by a hundred-foot tinted window with high polished gold railings craft on the docks. The ship was called "Becky's Buns," registered in the Cayman Islands. Forcing his eyes off the boat, Jay focused on the bike. Its neon handlebars stretched out to the side and curved up into twirls like an old fashion mustache. The lights were off on the yacht, but he decided to commandeer the bike.

Drawing out his MegaSmart, he realized that he finally had bars. He quickly decided to let the police know his location with a

182

text to the department, warn them of the inference, and register with Earth Corps that he was commandeering the bike if the owners searched for it. Although it was so hideous, he seriously doubted anyone would miss it. His megasmart phone vibrated, and he drew it out of his pocket.

*Hey Jay, Your sister is in the hospital right now.* He knew the number but could not place who it was at first.

Worry flooded the man, but he decided not to respond. *Was his sister really in the hospital? Was she ok?* Then it hit him. It was Colleen's husband, so he dialed and reached Steven. He repeatedly asked his brother-in-law, "Who did it?" and Steven answered he had no idea each time.

Jay's heart sank, hearing the details of the attack. Even though the man assured Jay that his sister was stable but in critical condition, Jay felt the urgency to get to the hospital.

Jay promised to be there very shortly. "Don't worry," he shouted into the phone as if speaking the long distance required him to cast his voice that far. "I just have to finish this one element of police business, and I will be there." Tears flooded down his face, and he did not bother to wipe them away. Anxiety filled his heart.

After, he leaped on the bike and kicked her into gear. His broad muscle exposed from the tears in his suit, he revved the engine and headed back to the hut. About two blocks from the shed, he saw the reporter out of the corner of his eye. She'd run out to safety but now, having seen him, she seemed to be returning. A rush of heat flushed through him, and his eyes pleaded for her to stay away. He hauled the bike next to her.

"Jay?" She asked.

"It's me," he stated. His face appeared twisted with pain. "Do you need a ride back?" Jay was Felicity's friend when she thought she couldn't have friends anymore, and it killed her to see Jay's pain, but she understood it had been a long night.

The reporter jumped onto the back of the bike, and her hands landed on Jay's broad shoulders, and then with some embarrassment, she wrapped them around his waist. "This thing is ugly," she said.

"Better than walking," Jay announced and secretly felt embarrassed. He'd be glad when he got home and showered.

~

183

The police hover landed, and squads of officers were marching toward the building. Officer Jay's motorcycle slid closer to the building.

Felicity rapidly explained the case to him. All the while, his mind drifted back to worrying about his sister. She'd always been there for him, and now he was blowing it with "police business." He needed to end this and end it quickly.

"Sure, the virus would be big business, but it takes time to spread. And the police were an ever-present threat. It would be best if the officers, or at least their machines, were blind, spending energy on wrong paths," Felicity explained, yelling from the back to the front of the bike. She wished Jay had picked up the communication headsets for the cycle, but he seemed oblivious to the concept. "Plus, Purt had no idea the Marked Ones were making the virus. Purt assigned them to steal the robots and then deliver all eight."

Soon, they hauled up on the bike, and Jay got off. He strolled over and said, "Take it easy, kid." and patted her shoulder twice

"You stay out here," Jay ordered the reporter. "It's just mopping up inside, and no need for you to take the risk."

"Jay," she protested.

"Listen, lady," he commanded. "You're are star witness. We need you not to get killed." He patted her arm.

*How could she argue with his logic?*

She noticed her bullet wound and reached out a hand to it. "Just grazed," Jay insisted. "I'll get it looked at after this."

"Promise you'll come back, Mister," she insisted.

"Police one o-one," he replied. "Never make a promise, but I got no plans to die. I got this." Blaster drawn and eyes keen, Jay announced his presence and roll and then filed into a V formation of officers entering the Hut.

~

Three police quad's swirled into the area, "Drop your weapons," the voice screamed out. "Hands in the air." The helicopter voice gave several moments to comply as the quads swirled around, encircling the gang members. The spotlights were like an invisible net of light holding the gang captive, much like fishing nets held in the day's catch. "On your knees and then assume the position," the voice on the quad called. Huge spotlights circled from the armed hovers scanning the gang members below. The positions were prone to allow for search without the worry of a suspect drawing a weapon. Several gang members scurried, but many complied, placing their heads to the side and giving the police no excuse to fire upon them. Hell, there was no need to risk lives. Their attorneys would have them released in a couple of hours.

Two more police hover entered the area, giving chase to the gang members who chose to run. They lowered enough to allow the strike teams to jump out in their squirrel suits and glide into the escaping criminals.

Felicity watched as officers slammed into fleers and smacked down the cuffs on them. In the distance, he caught the faint sight of the sky changing color. The black started turning to a purplish blue. Soon, she knew the sun would rise, and today would be a safer day. Then in the distance, she caught sight of it. It was a hover, and Renee held on to the outer door. The black clothing and crazy hair confirmed it. Her face still bled from where Felicity had scratched her. The woman was jeering into the crowd. Utterly frozen for just a second, the reporter heard a scream in her head, "Don't let her get away." How could she? Susan counted on her. The Marked Ones needed to come to an end.

After a quick blink, Felicity darted toward the quad. She covered two blocks in under three minutes.

Two things happened simultaneously. Felicity whipped around the blaster and fired. The gang leader's quad saw her and twisted, spraying the ground with gunfire aimed at Felicity. The spray of bullets flew simultaneously while the orange blaster balls charged toward the quad. The gang leader's hover exploded into a flash of white. Bullets sliced through Felicity. White-hot pain burst in every inch of her arms and legs. Large quad portions ripped through the air and rained down on the reporter, smacking into her. Through the pain, Felicity thought a body had been blown from the side, set ablaze. Then darkness

# Chapter 12

Three weeks later, Detective Johnson entered the precinct invited. On the phone, receiving his invitation, the staff sergeant told the detective not to bring his piece, so he left the Smith and Wesson home. Johnson passed by the front guard, who shot him a suspicious glance and double-checked his bag and bionic arm before letting him through. From a distance, he caught sight of Officer Jay and pulled a manila folder from the pack.

The officer approached him. "Are you ready," he asked as the detective handed him the folder.

"Sure am," he replied. "Does everything look in order?"

"I think it will complete the point," Jay said and then waltzed toward the captain's office and knocked. Mendez sat in his chair. The lighting was poor: a single lamp lit by a wall switch.

"Captain, sir. I need to speak with you," Jay stated, trying not to stare. Next to him stood Detective Johnson.

"I'm a bit busy," the captain replied, pouring over paperwork on his desk. His eyes fell back to the paper, scribbling a quick signature.

Jay's eyes turned icy, "You're really going to want to hear what we have to say."

With a frustrated expression, the captain's face shot up again. "Ok," the captain replied, lending the two into his office.

The sparsely furnished room contained a large oak desk in the center with a computer system with virtual reality ties. A large white board on the wall had scribbled in black marker the officer names who replaced others for different shifts over the next week. The captain sat in his onyx swivel chair.

"I'm listening," the captain said. His face was rather pleasant.

"Good sir," Jay reported. He scanned the captain's face. "It has to do with the case we just completed. Detective Johnson and I believe there is a mole in the department."

"You don't say," the captain leaned forward. "Who?"

"You, sir," Jay's voice dropped to a deadly pleasant.

The captain wasn't ready for the accusation and became indignant. "How dare you come into my office!"

186

"Excuse Officer Jay for going right to the point, but we have let you know what we found," Johnson reported, and you are going to want to hear this.

"Get that idiot out of my office," the captain seethed through gritted teeth.

Johnson licked his lips. "I'm leaving but let me say, I got suspicious when you okayed my plan," he said.

"It was your plan," the captain stated.

The detective swallowed and rolled his hand as if to encourage his voice out… "Sure, one that I stated more to keep the client happy than to execute. But I was surprised when you approved it, and Ms. Cruikshank cleared her psych evaluation. It frankly shocked me. So, I took some liberties to get the report."

"You hacked a departmental report," the captain stated. "That is a crime, Johnson."

"No, nothing like that. I expressed my concerns to my son Joe. He works for Earth Corps. We don't speak often, and I thank you for giving me an excuse to call him." The detective nodded his head, and a wry smile crossed his lips. "Anyhow, it appears she failed the psych evaluation."

"She did but going was my call, and I found reason to send her," the captain stated. "You got a problem with that?"

"I figured you would say that," Johnson reported. He swayed his head in the beat cop's direction. "So, I asked Jay about the flight schedule. The only people who knew the quad flights were you and the people in the room. For the electronic disrupter do have been geared up and focused as it was on the two quads, they would have to know we were coming." Jay drummed his fingers against the side of his neck. The tempo was fast with measured changes.

"You got nothing," the captain chided. "They could have had a general search on and picked up the ships.

"Your right, only speculation at that point," the detective replied, "which is why I turned over to Jay." The captain rolled back in his swivel chair. His hand slid under the desk.

"Well, sir," Jay's voice was flat as he began to inform, but there was a transparent element of pity in his mannerisms. "My sister worked undercover for the department for years. Her records were blocked. If anyone tries to draw them up, you cannot get the record for her address or pretty much anything about her.

The only people who could access that would be her captain, the diamond wing division's captain, who runs the undercover operations, internal affairs, or the commissioner himself. Well, sir, the fact they found her home and came as police led me to contact her friend on the bench. You know she has a friend who is a judge. It helped her a lot in expediting warrants and contacting internal affairs. He was shocked by her being in the hospital and really felt horrible about her kids. He granted access to those who looked at her records recently, and the only person who accessed in the last six months- was you. Interesting, it was the day of the attack, sir."

"Jay," the man's face pleaded. "It was a normal review of records for her performance evaluation."

"I thought it might have been, so I asked her judge friend if we could review your accounts. At first glance, sir, they appeared in order. You only had seventeen thousand credits in the account. A little high but not exorbitant, but, sir, Mr. Johnson was retained by the department for his computer expertise. You know the detective is always looking for work. Anyhow, he helped internal affairs out. Sir, it kills me to report- you have ghosts."

"I got what?" The captain asked, and Jay glanced at Johnson. The officer rose and strolled out from in front of the desk to the side.

"Ghosts are encrypted accounts. They disappear and only appear when summoned. Very tough to track," Johnson elaborated. "I noticed a transfer from the ghost into your regular account last week. I believe it was for your monthly alimony payment of one thousand six hundred eighty credits. The thing with ghosts is that while crypto-currency can funnel in from anywhere- the accounts are limited to where they send themselves. So, you have at least four ghosts, and I say this with no pleasure, Captain. The accounts received a total of one hundred twenty thousand credits just before and just after the community center bombing. Then the day of our attempt to take down the Mark Ones, they received thirty thousand credits prior and forty thousand after...."

Johnson never finished the sentence. The captain's shoulder's tightened. Like lightning, Jay leaped on him. His fists flailed on the captain. The blaster rolled out of the captain's hand as Jay's voice called. "That for my sister." Johnson let the first twenty, maybe thirty punches land on the captain and then grabbed Jay and drew him back. Mendez's bloody face twisted, and tears streamed from his bruised eyes.

Berger and two officers waltzed into the captain's office. "Arrest that man for the murders of Officers Thorpe and Thompson. Also, the attempted murder of Officer Colleen Jay-Yazzie. More charges will follow."

The officers grabbed the vile, unrecoverable blight of a man and hauled him up to his feet. Then they spun him and slapped the cuffs on his wrists. He'd stained the department so thoroughly that Jay felt it would never recover. Captain Berger glanced and nodded to officer Jay as they left the room. "I hope they kill him in prison," Johnson mumbled.

"No, we need his leads to catch Renee," Jay returned.

"Good point."

Johnny turned to Officer Jay, hopeful and excited. He knew Jay had spent the last few days with his sister. He hoped that she'd told him the truth about his genetics. "Jay," he stated, appearing expectant. "You were awesome. Lightening quick."

"Yeah, I was pretty good," Jay started. "I guess when the adrenaline is flowing, it really kicks you hard. Let's visit Colleen and then Ms. Cruikshank if she is awake." Hope died. *I guess some family members will take their secrets to death,* Johnny concluded.

The detective placed his arm on Jay's shoulder and turned him toward the door. "I guess it does. Hey, I got some flowers for their hospital rooms- and an extra set if you forgot." Jay turned off the office lights as they left.

~

When she opened her eyes, six people were around her in the room. Their bodies were outlined with green and red heat signatures. Shocked, Felicity blinked her eyes. Her heart fluttered as she unlatched them again. Nothing changed. In the room, the Psychedelic Furs *Pretty in Pink* played. She loved the song and figured Jay told the robotic doctors.

She glanced over to the intravenous line that ran into her arm. There was no pain this time, and she guessed that was good. "I got some good news for you," Jay stated, and he thrust a handle-held reader to her.

189

The reporter read the bi-line, "Unfinished Business on the 97th Floor by Jackson Newman." She scoffed. So, he'd stolen her story. Well, to hell with him. "How could you think I would be happy with this?" She asked Jay.

"Check out the footnote indicated at the top," Jay encouraged. The reporter twisted her head to the side. "Don't roll your eyes nor jerk your chin at me," Jay insisted. "Just read it."

Felicity read it, "This story would not have been possible if not for all the hard work done by Felicity Cruickshank. She is the true hero of this tale. Ms. Cruickshank would have written this piece if there were any justice in this universe. She is in all our thoughts and prayers. We hope she survives."

"He writes shit like that to make himself look good," she announced."At least it sets me up to write a book about my experience later."

"That a girl," Jay chuckled. "Always thinking of an angle."

The reporter scanned the article. "It does not mention the virus at all and suggests the only reason we went was for the robots."

"Corporate Council censored the parts about the virus. Besides, the Cyber Press is a tabloid that no one would believe."

"He made my injuries out pretty bad. What happened?" she asked. Her eyes scanned the room, but no one seemed willing to talk. They all appeared quiet. Johnson had his human hand thumb to the base of his chin with just an intense look of concern.

"We almost thought you weren't going to make it," Jay was the first to speak. His tone was solemn with a hint of frustration.

Behind him, the robotic doctor wheeled in to see his patient. "There was a huge amount of damage," he informed her. The shock engulfed her.

"Oh. How much of me did I lose?" Felicity asked, staring at the new bionic implants for her legs. Her mind reeled in anger. How could Jay and the others let the doctors do this to her. The microchips stacked in Buckey-ball designs in her hand sensed her discomfort and curled her toes.

"Nothing of you was lost," the doctor informed. She stared at him angrily. "Your soul is still completely intact." She rolled her eyes.

*Great of all the robotic doctors. I got the religious one,* she thought. Her heart fluttered, and she remembered her father once telling her that he wanted an atheist doctor if he was ever in a life-or-death situation. One was fighting tooth and nail for him in the present and not one who was making him comfortable while he waited to go to the other side. Frustration grew, followed by a sense of despair. She was alive, but as the metal attested, she was far from whole. It was all too much, and she felt unsure that she could go through it. The process of accepting felt impossible. She tapped her legs but could not feel anything in them like they were dead. She wondered just how much of her body had been removed and replaced.

The reporter concentrated. Her heart and mind were on their toes. The microprocessors sparking to life inside her legs created an odd feeling akin to a sensation of snapping. The gears in that portion rolled and ground. She'd seen Detective Johnson produce an arc light of electricity around his limbs in the past. She wondered if she could do that. Felicity stared down and blue metal electricity arced between her toes. *Okay, that was cool,* she thought, but her body jerked back as pain rose in her skull. Scar tissue marked her shoulder and neck.

In some ways, her whole life was gone. It vanished in the flash of light of her near-death experience. *Was she even human now?* Nothing could describe the rage she felt. Even with it, she had a weird sense of gratefulness. In some sick ways, she was even better than before the operation.

The reporter had a receiver placed in her inner ear, which increased her range of heard frequencies. Now though, it shrieked and crackled, causing her headache to worsen. The world around her and in her had changed, and she was helpless to change it back to the way things were.

Life had a weird way of destroying everything she built. They'd constructed a neural learning enhancer at the basis of her brain. Its connections fused into her hippocampus, stimulating it when she triggered it with a tightening of muscles in her neck.

She thought of the sweat notes her sister used to write her. She recommitted to the idea of bringing down Purt and their henchmen: The Marked Ones, once and for all. She'd finished some of the unfinished business on her floor. Still, much remained to be done, and now, she felt her healing would require so much more.

"Well, the good news is you got a story for the front page," Johnson spoke up this time.

"If they don't censor it," she replied.

"Even if they do," Jay offered. "People are going to want to hear something from your perspective. Newman's words have kind of guaranteed it." He patted her on the arm.

"Yep, I guess I do. "

"I'm thinking 'Local Gang with Delusional Visions of Global Domination, " Jay suggested.

"I was thinking more like More Unfinished Business." Johnson offered.

"Not quite right. I was thinking more to the story's heart, like the Marked Ones," Felicity offered.

"That too, I guess," Officer Jay shrugged and said.

"Whatever, I need to get home and dictate my case notes and want to spend time with Jackie," Detective Johnson finished up.

# Epilogue

It was the third time that Susan had called her sister and not gotten a response. The phone rang and rang, but nothing. Her heart fluttered in desperation as the voice mail came up. "Call me when you get this," she said. "I'm worried about you." On the television, stories about the attacks on the warehouse seemed on an endless loop: the problem with the twenty-four-hour news cycle was its ability to heighten existing worry and leave a person no options to escape it.

Initially, it was not a concern. The last time Susan saw her sister, she had headed to the police station, and Felicity was being heavily protected. Maybe she was still in protective custody. But the docks were the reporters beat. Her sister was always investigating the area, but what concerned her the most was one of her friends, Addison, said she'd thought she'd seen Felicity in one of the fighting scenes. She forwarded the video in a private message on social media, and the truth was, Susan couldn't tell.

Even without the attack on the docks, Susan was scared for her sister. This fear was especially true since the reporter had been so obsessed with the events at the ports, especially when it pertained to the Marked Ones. After meeting with her sister at the hospital, Susan felt her sister became focused on justice. All Susan could do was pray that her sister was okay.

Nervously, she straightened her clothes with her hands and stared at the applications on her MegaSmart. She'd texted her sister earlier but no reply to the text either.

Tired of the news and needing fresh air, the teenage girl decided to step outside onto the balcony. She leaned over the railings and stared down at the void below. The sky was pitch black, and the only light sources were minor blips of neon light of all colors.

# Bonus Short Story

## *The Juice Wars Begin*

Joseph Cautilli
Marisha Cautilli

Flanking the sky, New Cyber City's Maenianum Maxus Primum Colosseum was massive by any standards. When filled, this glass, gargantuan-scale structure boasted a capacity of over two hundred fifty thousand people, and tonight it was packed. Huge spotlights filled the hot night air with bright white light, and tiny insects danced in the beams. His show in New Cyber City was sold out.

A concrete grandstand formed in its center was a single platform bathed in multispectral laser light. The crowd cheered as three holographic images stood out front and center, dancing and singing. Behind these images, a four-piece band played Korean pop with a mix of old 1940s sounds and words like the Andrews sisters meet Billie Holiday. Tonight was the first performance of sixteen in a three-week scheduled run.

The holograms wore short shirts revealing their tight abdominal muscles with a long red skirt and bopped, slapping their butts and putting their hands to their knees. The dance ranged from cute to bawdy. In every sense, they appeared alive, and the audience did not care that they were just constructed images as they shifted their hands in front of the knees before whirling out into pointing first left and then right.

Blue, purple, and red lasers rapidly shifted over the stage. Next, they threw their hands in the air, circled them down, and ripped off what appeared to be tear-away skirts revealing sexy long legs and overly tight shorts. Fireworks exploded behind them. The ladies rolled their hips, slid to the floor, and swirled their legs open into a spin, just as they were programmed to do. The crowd gawked before going wild.

Everyone seemed excited as the dancers squatted and swirled- except for one man, who sat cautiously in a small back

194

room gazing at the screen, terrified that something might go wrong. This man was Harold Jones. He had created the *Bioelectrics* four years prior. The band was an instant success, with the sultry choreography and happy bouncing rhythms by his wife and his lyrics ranging from the soulful to the blues to the seductive.

Sadly though, many critics still attacked him, but would one expect that of culture and the media these days?

Of course, all these factors were secondary to the stage opera that themed a mass protest to a culture absorbed with the juice crisis. Inside, Harold hoped these concerts sparked a rebellion against the massive number of kids hooked on the streets.

The holograms were still thrusting their hips on his screen, and their unified voices hypnotically teased the crowd. Green and red laser lights swarmed around the holo-women. Wrinkles of rising heat poured off the stage. He remembered tabloids with him on the front cover, headlines ranging from "Harold Jones a Phony?!" to "Scandal Between the *Bioelectric's* creator and the government."

In his control room, the air was like melted iron. The room smelled of sweat and overheating electrical cords. Harold's fingers scratched his scalp under his short, tightly curled black hair. Sweat beaded over his fingertips and glistened over his nails. His eyes never left the computer screen. Around the stage, various stage crew and Paul Bentley's security team dashed to make sure no one in the crowd could get to the stage and mess up the show. Harold radioed instructions to the ground team to ensure that even minor obstacles were quickly fixed.

The light had turned golden on the stage and blinked very rapidly. The flashing light was one of the reasons the show posted a seizure alert for the audience. The holo-lady's receding images danced up a fire mountain, ready for the final volcanic explosion. Harold flipped the switch so that the smell of sulfur and lava would fill the stadium on cue.

Daring to glance over his shoulder, he caught sight of He-Ran: his wife of twenty years. Harold had married her a few years after the third Iraq war. She placed her hand on the dark brown skin of the back of his arm to give him support. A tingling sensation rippled down his spine. As much as he found it annoying, he still enjoyed the feeling. He cast her a deep loving

195

gaze but then reached into his pocket with his other hand, pulled out an inhaler, placed it in his mouth, and took a large puff to prevent an asthma attack.

Feeling like his lungs were releasing their grip, Harold turned to his wife, "I think we can put this one in the plus column." Firecrackers and explosions rocked the stage. Silver crackled into the air while fans gasped at the ending.

The roundness of her face belayed her Korean heritage, while the green markings over her shoulders made her a Green Sleeve, a genetically mutated child. The process was particularly appealing to parents, who were usually cyber-hippie environmentalists. The process was simple. In the blastula stage, a small virus was inserted at the parent's request into the path of cells. The virus would enter the cells that would form the shoulder and neck, depositing the working mechanics of chloroplast into the cell. Using a virus to change colors was an old practice. In the 17th century, viruses were used to alter tulip color.

With blastula, the practice of getting green sleeves was not much different. Many of the children had severe metabolic problems, but as the process became purified, the children grew up being less dependent on food and left a much smaller carbon footprint on the earth.

The skin around the neck, over the top of the shoulders, and down her arm was a fluorescent chlorophyll hue. They ate about one-third less than normal adults in the summer, but when their green sleeves turned a bark-like brown in the winter, they devoured as much as anyone else (if not more). Since the changes did not affect the sex cells, continued modification relied on the parental choice of each generation.

In a low-cut, black leather dress and a contrasting white, buttery cotton sweater, her face glowed at him. The shiny dress appeared as if it was poured hot on her body and then dried. Her pupils seemed to dominate her entire iris. Her eyes gleamed in the dimly lit room as her freakishly long aquamarine hair rested at the base of her knees. He loved her because of her contrasting (and sometimes clashing) features. Whenever she wanted to wear something red, she would accompany it with green apparel. Indeed, her clashing tastes were what made He-ran his first choice. He-ran was the inspiration for *Bioeletrics*. Indeed, early in their creation, Harold filmed He-ran dancing. He then modified each of the holo-singers to display what he referred to as shades of He-ran's personality.

He took his mirror sunglasses out of the pocket of his white work shirt, placed them over his eyes, then reached out and gently stroked her long blue dreadlocks. Instinctively, He-ran leaned in and kissed him. It was a small smooch, like those of kindergarteners that knew no better. He loved this woman partly because of some of her childish, playful qualities. He knew he still possessed the qualities himself. Holographic haepari (Korean for jellyfish) glided through the cloud as the audience's children reached out for the realistic holographic beasts.

As the warmth calmed his soul, Harold reflected on his affection for He-ran. They met first in Nantucket when he was just seventeen. They dated for two years, and then he enlisted for the third Iraqi War. Harold had wanted to make a difference.

Before leaving for Iraq, he felt she was bossy, and part of him struggled considering ending the relationship. He even told his commanding officer, Johnny Johnson, that he would leave her. After returning from the war, he was so far in his head, and she was the perfect therapy to keep him from being swallowed up by his mind. Still, at times, her diva routine frustrated and angered him. He learned to live with it. She was his inspiration. Her annoying features were a small price for not living his life in some sheltered room and never leaving.

A pleasant grunt escaped He-Ran's lips. "When can we get out of here?" It was clear that she was bored and wanted to be home. Her word ticked Harold off, but he caught himself before saying something he would regret later.

Harold felt a familiar pang in his heart. "I need to play the encore and break down the stuff, so figure 35 more minutes." Sometimes Harold wondered if there was anything more to him than being a slave to his work and wife.

Picking up her black leather purse from the ground, she mewed sadly, "alright, she finally agreed." She leaned in and granted him a kiss on his nose.

When the crowd was gone, there were no sounds at all. Indeed, the stage was empty, and part of Harold felt empty. Still, it was excellent exhaustion, the empty kind. He left the room and plunged through the seats.

A small grey animal scurried past his feet. It was enough to make him jump. "sorry little guy," he said out loud in case he had frightened the rat. Slowly, Harold inched to the stage. His heart swelled with joy. His eyes were drinking in the whole scene. If anyone had told him during the war that not only would he have lived but that he would come home to program the most successful Korean pop bands of all time, he would have broken out laughing.

Reaching the state, Harold placed his last hand on it. The tarp was still warm. His fingers smoothed over its roughness. Hopping on the stage, he went to the amplifiers. Soon, his crew would be here to remove them. He snickered to himself that he had a band, and then he heard a sound above, like metal bending. He looked up to see the scaffolding falling onto him. He screamed as he tried to jump out of the way. It crashed less than a foot from him.

~

Across town, Johnson sat in the enormous blue office. For the last five months, this was his residence. He'd given up the old one shortly after the death of his assistant, Daisy Bell. Johnny missed Daisy. She had a positive quality that seemed to give him hope, even when the bills were tough to pay. Missing her brought on the inevitable feeling of guilt that he had not taken out her killers. The old detective found it easier to call a truce with Lui and live to fight another day when given the opportunity. The self-loathing followed… It always followed.

Johnny reached over to where a small Japanese bonsai plant rested. He pulled open his desk drawer and removed a pair of scissors. Jackie had given him to a tree to help him relax. He clipped the branches.

For all his self-hatred, Johnny had to admit his life was on the upswing. The new office building was spectacular compared to his old brownstone. A smart building, the lavished office had a built-in biomechanical computer system with virtual reality capability and a Mega Flash router that gave nanosecond downloads of trillions of megabytes of information. Overall this place was much more extensive and massively higher in technology than his old place of work, as Jackie was helping some with the rent, and his street credibility had jumped up since the Eddie Whyte case. The detective had a whole floor, a nice waiting room with a reception desk, toilets rather than the old shared between the foundations of the building system, a small room he used for file storage, and a small camp bed for those late nights.

In the background, Johnny had Jackie's retro-Goth show playing. It was part of a revival style that she orchestrated for the station. He listened to her soft words, and then she placed on a song: The Sisters of Mercy's *This Corrosion*. He lounged back in his chair and closed his eyes. His office was a proper room, rather than a space within the room, partitioned off like before. Deep inside, something always felt wrong about the place, and often Johnny suppressed the sensation of being a kept man.

*Knock*. Johnny's eyebrows raised. It was five-thirty in the morning. Why was someone coming to him now? *Knock*. With no assistant to turn to, he slowly rose from his seat. The pants of his mauve suit fell into place. Belly pain from his old gunshot wound still rung inside him, but it was healing. On top of that, his joints ached.

Arthritic pain overcame him as he slowly shuffled to the door. It seemed as if time was catching up to him. He was far too old to be still working.

When he opened the door, an African American man stood with a shocked face. "Do I know you?" He asked.

"I dunno, do I? The eyes look familiar. The same empty glow behind them from the war." Johnny attempted to retort. "A-anyway, have a seat." Johnny showed the African American man to the seat. The guy stared at him like they had known each other before.

The guy sighed. "I like the Japanese fighting fish as I walked in," the man stated.

"Yeah, they are pretty cool. The aquarium was one of the reasons I chose to rent here...Mr...." Johnny let his voice trail hoping the gentleman would fill in the name. Instead, he just continued to scan the room.

A minute later, a second set of knocks landed on the door. Johnny got up to answer. It was a beautiful Korean woman. Johnny's heart danced. "I brought some bok choy," the woman announced.

Johnny broke out into an open laugh. "You two *still* haven't forgiven me for that."

"No," they said in unison. After the war, Johnny visited his old soldiers. He loved to spend time talking about the ancient war

199

days- well, except for his mission to the meadow outside the small village of Dabiq, Syria. It was a place they had no business being, and worse scared them all. The war had cost him his arm. The bionic replacement was working fine now, but for years it had caused him headaches both figuratively and literally.

On the visit to one of his soldiers, a Harold Jones, Johnny had met his Korean wife. They were so excited to see him that they rushed him into the house, and Harold told him his wife would make dinner. Johnny assumed it would be Korean food and stated, "I am not good with Kimchi and Bok Choy. Let's go out to dinner."

Obviously, he'd hurt his host's feelings. It turned out that several of his assumptions were just flat-out wrong. First bok choy was Chinese, not Korean. He felt terrible about that. Second, He-Ran, the wife's name finally returned, was born in America, orphaned, and adopted by an Irish family. She didn't cook Korean food at all. Indeed, she was proud to make haggis.

"Well, come in, and please, since I lost my favorite restaurant, let's share the bok choy." The woman walked in. Johnny noticed her dreadlocks and bit back the urge to ask her if they were real or hair extensions. But he remembered that He-ran, while primarily a joy was prone to go Full Diva on occasion. Out of one fire, he figured it best not to walk into another. Instead, the detective offered, "Hey, I got some pure water- real A1 grade. I'll get it, and I can contribute to the meal as well. I got some broken olives in lemon juice."

The two giggled, and Johnny ran, getting the water. Water was corporately owned and expensive in New Cyber City. Johnny got the water by possessing an illegal de-humidifier that he had scavenged after a job a few years back. Inside a minute, he brought out three glasses and a filled pitcher.

Pouring the three glasses, Johnny placed the jug on the coffee table, raised his pants legs, and sat in his armchair. "It is so great to see you guys," he added.

"So are you seeing..." Harold started.

"Long story, but Jackie and I are back," Johnny added, waving his hand toward the sound system. Jackie's voice hand just started speaking again, and then she placed on Siouxsie and the Banshees' *Spellbound*.

He-ran giggled, and Harold gasped, amazed, "That is awesome."

He-ran pulled out three boxes of bok choy, and Johnny passed around plates. "Are those mushrooms?"

"Yep," Harold replied. "And see the cherry tomatoes."

"Awesome!" Johnny replied, putting the container of green olives down, and He-ran scooped them onto the places as well. As she dug, Johnny noticed her rings. In addition to her wedding rings, she had four—two on each hand. The first of the rings on each hand were of little interest. On the one hand, it was a human eye, and on the twin finger, on the other, it was an Irish friendship ring. Johnny remembered it was the first gift Harold had given her. Harold told him about it during the war. Johnny spooned some bok choy and tomato into his mouth. He liked the mix, especially with fresh garlic. "Is that bulgur in it?"

"Excellent sense of taste, Johnny," He-ran offered. Bulgur was wheat often used as a substitute for meat, as global warming had gotten so pronounced that to combat, livestock kept to a minimal.

The second of the rings, black onyx, on each hand connected to a lacey black mesh bracelet. Centered on the bracelet was a black scarab encrusted with gold. Lettering marked the gold. "Egyptian?" Johnny asked.

He-ran pulled the glove back. "Yes, actually, the hieroglyphics from the Book of the Dead say, After I have created my own becoming, I have created many things that have come from my mouth." She turned the glyph over so Johnny could see the inscription on the back.

Pulling in close, Johnny looked at the engraving. "Very interesting," Johnny acknowledged.

"So, how the hell are you, Johnny?" Harold asked. For the next fifteen minutes, Johnny went on about his life and all that had changed.

"Johnny," Harold started. "it is always great to see you, but...."

"Business already, Harry," Johnny interrupted, and his eyes lit up.

"Johnny, they tried to kill him," He-ran chimed in.

Suddenly, the joviality of Johnny's look disappeared. He had lost so many friends over time. His heart twisted at the thought of losing another, even one he had not seen in a decade. "Who?"

"Not sure, buddy," Harry added, letting a spoon of bok choy return to the bowl. "Happened after a concert."

"Give me the whole story. Don't leave out any details or suspicions."

With that, Harold started to relay the details. Even though he had not seen Johnny in close to a decade, it was amazing how comfortable he felt. It was almost as if it were right to tell him. If anyone could keep him alive, Johnny could. In the background, Joy Division's "Isolation" played.

"K-pop always made me feel like throwing my hands in the air and dancing," Johnny said, "especially your stuff. I love how you program those riffs."

A little skeptical, but Harold stated anyway. "Good to know."

"You know I still listen to it," and then Johnny rolled off a list of songs with his analysis from the *Bioelectrics,* and Harold was shocked that he had paid so much attention to his work. Even more shocking was when he said, "I would be really honored if the two of you would spend a day or two with Jackie and me until this case is sorted out."

Stunned, Harold glanced at He-ran. She blinked. "We could not put you out like that," she finally said.

"Not a problem," Johnny replied. "It is the best way to ensure that you are safe over the next few days, and Jackie would love the company."

"How would I work?" Harold asked.

"Only be a few days while I run down some leads," Johnny replied.

Both He-ran and Harold looked at each other, and finally, Harold said, "Well, if you are sure, it will not put you out. Let me head to my place and pick up some stuff, and then we will be there."

"Good," Johnny replied.

~

Stormy was how most would describe Johnny and Jackie's relationship in the past. Not now. In older age, they had become entirely simpatico. As the doorbell rang, she playfully teased Johnny about slamming the door in his friends' faces. He giggled as she waltzed to the door.

Outside she heard some laughter and then a scream. With a huge smile, Jackie opened the door to find Harold holding He-

202

ran in his arms. She was stabbed in the chest. The laser knife hilt was fixed at her breast plate. Harold was crying and calling for help.

Jackie wailed. Johnny dashed to the door. Harold pointed to the bushes, and Johnny charged into them full force. He bolted into the wooded area. His pants ripped, and his legs were scraped by hedges. His eyes searched the area for broken limbs and the ground for footprints. Which way to go? Finally, he caught sight of broken branches to his left and charged about forty feet to a clearing. While the muscles in his legs burned from his mad dash and he heaved heavy breaths, his eyes assessed the area.

Doubling back, Johnny reached his front door to find Jackie already on the phone with the police. Harold was kneeling now next to his unconscious wife. "Harry, what happened?" Johnny questioned.

Blue corn-rolled hair scattered out onto the street, and the woman's face was pallid. The laser was so hot that it had fused around He-Ran's skin. Maybe it was keeping the blood inside. Johnny saw very little overall. "I don't know. We were on the step-joking and kidding. I heard something on my right, like a cracking twig, and spun toward the bushes. When I turned back, she fell in my arms. Come on, baby, hold on. Don't die on me," he began to chant, repeated the last phrase.

Scanning the scene, Johnny caught sight of the black mesh bracelets again. This time he focused on them as if seeing them for the first time. Johnson placed his hand on Harold's shoulder. He was surprised when Harold grabbed his head. It was as if the man was desperate for support. Johnny bent further and reached for the bracelet. "I know this is an odd question," he started. "When did she get these?"

"Johnny, my wife man!"

"Sorry," Johnny reached and touched the black scarab on the left hand with his bionic fingers. He removed it from her wrist.

Within three minutes, a blue and black police quad and a red and orange ambulance quad pulled up with lights blaring. The screaming siren echoed in the neighborhood. Most of Johnny's neighbors were now out of their houses, staring at Johnny's place. Within one minute, the ambulance medical robot slid a gurney under He-ran, and slowly she rose. The scan showed the laser knife was lodged in her heart. They needed to get her to the hospital for surgical removal.

203

Eyes red and puffy from crying, Harold held his wife's hand as the surgical bot pressed the button on the gurney. It raised and rolled itself to the ambulance quad. They bandaged the wound and cauterized the wound. Harold began to tear up, his wife's face slowly graying as the life drained from her. Harold walked in, but a man stepped in front of her.

"Oh, no, you don't." the police detective-looking man said. "I'm afraid I can't let you pass!"

"Wh-what?!" Harold whined. "That's my wife, thickhead! I should be in there with her!"

"Officer Jay. I need to interview you before you can see your wife."

"I didn't hurt her, I swear!"

Johnny watched as the fight went up and back. He watched Harold sob and begged to be let in as the hospital drove away. "Hey Jay," Johnny's voice was buttery soft.

"What do you want, Johnson?"

"I know this is your gig. You're the albatross. You're in charge, but I know this guy. I like to fly second on this."

"You ain't police Johnny,"

"I know, but I think I can help,"

"Johnny, let me do my job,"

"Sure,"

For forty-five minutes, Jay interrogated and finally stated, "I will take him downtown for questioning."

"Why, Jay?"

"Johnny, he was alone on the step with her. By his admission, he's got anger troubles," Johnny went to interrupt, but Jay waved him down, "I know from the war, but still."

"Jay, studies show that vets are less aggressive than non-vets,"

"True, except the ones that seem to find their way to you," Jay paused to let that sink in and then added, "Besides, he even admitted that his wife was a total diva, and he had moments of intense anger when he felt like killing her."

At that moment, a dejected Harold walked into the room. He put out his hands, waiting for cuffs. As he did so, Johnny interjected, "Wait." Both sets of eyes darted to him.

"I want to show you something," Johnny said, pulling out the bracelet.

"Did you take that off the victim, Johnson?" Jay grumbled menacingly.

"Yes,"

Livid, Jay's face locked on Johnny's. "You know I should run you in for tampering with evidence."

"I have not tampered yet,"

"Is it more than a bracelet?"

"I think so. I think it's a transmitter. I think she was being tracked." Johnny's finger explored the outsides of the gem, and his thumb flicked it open. Harold's eyes widened in shock. "Is that why you asked me where she got it?" Harold questioned. Johnny nodded. "She has a friend on the east side of New Cyber City. Her name is Francesca Laredo. She just bought it this month. I can't believe this is happening. I am going with you two."

"Going where?" Officer Jay asked.

"To interview her!" Harold barked.

"Now, wait a minute!" Officer Jay barked. "You are not going anywhere. At best, you're a grieving husband, and at worse, you are involved. Either way, no!"

Shooting Harold a sharp glare, Johnny said, "Jay's right. You go with Jackie to the hospital, and I will go with Jay." Harold went to protest, but Johnny added, "Your wife needs you."

Stepping into the night, Johnny and Jay went to find one Francesca Laredo.

~

New Cyber City reminded Johnny of the circuits on a computer motherboard from the sky. He stared at the highways and stacked buildings as if looking at the surface of computer chips. A quarter of the way there, Jay dipped the quad down into the lanes between the city streets. The black and white quad pierced through the neon blue, red, and green lights like a fish darting through water in a stream.

Giant billboards close to a billion pixels played the video of the most wanted with cut-away shots of their victims, alternating with advertisements from sponsors. Giant holographic images danced in the sky, testifying that women and men could be more. *When you could get the latest upgrade and be so much more, why be you?*

Inside Jay's hover, black and white, Jay placed on some old opera music. The aria Mozart's Der Hölle Rache Die Zauberflöte. The music was voracious, and the sound bordered on the divine. The harmonious textured vocals filled Johnny as he shifted to gain comfort in his seat. They say opera can inspire brain parts to work, and Johnny deeply felt his forebrain was obeying this rule. "This is a challenging piece," Jay explained.

"I'm sure," Johnny replied as he searched around the quad. Maybe nothing was inspirational, and it was just his hype. He was not used to flying in the front of a police quad. "Did you call in the warrant?"

Outside the window, they passed hover cars on either side. Behind them, the transparent tube served as a mode of transport mainly for poor workers who could not afford a hover. Company logos danced in the sky as if to be worshipped. On either side, massive glass buildings painted in sharp neon glowing lights had scrawls of news rolling on the sides. Below, the streets of New Cyber City were like carnivals of old. Various oddly dressed spectacles lined the ground, from hookers, both human and robotic, to performers and derelicts. Street jugglers tossed fire or pins in the air to entertain. Above, more hover quads. "Yes, it will take a few minutes for the information to get to the judge and for her to authorize it," Jay replied.

"City has whatever will tickle your fancy," Johnny commented, as his eyes fell on the alleyway that connected between skyscrapers. He imagined the smells from bad to worse, and juice addicts lay beside dumpsters. When did this city get so bad? Had the juice epidemic won? His mind flashed back to years before. He remembered a young woman he had helped escape the city. It was her blood they were using as part of the juice (the most addictive part), and he had always hoped her blood would provide the necessary ingredients for the cure. He had heard rumors that Silversoft in Chi-Pitt was working on it.

Jay fidgeted in his seat and reached into his shirt, adjusting his vest. " I know the neighborhood's bad but are you wearing a laser-proof vest for protection?"

"Yep, I've been since Mikolaj" Jay's voice was monotone. It ticked Johnny off because Johnny knew it covered up so much. Mikolaj was both their friend, and Johnny swarmed with a hundred emotions and reactions around the death. The vest told Johnny that Jay did the same.

Jay looked uncomfortable as he struggled to fly the hover and fix his vest. Johnny decided to get a jab in. "Jay, you know it might signify that you are gaining a few pounds that the vest fits...."

"I ain't gaining no weight, Johnson," Jay interrupted. Jay was always vain about his appearance. Johnny just chuckled to himself.

Reaching their location, Jay careened his quad toward a lot. Johnny's MegaSmart rang. It was Harold requesting a video call. Johnny knew it was a bad idea, but he decided to answer in the small case that Harold had something legitimate to offer. "Harold, we are still on the way," Johnny barked. Rattling off many questions that Johnny already knew to ask, Harold went on about how he should be there and that he was the best person to interrogate Francesca. Johnny tried to reassure him that he could handle it and that this was just one of those instances in life where he would have to learn to trust another. On that note, Johnny clicked off the screen. "Well, at least you know he is at the hospital," Johnny stated to Jay.

"I just hope that we are not on a wild goose chase. I am thinking of sending a quad to the hospital to pick him up." Jay raised his hand from the wheel and pointed a shaking index finger at Johnny. Johnny felt it was no use to argue with Jay and instead pointed to a spot for landing.

The black and white quad descended, landing in front of a bail bond office. Its vehicle's doors rose, and Johnny stepped out. After Jay emerged, he placed the quad on an anti-theft shutdown. The metal covering emerged and folded over the top of the car protecting the windows and doors. They headed to the other side of the street and passed an all-night convenience store and then a pawnshop before arriving at the destination.

Thick white steam emerged from street grates. While most cities are heat pockets, New Cyber City had a reputation for its nighttime humidity. This night did not disappoint. The moisture added to the reek of rotten trash awaiting pick up in the dumpsters. The blended stenches assaulted Johnny's nose. The neighborhood was horrible for such a famous and successful designer. Johnny doubted she would even be at the store.

When they arrived at Francesca Laredo's address, they rang the doorbell, and Jay stated their credentials to the robotic security voice that answered. A voice replied, "Let's see them," and Jay held his badge to the security scanner. After that came, a loud buzz and Johnny yanked the door open. "Any word on that warrant?" Johnny questioned.

"Should be any minute," Jay replied.

Once inside, Johnny noted the walls were photosensitive plastic. He wondered if they were arranged to provide a counterattack if any electrical or laser weapons were used. The display cases offered a wide array of glowing spiked leather bracelets, mechanical pendants, and watches. The Egyptian styles caught Johnny's eye, mainly the scarab-lined gloves.

Several women stood behind the display case. Johny's eyes assessed them. Wearing a studded black leather body suit, the lead woman approached. Johnny pegged her as the muscle.

Behind them was a separate wall covered with mirrors and a tiny shelf that ran the gamut of the room. Johnny surmised the stand was for work and that the group might need to modify the jewelry to suit the customers' tastes.

Overall, the place reminded Johnny of a vacation to Osaka that he and Jackie had taken just after the Eddie Whyte case. When they were there, they shopped at many fancy jewelry boutiques.

Jay asked to speak with Francesca. A woman with heavy black mascara-covered eyes and in her mid-twenties emerged from the back in a long black leather military blazer with a hood. The sleeves had four gold bands on either arm. The bottom back of the blazer was gothic black lace. "You are looking for me, officer?"

"Yes, ma'am," Jay replied, "Can we speak in the back?"

"Sure," the woman said as she sashayed into the back. Jay followed. Johnny headed back and caught sight of a letter from Moncore Bank on the corner of the work shelf. He stored the name.

In the back, the woman poured herself a glass of fresh water. She did not offer any to Johnny or Jay. The water of every grade was expensive. "So, what brings you here?" Francesca asked with a buttery sweet voice.

"A piece of your jewelry," Jay said.

"I did not know that the police were fans of my work,"

Jay went to protest, but Johnny cut him off. "One piece in particular, ma'am," he said, yanking the scarab from his pocket. "Does this look familiar?"

Francesca's eyes glimmered, "That is my work."

"Who did you make it for?"

"An old friend and a loyal customer, He-Ran Jones,"

"Did you know the piece had a listening device implanted?" Jay asked.

Francesca appeared genuinely shocked. "A what?"

Johnny opened the scarab on the glove, "Yes, ma'am. See, it opens to some sort of tracking mechanism."

"Officers," she started.

Jay interrupted, "I am an officer. This man is just a private detective."

"Well, gentleman. I am sorry to disappoint such a gorgeous gentleman as you, but electronics are not my Thing. That must've been done outside of here. I do not know."

"Was your shop always located here?" Johnny asked.

"This was the original store,"

"Famous jeweler as yourself has just the one shop?" Johnny questioned.

"Used to have two, but we had a problem with the other shop on twelfth and Market," Francesca admitted and had to close it down."

"Pricey neighborhood," Johnny gawked.

"What kind of problem?" Jay asked.

"Burglary. The crooks came in and took a ton of inventory a month or so ago. We are waiting for an insurance payment before re-opening."

"You mean the shop in the expensive neighborhood got hit, and this one was not touched."

"Oddest thing. It was hit twice, and this place has never gets hit. You think with all the juicers here, this place would have been robbed."

A ping went off in Jay's pocket. He pulled out his phone, but Johnny knew the warrant had arrived. "Well, we have a warrant to search this place," Jay showed him the phone. He scanned the picture of the warrant.

"Search for what?"

"Probably nothing," Johnny reassured. "He-Ran is in the hospital."

"That's horrible. Is she ok?"

"For now, I need to use your phone."

"Out-front," Johnny rolled into the front of the shop. He pulled two wires from his bionic arm and inserted them into the phone. Inside a microsecond, the detective was inside Moncore bank. He sifted through the company records, looking for massive deposits or anything outside of the ordinary. Surprisingly he found nothing. He went back a month and did not find anything. Finally, he sifted through the checks and credit card payments. This was interesting because he found no record of a bank check from He-Ran Jones or her husband.

"Do you have the sales receipt for Ms. Jones's purchase?"

"Yes, it would be in the drawer." Johnny searched the drawer. Nothing. "Ma'am," he said softly as the muscle girl peered over his shoulder. He could feel her breath on her neck and the studs from her leather jabbing his skin. "I don't see the receipt."

"It should be there," then Francesca paused as if remembering something. "She didn't pick it up."

"Excuse me?" Jay added.

"Sometimes, she and her husband are too busy to pick up what they buy. I believe they sent their security guy, Paul Bentley, to fetch it this time."

Suddenly Johnny felt his face flush red with anger. He hated being played. He pulled out his MegaSmart and tried to call Harold. No answer. He called Jackie. "Hey, babe," the soft voice on the other side said.

"How is He-Ran," Johnny asked.

"She got out of surgery a little while ago. She's stable but still asleep."

"Good to hear. Hey love, I'm at the shop. Is Harold there?"

"No," she said. "When he got off the phone, he said you asked him to come down and meet you."

"He is coming here?"

"No, at the concert hall."

Johnny felt better. At least he knew that Jones was sending him a message of his destination. This was slightly relieving. "Jay, we got to go."

"Where, Johnny boy?"

"Concert hall," Johnny replied. "Thank you, Ms. Laredo."

"Glad to help. He-Ran is one of my oldest friends. She trusted me when no one else would. Anything that I can do to help."

Leaving the jewelry shop, the pair headed for Officer Jay's quad. "What's up, Johnny?"

"Well, it seems like Harold knew that his security guy picked up the piece and sent us here on a wild goose chase so he could confront his security guy."

"Damn it, Johnny!" Jay yelled, "I knew I should have taken him in."

"He is at the concert hall,"

"No, that is what he told Jackie,"

"I doubt he is lying,"

"He has been lying all night as far as I am concerned."

The two jumped into the black and white. Jay put the sirens on as they bounded into the sky.

~

For eight years, Harold Jones employed Bently. Unfortunately, Harold trusted him completely, so the betrayal was beyond comprehension. It pulled at Harold's gut and riveted his mind, which fumbled for an answer. Besieged by a mixture of raw rage and embarrassment entered the stadium. The word: *Why?* Repeated in his mind.

Harold landed his hover in the parking lot and pulled Light Ion Blaster (LIB 12) from the trunk. Thrusting the gun into its holster, he searched the trunk for his Bushwacker scanning and sequencing laser (the Monster 5, as it was called). Finding it, Harold ran his and over its metal surface, lifted it from the quad, and swung it over his back. He flipped open a final compartment in his truck, pulled out two small laser knives, and hung them on his belt just over his hips' left and right sides.

Surprisingly, Harold had no remorse for what he was about to do. He knew it and fully accepted it. He also knew there would be consequences for his action, but this did not faze him. Indeed, it felt like his mind was locked off from his body at this point. The questioning and indecisiveness had all disappeared.

A few years prior, Harold had spent so much time involved with his work, He-Ran had threatened to leave him. He spent more than one night lying in bed, searching for his priorities. With her lying in the hospital, his priorities were crystal clear: Kill the man who put her there.

Moving past a loose collection of buildings referred to as the coliseum city, Harold picked up his pace. He had performed over a hundred concerts in this stadium over the past twenty years. His body was at home in the darkened complex. He eased himself through the turnstiles and past the security checkpoint. Surprisingly, no one stopped him. Perhaps because he was so recognizable, security may have believed that he had forgotten something in the control room and was just returning to pick it up. Harold stalked three hundred meters toward the stairs. His eyes gazed out on the open area of the arena.

An eerie feeling crept over Harold as he realized this would be an excellent place for an ambush. He needed to remain focused. His eyes scanned the area. His best bet was to make it to the corridor below and examine the place with the computer equipment in the control room.

Advancing down the steps, he went down five levels, a total of fifty meters, and stopped. Terraces arched back and climbed as high as he could see. The arena was huge but empty. The sound of a can falling caused Harold to spin. He swung his Monster 5 from his shoulder to rest in his hand but managed to catch himself just before firing.

A furry grey rat ran into a trash can. *'I should have killed him the other day,'* Harold thought while circling far away from the can. He headed through the rows of bleachers toward the more expensive seats at the ground level. Once he passed them, he darted under a bow arch and into a corridor just off the side.

The hallway was lined with an eggshell-colored tile. Yellow neon lights lit the passage. Its floor was a hard-alabaster enamel-type substance called forenzocite, invented only thirty years prior. The old military man's heart pounded loudly in his chest; still, he felt no fear. At any point, He-Ran's attempted killer could emerge. Harold needed to be in position. Silently, Harold placed his hand on the tunnel wall and used to smooth surface to aid his dash.

For the first time since his arrival, he heard voices in the hall. Laughter came from the group. Harold made out three males. None sounded like his target. Harold decided it was best to keep away from whomever the voices belonged to, as tagging along his weapons would surely lead to an arrest.

With his Monster 5, Harold dropped to a slow march in the dark hall, searching for Paul Bentley. He knew the security guy worked late and was sure he would find him at the place. The theater was dark and eerie. Harold called out Bentley's name.

The air grew foul. It was the smell of the men's and lady's rooms that he found himself passing. Still, Harold found no sign of

Bentley. He arrived at the operations control room and pulled out his key to open the door. Inside, the room was lit with a putrid fluorescent shade of green lay a dirty couch and several beer cans on the floor.

~

Officer Jay and Detective Johnson arrived at the front of the stadium. Jay landed the black and white. The two jumped out and headed toward the gates. "He better be here, Johnny, or I will arrest you for conspiracy and hindering an investigation," Jay announced.

Reaching the gate, Jay slapped the turnstiles with his nightclub. "I thought you called security," Johnny asked.

"Yes, I told them we were on the way, and we needed to question Mr. Bentley."

"Well, where are they?"

The two pushed past the turnstiles. Just beyond them, a black mass of forms approached. As they got closer, Johnny made out three people. They looked like gangsters with their spiked blue-black dyed hair and tattoos. One lit a cigarette. His face glowed as he struck the match. It was not just a disgusting habit but mostly discarded through mass community-wide behavior modification programs in the forties or at least socially replaced by the equally disgusting habit of vaping and e-cigarettes some twenty years earlier. The "juicing" habit, vaping exotic flavors, was limited to the lower social classes.

Concentrating, Johnny saw the man was wearing optical implants standard for hitmen. Johnny's hand dropped to the inside of his suit jacket where he kept his Smith and Wesson Cannon holstered. The man placed it in his mouth. "Police," Jay called. "You were expecting us?"

The first guy pulled a rapid laser particle weapon and began to fire. Singing Johnny's hair, energy waves exploded through the room. Lightening quick, Jay and Johnny drew their blasters and returned fire.

~

Viewing over the computer screen, Harold caught sight of the battle between Johnny and his assailants. Blue and orange laser fire ripped through the room. Jay had ducked behind a corner on the wall, and Johnny was partially behind a door.

At first, Harold wanted to rush to join them, but then he caught sight of Bentley on a second screen. He was in the deluxe box three floors above. Bentley had tied off his arm and was placing a needle in them. Harold stared in horror to find Bentley on juice. He really knew nothing of his security guy, after all.

His mind assessed whether to take the elevator or stairs. In addition, he wondered if Bentley had access to computer screens. If he did, it was clear that Bentley would head to the scene where Johnny and Jay were. *What was the play?* Jones wondered, but Bentley rose and grabbed four juice needles off the table and his ion gun. He staggered for the door.

Harold rubbed his face. There was only one play now. Taking a deep breath, he shot to the door, grabbed the handle, and quickly marched his way to the stairs.

~

Electricity sizzled in the air, and the laser fire sounded like striking an aluminum pan. The air smelled of fresh ozone. The shots pinned Johnson and Jay.

Griding his teeth in frustration, Johnny pushed off the wall. He fired, but then a return series of blasts forced him to back up. Multiple volleys of shots ripped through the hall. They simultaneously returned fire. Badly outgunned, they needed a plan quickly.

Sweat beaded over Officer Jay's forehead. He motioned to Johnny to cover him, and he pointed to a way around the corner. Johnny knew if he did not run quick enough, they would be picking up his dead carcass. He jumped out. As he did, he noticed a man roll out on the floor. Jay targeted the man immediately. His shot was dead on the mark. Killing the guy instantly, he felt a wave of relief flood through his body. A second shooter circled out at that point and fired a shot, and Johnny dove to the side, letting the shot go over his head.

Jay swung and fired at the second shooter. His shot hit the man as the man's shot struck him square in the shoulder. Jay flew back into the wall. His body slumped to the ground. Johnny hoped Jay's vest absorbed most of the blast. Still, he worried that Jay was dead. He skirted behind a beam and then advanced to a second beam closer to his foe.

The last shooter's breathing was labored. Johnny could hear him as Johnny circled slowly around the poll. He needed to get a clean shot before his target took him out. He rushed to the next pole in line.

214

~

Harold advanced to the battle scene. From the corner, he saw Johnny struggling in a shootout with his assailant. Aiming the Monster 5, Harold tried to get an open shot. As he did so, Johnny kept drifting into the way of his scope. Harold tried hard to stifle a gasp. He wanted to call duck to Johnny and just fire, but he doubted Johnny would hear him at ninety meters. He decided to half his steps and quickened his pace to a full run.

Rushing, Harold caught an image out of the corner of his eye. It was Bentley moving toward a downed Jay. Harold rushed to aid the officer.

Bentley drew one of the needles from his pocket and rushed to inject the juice into Jay. Harold knew that the substance was almost instantly addictive and turned Jay into a drug-crazed robot. He had but one move. Leaping in front of Jay, the needle hit Jones dead in the chest. He managed one shot of his Monster 5 and, at close range, blasted Bentley back twenty meters.

Jones expected a pleasant high, which would be so intense that it would zap away his freedom. Instead, it seemed like his body rebelled. He had an extreme adverse reaction. His entire body seized. His mind thought, *how the hell could anyone enjoy this or get hooked*. There was no high, just pain.

~

Twelve paces and round the pole, Johnny smelled the nervous sweat off his assailant. He heard the man's footsteps and labored breathing. If he spun out and did not get his shot off quick enough, he would be fried worse than Jay because he had no vest. His heart beat rapidly. He would only get one chance: Live or die would be decided when he stepped out. He prepared his strike.

The Smith and Wesson's cold metallic feel helped Johnny concentrate. His bionic hand taped the side of the ion cannon. Withdrawing his bionic hand to his pocket, Johnny pulled out He-Ran's scarab. He tossed it off to the side. As it struck the ground, he spun. He was face to face with the assailant. The clunk of the scarab had bought him the second he needed. He fired, and his opponent tried to dodge and fire. The proximity bought Johnny's opponent no time, and the jerking of his move caused the shot to hit Johnny's bionic hand. The hand fried, but Johnny's shot was dead to rights. The blast seared his opponent.

215

There was no time for Johnny to savor his victory. He saw Jones supine on the floor. His body twitched and jolted. Johnny rushed to his friend. Jones's muscles strained, and his eyes bulged from his head from the effort, but still, he dragged his torso off the ground. "Johnny, I need to know why he did it?" Harold said. His muscles still strained from the drug reaction. His face contorted with agony. Jones collapsed back down.

Placing his Smith & Wesson Ionizer Cannon back in its holster, Johnny's soft eyes met Harold. "Sure, buddy," Johnny said cautiously. "I think I can get him to talk." Johnny uncurled the wires from his arms and went to Paul Bentley's unconscious body. He was sure the man would never tell a soul why he tried to kill He-Ran. Johnny placed the wires to the cyber implants on the back of his neck. The implants Bentley used to override security codes.

Twice before, Johnny hacked into such human implants. They were designed to go directly to the hippocampus, amygdala, and neostriatum. The brain remembered many things, from processes and procedures to images, emotions, sounds, and smells. The difficulty was always getting the information to come back as a unified whole that made sense. The last attempt Johnny made at such a hack almost killed him. His body cringed with the idea of trying it again. He glanced at Harold. The man was in such pain, and he would never get closure from Bentley, but Johnny could give him closure.

Johnny placed his wires to the base of the implant. His thick fingers threaded the wire inside the jack and then twisted it around. The old detective took a deep breath, closed his eyes, and willed his mind to draw out the images. Rivers of information painfully flowed into Johnny. His hands tightened, and his neck strained as jumbled impressions scurried into his consciousness. The sensual assault was massive. It was a hundred thousand times worse than the sensual assault of the streets of New Cyber City. His mind integrated electrical signals of sensors, connections, transmissions, processors, and controllers in Bentley's implant and brain.

Immediately, Johnny felt a piercing feeling between his eyes and a gripping sensation at the back of his brain. His heart rate surged, beating so fast he thought that it would leap from his rib cage any second. Sweat poured from his skin. He coughed as if the transfer was stealing lungfuls of air away and felt like he would vomit. Maybe it was panic, but Johnny thought that he could not breathe. He felt himself foaming at the mouth.

Cold, harsh images and broken sounds flowed. The memories were jumbled and sporadic. His mind leaped from scene to scene. At first, Johnny was unsure if he could filter or even slow down the images. They moved with incredible speed into his consciousness, and then he realized his brain was trying hard to retain the memories as if they were his own. The effect made him vomit, and he felt a convulsion coming over his body as his eyes rolled up into his head.

Blood pressure rising like a massive headache, Johnny's body fell to the ground. Overstimulated muscles around his arms began to seize. Vaguely in his mind, he was aware that his heart and lungs might eventually follow suit.

Shocking images in corporate rooms of meetings with senior management of Purt Network. The steps are taken to kill or at least discredit Harold Jones. The sights were horrific, but even these images contained other details. Details that Bentley might have been only vaguely aware of. Information was vital to end Purt itself: Computer codes and computer screen access codes reflected in mirrors.

An eternity of time seemed to pass. Finally, Johnny felt the connection break. He was not sure how long he lay in darkness, but he saw Officer Jay above him when his eyes opened. The old officer's nightstick touched Johnny's shoulder. "You alright?" Jay asked.

In all his years working with Jay, Johnny was surprised by the gentleness of Jay's tone. It was clear that either Johnny's spasm or Jay had broken the connection. Johnny was afraid to ask, which occurred. Instead, he replied, "Yeah," and followed it with an extended exhale. Even disconnected, Johnny's heart was still pounding. He took several long slow breaths to relax.

"You're a lucky man, Johnson," Jay rumbled. "Had I not managed to break your wire, I shudder to think about what would have happened. That was some crazy shit."

"Jay, I saw it," Johnny said.

With Jay's assistance, Johnny rose from the ground. His legs were unsteady, and his knees felt like they could buckle at any minute. "What'd you see?"

"Purt Network hired him to kill Harold. They wanted him gone because he is bad for the juice business."

"Johnny, your little mind was probably miscomprehending the scene. Purt is involved in getting addicts off the street, helping tens of thousands of them find a spiritual way."

"Jay, not only do I know what I saw, I can prove it."

A smile crept over Jay's face. "Actionable intelligence?" Johnny nodded. Exhausted, he felt something he had not felt in a long time around Juice- a sense of hope. "To get the juice off the street." Johnny nodded again. "Alright, let's get you and your crew to the hospital, and when you are released- I want this intel!" Jay cuffed Bentley and ripped him from the ground. "This one is going to jail for a long time." Jay pulled out his cell and called for backup and an ambulance to get Harold to the hospital.

Jumping to Harold's side, Johnny grabbed his hand. His hand seized tightly around Johnny's. The pressure increased, and Harold's muscles kept growing in their contractions. Painful and uncomfortable, Johnny bore it. He whispered to his friend, "Bentley did it for the money. He was hooked on the juice, and the Purt Network put him up to this."

Harold's face strained, and he appeared to be having difficulty breathing. Johnny yelled, "Jay, where is that ambulance man!"

"On its way, Johnny- boy," Jay yelled back. Harold's lips moved as if trying to speak. Johnny instructed him to rest. Jay walked over and slumped at Johnny's side. "He saved me," Jay said. "Jumped in front of those needless. I could have been a slave to that crap if not for him."

"Yeah," Johnny replied. "He is a good guy. Always has been."

~

Three weeks later:

Harold handed Johnny a check. Johnny refused, saying, "Look, I know that you just missed three weeks of shows, and I don't want to take this and leave you in a lurch."

"Not a problem. I got insurance to cover the ticket losses on the shows, plus we just reschedule them for after we get back from touring in the Chi-Pitt region. Besides, it could have been worse. I could have gotten hooked on that crap."

"The juice is a killer. I will be glad when it is finally off the street," Johnny replied, stuffing the check into his jacket pocket. Johnny pulled out a pen and wrote a name and address on a

218

sheet of paper. He handed it to Harold. The man glanced at the name. "Willowson?" he asked out loud. Johnny nodded.

"Very addictive stuff," Jackie inserted. "Maybe she has the latest news on how to defeat it."

"For me, it was not addictive at all. I am glad never to have it again. Not sure why the Juice affected me so badly," admitted Harold, still holding his wife's hand in the hospital. "Part of me is glad it did, else I would be addicted to the stuff now. Maybe it had something to do with the Harris-Rutledge serum we took in Syria."

Mentioning Syria caused a wave of nausea in Johnny, and he got defensive, "Let's not talk about that. We have a promise." Harold bit his lip hard enough that blood seeped out over it.

Sensing the tension, He-Ran spoke, "Well, thank you for bringing in my attempted killer. Now, I plan to meditate every day to help heal myself."

"Well, just try to rest," Johnny offered, "Too much of that nam yo ho renge kyo stuff can cut off oxygen to your brain and slow down healing."

"See, Johnny, why did you have to go there. The chant is Japanese and Chinese. My wife is Korean. You are like the worst. Also, you know she ain't even a Nichiren Buddhist."

Johnny protested, but Jackie took him by the hand. She smiled and, with a chuckle, said, "Well, guys, it looks like you have something to hold over him for the next ten years."

The group laughed. Harold felt invigorated with new ideas for music to condemn the juice. He was ready to return to his work to lead a civilization from the drug with He-Ran. Her soft hands touched his arm. That tingling sensation blasted down his back as he leaned in to kiss her.

*Marisha Cautilli* is an established writer. She has authored more than a dozen books. Diagnosed as gifted in kindergarten, she has dominated the education setting and is presently taking college courses at PA cyber. Her interests range from swimming to robotics. She has taught two courses, one co-taught and about writing, and one in strategies and tactics in gaming settings.

*Joseph Cautilli, Ph.D., MSCP* is a licensed psychologist in PA, DE, and NJ. He has authored over fifty scientific and theoretical articles. He founded seven journals in behavior analysis, which he sold to the American Psychological Association back in 2011. He has co-authored over a dozen books with his daughter, which deal with cyberpunk, biopunk, and horror themes. Presently he owns a mental health company, Behavior Analysis and Therapy Partners, which services children and families in Montgomery, Bucks, Delaware and Philadelphia Counties.

Made in the USA
Middletown, DE
14 October 2022

12669835R00124